THE COURTING SEASONS

A KINGDOM OF PROMISES AND LIES

N. F. SCHMITT

A Kingdom of Promises and Lies

Copyright 2024 by N.F. Schmitt

ISBN 979-8-9899584-0-5 (paperback print)

ISBN 979-8-9899584-1-2

First Edition March 2024

Dedication

To my beloved Grandma Janet,
If it was not for you buying me "Dick & Jane" when I struggled with reading as a child, I probably never would have found my love for reading and written this book.

Books by N.F. Schmitt

A Kingdom of Promises and Lies

A Queendom of Heartbreak and Deceit – *coming spring 2025*

A Queendom Book 3 – *To be Determined*

A Kingdom Book 4 – *To be Determined*

KINGDOM SHEDIWARK
KINGDOM T'CUDTER
KINGDO THEORIN
QUEENDO GREWT'E

KINGDOM HAYVERTON
KINGDOM T'LOVONESS

PRONUNCIATION GUIDE
Monarchies:

Grewt'en: Groot-N

Hayverton: Hay-Ver-Ton (or) Have-Er-Ton*

Shediwark: Shed-E-Wark (or) Shed-Uh-Wark*

T'Cudter: Tu-Cud-Ter

Theorines: Theo - Rhines

T'Lovoness: Ta-Love-Oh-Ness

**Depends on monarchy of how they pronounce it*

CHARACTERS:

Deveroux Theox: Deh-Vr-Oo Th-Ox

Eloise: El-Oh-wheeze

Esame: Ez-Uh-May

Fairness: Fair-Ness

Gideon: Gi-Dee-Uhn

Grace Lily: Grace Lil-lee

Iryse Skyvien: Er-Reese Skiv-E-N

Killien Knox: Kill-E-N Knocks

Lydia: Li-Dee-Uh

Montgomery Victory: Mont-Gum-Er-Ree Vik-Tr-Ee

Myrese: Mehr-Reese

Olivia Jade: Oh-Liv-E-Uh Jade

Opal: Oh-Puhl

Percival Chivarly: Per-civ-val Chiv-Er-Lee

Persamina Rowena: Purse-A-Mean-A Rowe-N-A

Rachelle Mortese: Rah-Shell More-Teese

Rafael Baylor: Raf-A-L Bay-Lore

Regalius: Reh-Gale-E-Us

Regina Isadora: Reh-Jean-Uh Iz-Uh-Door-Uh

Rohanna Mrycella: Roh-Ahn-Nuh Mer-Sell-Uh

Serenity: Sir-Ren-Nit-Tee

Stella: Stell-Uh

Tearani Ryver: Tear-Ron-Knee River

Tiviola: Tiv-E-Oh-La

Voltaire Edric: Vole-Tear Ed-Rick

NICKNAMES:

Irysey: Ers-See

Bay: Bay

Livvy: Liv-Vee

Mina: Mean-Nuh

Monty: Mont-Tee

Reggie: Redg-Gee

Tea: T

HOUSES:

Wandern: Wan-dern

PETS:

Pumpking: Pump-King

Sugarplum: Shu-gar-Plum

Prologue

"Y̲ou have one goal in life, Persamina" Mother paused mid-brush stroke of my raven black hair. Her piercing silver eyes met mine in the mirror as she continued, "and that is to marry Prince Rafael Baylor of T'Lovoness."

I nodded to confirm I understood before she resumed brushing my hair. With her attention focused, I took a moment to admire her reflection in the mirror. Today, her fawn hair was let down in loose waves that fell to her waist, and she wore a serene smile. When I was six years old, I had already known I was her opposite in every way. Nothing has changed in the last five years.

My mother was the pure image of elegance and grace wherever she went. I, on the other hand, was a disgrace as a princess. At least, that is what I was told almost daily. I did not share the same beliefs as my mother. I did not believe I was worthy to marry the wealthiest bachelor, Prince Rafael Baylor of T'Lovoness.

Maybe if I had the same courtship as Mother did with Father, I would be more likely to share her beliefs in my life's goal. Her favorite bedtime story to tell me was how my father was looking for his future wife and queen. He had been dancing with another lady when he saw Mother enter the ballroom. Father stopped mid-step with his dance partner; he left her to walk across the room to claim mother as his beloved. The rest, as they say was history.

I, personally, already knew my life was not some magical fairy tale. I was not my mother. I would not be as lucky. I had eleven years to become perfect until I would be sent to live at T'Lovoness castle. When Prince Rafael Baylor turned twenty-five, it would be his turn to host The Courting Season in search of his future queen.

If I failed, my kingdom would crumble, ceasing to exist. The coffers have already begun to run dry. My kingdom's fate and salvation rests in the matrimony of my hands. If I do not secure my hand to Prince Rafael Baylor, I fear for what will become of my home.

My parents could have set their eyes on a smaller monarchy for my marriage, but when Mother dreamed, she dreamed big. She was partly why we were in this predicament with the lavish parties; the castle remodels, and all the dresses my mother had demanded over the years. If I am being completely honest, I am terrified of failing in eleven years.

Chapter One

I had spent the last two weeks of my twenty-two-year-old existence jostled around in this small, cramped, pathetic excuse of a carriage. I wished my parents would have sent me in the more luxurious one. However, they insisted they may have a need for that carriage.

This carriage was the spare. As a matter of fact, it was the servant's carriage and was only utilized when my parents required servants to attend an event with them. Aside from the exterior that matched their luxurious one, that was where the similarities ended.

The interior wood was splintered and cracked from lack of care and age. The wood held no shine, nor were there any beautifully painted designs on the interior walls like the other carriage. The seat cushions on the hard wooden bench were either lumpy or flat, depending on where I sat. The curtains must have been made from the roughest material to be found in all the kingdoms and queendoms. Whenever I moved the curtains to view the outside world, they would make me itch.

The horseshoes began to click-clock on cobblestone. Eloise, my handmaiden, bolted upright to hastily move the itchy curtains out of the way. I scrunched beside her as we took in the view. We were approaching the Kingdom of T'Lovoness.

"Finally," she sighed as her shoulders sagged with relief. I nodded with mental exhaustion in agreement. This trip was finally coming to an end.

We were beginning to pass cute little shops with bustling people. Kids began to run alongside the carriage, yelling and laughing, as onlookers started to point and talk to each other. I jerked back away from the window when the eyes belonging to a townsfolk male caught mine. Eloise dropped the curtain, rubbing her hands together.

"Probably best we don't gawk at them like they are us," she supplied sweetly to ease my embarrassment. I nodded again.

"You have been awfully quiet, coin for your thoughts?" She flicked a silver coin my way, which I barely managed to catch. I flipped it back to her immediately.

"Return the coin to keep my thoughts," I replied. Usually, I shared everything with Eloise, but my stomach was in knots. Eloise, refusing to accept my wishes, tossed it back to me.

"I insist to buy your thoughts." She smiled, daring me to give the coin back.

"How about I buy your thoughts instead?" I tossed the coin back. She caught it with ease and an amused look.

"You cannot buy my thoughts with my own coin. Stop trying to play like a T'Cudterian." She tossed it back at me. When I caught it again, I looked down at it, fiddling with the coin repeatedly in my fingers. I could not even buy anything with a silver enny. I would need at least five silver ennies to buy a simple roll from a bakery back home. Who knew how much a roll here would cost?

Sighing, I gave in to her buying my thoughts. "I am so grateful to finally be done with this journey, but scared of what is next." I flicked the silver enny coin back to her.

"That is understandable. I think we are both relieved to soon be out of this carriage." She glanced about it, wrinkling her nose, unimpressed. "Your parents could have at least given us the royal one or fixed this one up before departure." I sighed in agreement. "As for being scared, I would believe you to be a liar if you told me you weren't." She tucked the coin back into her pocket.

We heard the guards shouting as they opened the gates to Castle T'Lovoness for us to enter. Once our carriage made it through to the interior of the castle walls, they began closing the gates immediately, and the noise from the city faded along with it. I put aside my disdain for the curtains to take in the breathtaking view.

The imagery looked like something out of a painting. Everything was perfectly placed with utmost care. We were riding alongside a tall row of neatly groomed hedges with not a single leaf out of place. The cobbled roads were smooth with little to no stray bumps, and the sound of the horse's hooves danced in a melody with the whirling of the wooden carriage wheels. We began to turn a corner, and at last, the castle of Kingdom T'Lovoness came into full view.

"Oh, Mina! It's beautiful!" gasped Eloise. I nodded my head, unable to form words. I knew my Kingdom Theorines was falling more into bankruptcy, but until today, I had no way of knowing how far we had fallen. I was used to gray exterior block walls with dead vines clinging to them. Here, the walls were a pearlescent white, glimmering a soft pink, as if blushing under our gazes. Healthy green vines climbed up the towers until they peaked into a kaleidoscope of jewel tones on the roofs.

The lane was lined with young, healthy trees perfectly straight in two rows on each side. There was not a single dead branch or tree in sight. Kingdom Theorine's trees were older, sometimes dead, and I always thought it gave them a romantic, nostalgic look. The trees here were in full bloom with bursts of flowering colors between pinks, yellows, and whites; the sweetness of their scent brought a smile to my lips. Kingdom Theorines did not have flowering trees; they really did not have flowering anything. During my lessons, I had seen drawings of peonies and had desperately wished as a kid to have them growing in our gardens. To see all these flowering trees made me envious of Kingdom T'Lovoness. They probably did not even appreciate what they had.

If I could secure my hand in matrimony to Prince Rafael Baylor like Mother wanted, I would never have to leave. This would be my home, I thought giddily to myself. But the thought of Prince Rafael Baylor made me nervous. What was he like? The only rumors I ever heard about T'Lovoness Kingdom were their riches.

When Prince Rafael Baylor's grandmother, the late Queen Opal, had passed away, his parents, King Regalius and Queen Serenity, announced to pausing The Courting Seasons until their heir turned twenty-five. Their announcement had put the six monarchies into a tizzy while simultaneously making their eldest son the most anticipated, eligible bachelor on the market.

His younger, reclusive brother, Prince Killien Knox, would also join him in this Courting Season. The little bit I knew about the younger heir was he apparently did not attend many events for gossip to be collected from, and even those tidbits were said in hushed whispers from fear of his name.

The carriage pulled up to the front of the castle, where white pillar columns with ivy climbing up them, were shadowing the dark mahogany red doors. From my small carriage window, I barely managed to make out how intricately detailed the doors were; there were elaborate swirls, and a forest scene with critters carved upon each door. I could have sat before these doors for hours, marveling at the details.

As we finally came to a stop, the carriage door was opened, and a castle staff attendant offered me his hand. I passed a quick smile to Eloise that she returned. We were done with this carriage, hopefully forever. Standing up, I took the staff attendant's hand. As I stepped out of the carriage, a breeze caressed my raven black hair as if welcoming me to my new home.

"Princess Persamina Rowena of Theorines, we have been awaiting your arrival," he said indifferently.

Well, not the most incredible welcome to my new life, but I would not let it damper my mood. I nodded at him and let go of his hand, making my way to the front of the castle doors. Eloise trailed behind me, as was appropriate for a handmaiden. I was not too fond of her inability to walk by my side, but we would do what society deemed correct for the sake of appearances.

We made our way to the front stairs of the castle, my heart hammering in my ears. Breathing sharply through my nose, I placed my foot on the first step. I tried to take each step with as much elegance and grace as I could muster. I tried not to trip as I channeled my mother's teachings.

Head held high, I kept climbing until I was standing before the towering double doors. A servant stood on each side, opening the double doors simultaneously and allowing me to take the first steps into my new home.

The castle foyer took my breath away, and Eloise gasped behind me. The first thing that captured my attention were all the people located in this one room. There were dozens of servants flitting about between guests and disappearing behind doors. My eyes drifted over the other guests in the room, picking out princesses and princes with their tiaras or crowns.

"Mina, there are so many people here," Eloise whispered. I nodded my head. I had never been in a room with this many people; it was exhilarating and frightening all at once. As my vision sifted through the people, I took in the room details. There were exotic blood-red carpet runners on top of marble flooring. An imperial staircase led up to a second level, with the stairs wrapping back around towards me to indicate a third level. Cream pillars swathed in royal blue silk held up the third-level interior balcony. I gasped when I looked above and saw the magnificent chandelier hanging in the center of the room. The lights twinkled through the diamonds, sparkling against the ceiling mural that depicted what I suppose was Kingdom T'Lovoness's history.

"Mina, stop gawking and close your mouth," Eloise scolded, bumping my shoulder. I clamped my mouth shut and quickly looked at the other guests to see if anyone had seen me. My eyes landed on a prince with black hair and silver eyes, giving me a devilish smile. I stepped back, bumping into Eloise and accidentally stepping on her foot.

"Ow!" She hissed.

"Sorry," I rushed out, breaking eye contact with the stranger. I turned around to check if she was okay.

"Don't fret about me; keep walking. You're blocking the doorway, Mina." I nodded and began walking forward. The prince that had smiled at me headed my way. I glanced at Eloise.

"What do I do?" I asked, panicked.

"You curtsey and say hi," she rushed out. I was unable to ask another question as the prince stood before me.

"Hello there, Princess Persamina Rowena, you are quite lovely," he complimented with a bow. I took a step back, not anticipating he would know who I was.

Eloise hissed in my ear, "say thank you . . . and don't forget to curtsy!"

Closing my eyes, I dropped into a curtsy. "Thank you . . . Prince?" There was a long pause as I awaited his answer.

"He left Mina," Eloise replied, bored. My eyes sprung open as I glanced about, noticing we stood by ourselves.

"Where did he go?" I asked as I straightened.

"A red-haired princess dragged him off."

"You don't suppose. . ."

"No, I doubt it. Now let's move." I barely walked two steps before a servant was at my side.

"Princess, your rooms are ready; please follow me," she announced.

My new rooms were everything I always dreamed of but never had. When the servant who led me here opened the door, I was sure she had taken me to the wrong room. It was quite an embarrassing blunder as I thought to correct her until Eloise touched my arm. She reassured me that the servants here would not make mistakes for this event and to accept the room with gratitude. I graciously thanked the servant with a curtsey. The servant gave me an uncertain expression before returning to a neutral, friendly smile.

"Do you need anything else, Your Highness?" She asked. I could tell she was still uneasy with my behavior. Eloise stepped to my side, placing her hand on my left arm.

"If Princess Persamina Rowena needs anything, I will attend to her. You are free to go." I glanced at Eloise, surprised by her giving someone else orders. The servant curtsied, excusing herself. When the door clicked shut behind her, I looked over at Eloise with a raised brow.

"These T'Lovoness servants need to know that I am your

handmaiden," she bit out. I sensed a bit of jealousy, and maybe Eloise was trying to secure her place within the castle. I was not sure why, though. It was not like I would allow anyone to replace her, especially not some strange kingdom's servants.

I guided us to turn back around to face my new living quarters. The first thing I noticed about the room was the emerald green curtains hanging on the wall in contrast to the golden-painted walls. I had never seen a metallic gold wall until now, and it made me feel more like royalty than I ever had in my life.

All the sitting furniture was in hues of a light sky blue with lavender and soft yellow throw pillows. The coffee table and end tables were all a light gray coloring. Arm in arm, Eloise and I walked to check out my new bedroom. While the main room was hardwood floors with area rugs, the bedroom chambers had silver blue carpet. The walls within the bedroom were light mint green, draped with white curtains that shimmered silver.

I took in my new canopy bed. The bed itself was predominantly in creams with accents of rich shades of violets and blacks. The canopy was made of matching shades of violet as spiral spindles of oak wood held it up. There were elaborate oak dressers and a vanity to match.

We exited my bedroom to cross the hallway to Eloise's bedroom. It was not as large as mine, but nearly an identical copy. Mine had a balcony on it, while her bedroom exterior wall was against the corridor hallway.

"It's far nicer than the one back home," Eloise commented.

"I definitely could say the same for me as well."

"Well, let's get you ready for tonight." She led me back to my bedroom to stand in front of the large mirror. Eloise dropped her arm from mine to stand behind me, and she began to undo the corset lacings of my dress. She helped pull the dress over my head when it was loose enough.

"I'll send this down to get washed later on," she commented, scrunching up her nose. Neither of us had fared well from traveling, and there had not been enough funds to support us staying at an inn. We had to camp each night, and I could not risk bathing in a river for fear someone's unwanted gaze might fall upon me. She draped the soiled dress over the nearby chair in front of my writing desk. Crossing the room, she opened the armoire full of my clothes. The servants had efficiently put away my belongings before we had reached the room. I watched as she pulled out a dark blue dress. It was the one mother had picked for the first night. She claimed it was an exact match to Prince Rafael Baylor's eye color. I highly doubted he would notice, but who was I to go against what Mother deemed correct?

"Go soak in the tub; no sense in wearing this pretty thing if you are going to smell like a day-old fart." Eloise scrunched up her nose even more.

"What did you call me?" I asked, bewildered.

"You heard me; now go and git!" She bossed.

I rolled my eyes, shaking my head with a laugh, as I walked into the bathing room. It was just as luxurious as the rest of my rooms. The whole room was a pink pearlescent white from floor to ceiling. It had four pillars surrounding the bathing tub in the middle of the room, with a gilded design etched along its sides. There was already hot water steaming from the tub, and it did not take my mind much convincing to sink into it. I began lathering myself and my hair with soaps and oils until my nose was a titter from all the scents.

I stayed there until Eloise ordered me out to help me dry my hair. Once my hair was dried, she made me stand back in front of the mirror for her to dress me. Eloise lifted the dress over my head, tugging it down onto me. I began swaying, loving the way the dress shimmered as it swished back and forth.

"Hold still, Mina," Eloise ordered as she tightened the new laces on my back. The temporary relief I had felt was slowly being taken away with each yank Eloise gave.

"I cannot help it, Eloise. What do you think Prince Rafael Baylor is like?"

"If I had to guess, he probably could stand still," she replied in a huff of irritation, causing me to break out in laughter.

"No, seriously, Eloise," I prompt.

She sighed, looking up and catching my violet eyes in the mirror. She wrapped her arms around my waist and rested her chin on my shoulder, squeezing me tightly. "I am sure he will be quite smitten with you. I bet he will declare his love for you upon first sight," she teased. I rolled my eyes, trying to escape her embrace, but she held me tightly close to her as she scolded, "Uh-uh! You asked, so I shall answer, Princess."

"Oh, here we go with the princess stuff," I laughed.

"Well, are you, or are you not a princess?"

"Yes, I am a princess."

"Then I shall give you all the answers you want to hear . . . regardless of the merit of truth." She winked at me before releasing her arms from around my waist and went back to lacing me up.

"You are incorrigible, Eloise," I chided.

"Only because you are a bad influence," she replied as she tightened a part of my waist extra hard, causing me to gasp.

"Oops! Too tight?" Her voice tilted higher as she widened her eyes to give me an 'I did not mean to do that on purpose' look before we both broke out into giggles.

She finished lacing me up, leaving me to stand there to swish the dress back and forth. When I began to walk, I noticed how the lightweight layers flared out from just a subtle breeze, and if I twirled, it became even more pronounced. The dress had simple straps and a sweetheart neckline.

Regardless, Mother had picked out this dress to be worn tonight. She claimed the heir's mother, Queen Serenity, had an eye for detail. According to Mother, she would most likely take notice of my dress. However, with all the single princesses, high lord daughters, and respected merchant daughters, how would I even have a competing chance of standing out? I was nothing more than just another princess to fawn over the eldest prince.

I continued swishing back and forth, pondering how tonight would go. I wondered if the reclusive Prince Killien Knox would be in attendance. I shook my head at the notion. I should not fret about such trivial matters. I needed to focus on my mission, Prince Rafael Baylor.

<h1 style="text-align:center">Chapter Two</h1>

I was late for my first ball. I had become lost in the confusing castle hallways. Despite all the guests and servants I had encountered earlier, the corridors were empty now. When I finally found the ball, it was already in full swing, with guests mingling and dancing. I noticed a servant introducing a line of guests to The King, Queen, and one of their sons, who had silver hair matching his mother's. I noted the empty chair next to where the handsome prince stood and I assumed he was Prince Rafael Baylor, and that the vacant seat was for his brother, Prince Killien Knox. I had not the slightest idea of what either brother would have looked like and only hoped when I came face to face with the missing one that I did not pass him without respectful acknowledgment.

I took in the view of the ballroom. Massive white columns rose to the high ceilings. They were wrapped in Kingdom T'Lovoness's colors of red and gold with touches of blue weaved within. There were planters of blossoming flowers everywhere around the room. Servants were flitting about while carrying platters of wine and food.

I could smell sugary sweet desserts, especially chocolate and maybe a hint of vanilla.

The number of guests in attendance was overwhelming, it was more than the initial amount I was greeted by when I had arrived. The female's dresses made mine look drab in comparison. I began to doubt my ability to stand out. My tiara, encrusted with dark blue sapphires in gold to signify my kingdom's color, began to weigh heavily on my head as I picked out the princesses in the crowd wearing their respective tiaras. I began to note the other female guests whose heads were unadorned, deeming them as either ladies or respective merchant daughters.

I tried to remember my history lessons about the various monarchy colors, but all my studies seemed to have slipped my mind once I walked through the ballroom doors. I could not determine which princess belonged to which monarchy, and I was afraid I would make a mistake if one of them began talking to me.

It was the beginning of The Courting Season, and Kingdom T'Lovoness was hosting it for all the princes, princesses, high lords, and ladies' children to attend and find their future spouses. We were all here for the same reason as our eyes roamed to the other singles in the room. We were all here to secure our hand in matrimony, and many of us females had the same male in mind: we wanted to become the wealthiest queen.

Arranged marriage couples were present as well, I noted. They were easy to pick out from the crowd; they were all wearing matching sashes to each other. I always thought it was a silly custom for arranged couples to wear matching sashes at events until they married. But now I found it easy to pick out the couples as they mingled with other guests. They were here to show the appearance of their relationship in front of all while simultaneously forming close alliances with the other monarchies. They were already preparing for their future roles when the respective parents stepped down, and the arranged couple accepted their new titles.

I approached the dwindling line of attendees before Kingdom T'Lovoness's royals. I passed by a group of mingling princes who were all laughing, a few catching my eye and smiling, causing a warmth to spread through my body. The dark-haired prince who had talked to me earlier was amongst the group. He winked at me, and I glanced away immediately. I was not accustomed to this kind of attention.

The servant at the bottom of the stairs announced the T'Lovoness's royals to the guests before them, and I had been correct on the son standing with them being Prince Rafael Baylor. He honestly looked nothing like I anticipated. His silver hair was short with a bit of flare to it, and his eyes were as deep blue as the ocean. The closer I became to him, the more attractive I found him. Instead of wearing his Kingdom's colors, he wore a smoke-gray suit with light gray patterns weaved about it.

King Regalius had dark black hair that led into a neatly trimmed beard and mustache. He wore his kingdom's colors of blood red with elaborate gold swirls amongst the sleeves and jackets. His legs were clad in matching accent blue trousers that ended with polished ebony shoes. His crown was the most extensive and most elaborate I had ever seen in my life. So many jewels were encrusted in it, all white and sparkling brilliantly against the gold. He had various gold rings with blood-red rubies and dark sapphires worn amongst his fingers.

Queen Serenity's silver hair had been done in a half up-do; there were small braids amongst her hair as the rest fell on her shoulders and down to her midriff. She had gorgeous high cheekbones, a straight, small nose, and pert pinkish-red lips. Her crown was dwarfed next to her husband's, as it sparkled with carnelian stones sprinkled about. Her golden dress had red swirls playing their way from the bottom up to her waist and resumed swirling down her long sleeves. She was quite beautiful.

Prince Rafael Baylor made slight eye contact with me before his attention was turned toward the gaggle of gorgeous girls approaching him. They were not princesses by their lack of a crown or tiara upon their heads. They must be daughters of high lords or respective merchants. I sighed to myself. It was only wishful thinking Prince Rafael Baylor would see me and instantly fall in love like Father had with Mother. I began questioning how an alliance with my kingdom could benefit Kingdom T'Lovoness.

The closer I approached the throne, the more uneasy I became. My parents did not give me the same fighting chance as the rest of these females. From the snippets of conversations I heard around me, everyone sounded like they knew each other quite well. Yet, I did not know anyone here.

My breathing became a little shallow as I realized no longer anyone else was in front of me. Whatever the girls had said must have annoyed Prince Rafael Baylor because he looked away, rolling his eyes as he waved them off in a huff.

They darted past me in a flurry, trying to keep their tears from falling onto their beet-red cheeks. This did not help build my confidence to talk to him, but I did not foresee a better opportunity to be introduced as his gaze fell upon me standing before him.

I approached him, my heart thundering in my chest, trying to remind myself to keep breathing. I was going to trip or stumble. I just knew it. *Breathe, Mina, breathe.* I managed to not physically embarrass myself yet . . .

A servant stood at the base of the marble platform, prattling off introductions. I cursed myself out; I should have paid attention to who the three girls were before me. I heard the servant begin my introduction, "Princess Persamina Rowena of Theorines." I curtsied in front of the throne.

"Prince Rafael Baylor," I timidly said to get his attention. I glanced up through my sooty black lashes to find him staring down at me over the goblet he was drinking from. He did not respond to release me from my curtsy.

How long would he make me stay this way? Thankfully, I had been prepared for this. Mother made me curtsey for an hour sometimes if I did not do it properly. I stole another glance up, and his goblet was now being turned various ways in his hand as he continued to stare down at me. I could not tell if he was bored, disgruntled, annoyed, or intrigued by his stoic expression. I decided not to go with intrigued because his eyes held no warmth.

A minute ticked by, and I was still not released from the curtsey. I wish I could say I was not starting to become self-conscious, but I could hear giggling as others took notice of me.

It was one thing to curtsey for an hour in front of Mother and passing servants that I knew; it was a whole other experience to do it for over a minute in front of strangers.

As another minute passed by, I again stole a glance to see the prince had a smirk on his face. This probably was not going to be good for me. As slowly as possible, I took as deep a breath as this tight dress would allow at this angle. The familiar ache in my calves began to form from the strain. I suppose smirking was a better sign than someone with an unreadable expression.

Another minute, the tension in my calves caused my legs to shake slightly. I began to feel myself sweat from the warmth of my dress and strained muscles. I could feel the eyes on me, the giggling and whispering increasing. Another stolen glance to see the prince was giving me a toothy grin, but his eyes barely held a trace of warmth or happiness in them.

I realized I was nothing but entertainment to him, a plaything at this point, and we did not even know each other. Even though it angered me, I could not fail. *Suck it up, I cannot go home this soon.* King Regalius and Queen Serenity's gaze had joined their sons looking down upon me.

"Rise," he finally commanded. There was a twinge of humor in it. His voice was not quite as deep as I had expected, but he sounded like someone who was used to being obeyed by the way power exuded from the command. I rose slowly, my calves protesting from the new movement; breathing became easier as the corset no longer dug into my abdomen. My lower back began forming a new throbbing pain from the muscles that had been used as tension began forming in my shoulders at the base of my neck. Despite all of this, I kept my face slightly turned down to not show disrespect.

"Who are you, and look at me when you speak." I was not anticipating this type of treatment and almost faltered, but I quickly caught myself as I looked at him, feeling a new warmth rushing through my body and hoping my cheeks were not too flushed. He never even heard what the servant had said when introducing me.

"Your Highnesses, I am Princess Persamina Rowena, daughter of King Gideon and Queen Lydia from Kingdom Theorines."

"Ah, you are The Princess they sent. *The Locked Away Princess*," he tacked on. I tried not to ball my fist at the comment. A comment I had heard often enough while I was supposed to be locked away in my room when guests were in the castle. Sometimes, Eloise used to sneak me out temporarily when we knew it would be safe. I never had been caught by my mother, but I did hear my fair share of people calling me The Locked Away Princess. They would muse over whether I was as beautiful as Mother boasted about or if I was hideous. So hideous that my parents kept me locked away for the kingdom's safety; no one wanted an ugly princess. Many speculated that my parents were going to arrange a marriage for me to be stuck with some unfortunate soul.

"Yes, Your Highness, I am she," I replied politely, dismissing the thought despite my embarrassment.

"Peculiar." He stroked his smooth chin. "Your parents have kept you locked up for all never to see, but yet here you are during *my* courting season. You were not even allowed to attend their parties if the rumors were true." He took low blow after low blow at me. My focus shifted from my red cheeks to not allowing any tears even to form. The crowd that had been whispering and giggling during my curtsey was all hushed as they hung onto every word, savoring every detail that I speculated would be gossiped about later on.

"Yes, it is true, Your Highness." My voice thankfully did not crack, but I gritted my teeth nonetheless.

"Well, then . . ." His eyes swept over me, and I felt vulnerable like he could see right through me. He made me feel naked with the way his eyes roamed over my body, ". . . I hope you enjoy yourself after a lifetime of being hidden away. I must admit you are far prettier than the rumors suggested." He smiled again, and I almost believed it might have been genuine. The people within earshot started whispering to one another as the fans in their hands picked up speed from the juicy gossip.

I bowed my head. "Thank you, Prince Rafael Baylor." Feeling that I had been dismissed, I did another curtsey. "King Regalius, Queen Serenity," I said out of respect and began to make my retreat before he spoke again, "you are most welcome, Princess Persamina Rowena."

I turned back at him, flushed for dismissing myself by the assumption that he had been done with me. He waved his hand lazily, smiling in a way that assured me I did no harm and to go enjoy myself. My heart fluttered, and I quickly curtsied again before walking away with my head held high into the crowd of people. I wanted to scurry, to run away with giddiness, but I needed to keep it together and not embarrass myself or my kingdom. I needed to stay calm and collected.

I found myself at the beverage table, not realizing I had aimlessly walked to this side of the room. I told myself that it would be okay; a drink could calm my nerves. I went to grab a goblet that had already been prefilled with wine when another hand also grabbed the same one. The stranger's hand covered my own. I jumped, startled, as my eyes followed the hand on mine, up the arm to the owner's face.

I could find no warmth in the stranger's face; his cold green eyes glared into mine. I tried to take a step back, but my hand was still trapped within his. His gaze traveled down my body and back up to my face. I was conscious of how new I was, but did everyone have to do this?

He had not released his hand from on top of mine, and I would be trapped by his grip until he did unless I had wanted to make a scene. Which I certainly did not after that extended long curtsy.

He had shaggy black hair that was adorned with a simple black crown, indicating he was a prince. I could not recall in any of my history lessons of a kingdom with a black crown, leaving this prince shrouded in mystery. He was clean-shaven and was decorated in very rich black clothing. He continued staring at me intently as I finished taking in his details. *Who was he?*

"Um, may I have my hand back, Prince . . . ?" This was becoming a tad awkward, and I did not need to add to the rumors that were probably already beginning to circulate about me. If there was to be any rumor I wanted to spread about me with a prince, it better be with Prince Rafael Baylor and not this handsome mystery prince with his cold green eyes while being shrouded in complete black.

He released his hand as if I had burned him without saying a word. I watched as he grabbed a different goblet and stormed off; guests began parting out of his way in fear before they looked to see where he had come from. Their eyes landed on me. Just lovely for them to see me standing here and how strange his reaction and their reaction to him were all at the same time. I could barely comprehend the interaction before a girl with straight, icy blonde hair was at my side, beginning a conversation.

"My, oh me, oh my! You sure are going to be the talk tomorrow," she chirped out. She had a very high-pitched voice. She was one of those flawless beauties, with blonde hair, blue eyes, and a splash of freckles across her high cheekbones. Her tiara was silver with inlaid sapphire stones. She was adorned in a silver dress with ice-blue filigree weaved intricately throughout the skirt, growing denser around the edges. She reminded me of an ice princess.

"Hi, I'm Princess Iryse Skyvien of Hayverton, and you are about to become the most popular and hated girl here." She gave me a knowing look like a cat who had just eaten the canary. I gave her a puzzled look in return, unsure of what she was hinting about.

"Princess Persamina Rowena, first off, no one knew what you looked like. You are a knockout," she complimented me, "so it puts all these vicious vipers at unease." I secretly preened under her compliment. "Then, to add insult to injury, The Prince called you pretty to back it up." She flicked her eyes at The Prince and then back to me before leaning in to whisper, "*he. Does. Not. Compliment. Anyone.* And you just took his brother, The Reclusive Prince's drink." She giggled, my heart dropping into my stomach. That was Prince Killien Knox, the second in line for the throne, and I had not the faintest idea.

"If I were you," Princess Iryse Skyvien prattled on, paying no mind to my reaction to this news. "I would be sleeping with one eye open." She winked before sauntering off. I could not determine if she was a friend or foe, and I guess only time would tell. I sighed to myself.

The Reclusive Prince. . . the spare. From the little bit I had gathered about him, he rarely was seen. There were rumors that he had a nasty personality. There was speculation that since Queen Serenity was from Queendom Grewt'en, where they valued the meaning of a name to hold weight in a name bearer's life, that she purposely named him with the word 'kill' in his name. I speculated she did it on purpose to be a protector for his older brother, and of course, as a prince of the wealthiest kingdom, he could get away with it all.

As my mother was giving me lessons on how to woo the prince heir, she was also instructing me to stay away from his brother. *"He will become your brother-in-law, but do not cross him,"* Mother would drill into me. I had just taken his drink. Would that be grounds for crossing him? Oh, dear me, I may have failed on the first night. If I made an enemy of The Reclusive Prince, did that mean I had eliminated myself from the competition? I fiddled with the goblet in my hands as I pondered this new problem of mine.

The rest of the evening blurred together. A countless number of people introduced themselves to me, and I lost track of names to faces. The prince who had winked at me when I arrived had not come up to talk to me, and I wondered if he would stay surrounded in mystery. Being the isolated princess caused all the nosey people to come out of the woodwork, it seemed. Everyone wanted to have a chance to talk to the girl who had been locked away all her life. I began to feel quite overwhelmed.

While my mother taught me names, relations, and countries, I never had a face to put to the name. Everything became one big jumble in my mind, and all I could hope was that they would wear their respective monarchies' colors on their crowns and tiaras. The only ones I could most likely continue to place by location would be the high lords, ladies, and their children. They all wore either a pin or had their family crest, which included kingdom location, on their attire. Everyone would know who I was; I just needed to navigate that I did not know who they were.

I caught glances from the prince heir here and there throughout the evening, but he never looked at me long enough. A couple of times, I saw him give a small smile when we caught each other's eyes, causing my heart to flip. I began to fantasize that he would cross the ballroom to talk to me, but of course, he did not leave the throne. Even though I desperately wished he would. His brother's chair remained empty.

Already, the guests who came to talk with me claimed I was marked by each brother. They determined who I was marked by depending on which event they either witnessed or heard about. I was completely surprised by how open these people were, not even the slightest bit afraid of being overheard. While everyone was happy to talk openly, nobody had asked me to participate in a dance.

I remained with my back against the wall, watching the others dance until King Regalius announced the ball had concluded. I followed the crowd, trying to navigate my way back to my room. After a few almost-failed attempts at opening the wrong room door, I finally managed to find the correct one. Thankfully, no one was in any of the unlocked rooms when I had guessed if it was mine or not.

Upon seeing Eloise waiting up for me, I relayed everything that had happened while she helped me undress before finally crawling into bed. I was ready to see what the following day would bring me.

Chapter Three

I awoke in a panic. This was not my bedroom; this was the most comfortable bed of my life. I had never slept this well before. It took me a moment for the memories from the previous day to flash through my mind. I was finally in Kingdom T'Lovoness. If I recall the itinerary given to me upon arrival to my room yesterday, I was invited to tea after breakfast today.

The itinerary stated that today's breakfast would be served in my room. The following days, I could choose whether to join in a communal breakfast with everyone in the banquet hall or have it served in my rooms. Growing up, I had breakfast served frequently in my bedroom. I had rarely been invited to dine in the banquet hall with Mother and Father; there was almost always someone visiting at any given time, and Mother did not want anyone to see me until the time was right. Tomorrow, I wanted to join in a communal breakfast. There would be no more meals in my rooms from here on out.

I was under the assumption that the tea would be a meet and

greet as I took a bite of my toast. Eloise worked my hair into intricate braids of various sizes without hindering the true length of my locks. A Theorinian's hair was their pride and must never be cut. To be cut was a great dishonor amongst my people. Eloise's creation was more lavish in style than I was accustomed to. I never had an inkling that she had the talent to do my hair like this; she had never done so in the past.

She claimed she wanted me to stand out at the tea party when I asked about it. I was beyond grateful for her confidence in me as she pushed me to wear this gorgeous lilac dress. It had more layers to it than I could count. The tulle layers were elaborate with what looked to be diamond dust as it sparkled in the light. She finalized my look with a simple single pearl necklace on a gold chain. I truly felt like an elegant and beautiful princess ready to face the world as I swished my dress left and right in the mirror to catch all the twinkling sparkles.

I hurried down to the tearoom alone; I felt exceptionally excited and nervous to meet everyone. I officially would be meeting the other princesses and attending girls. My main goal was to begin forming alliances with the other monarchy's daughters, but secretly, I hoped to form new friendships. As a servant, Eloise could not attend these, and it would be nice to have a friend to socialize with, giggle at various things, and gush over Prince Rafael Baylor. Even though I knew most of us were each other's competition, I still hoped to find some form of kinship.

I caught up to the other princesses and ladies milling into the tearoom. Many were talking in hush whispers to each other and giggling. I tried to show interest in joining their conversations. However, they did not make eye contact, indicating that I could participate in their conversation. *Brush it off, Mina,* better luck while sitting down at a table.

I scanned the room and saw a few open seats at a table where a red-haired princess with elaborate braids and a blonde princess with wavy hair sat. They seemed friendly as I made my way over to one of the available chairs at their table. I curtsied before sitting down in an empty chair. Both girls were wearing tiaras and smiled at me.

I decided to politely introduce myself, "Hello, I am Princess Persamina Rowena of Theorines." Smiling, I waited for them to introduce themselves.

Both girls did a quick, non-discreet look at each other before the redhead decided to take the lead in introducing herself, "Hello, Princess Persamina Rowena; I am Princess Regina Isadora of Grewt'en. A pleasure to meet you." She had drawled out *Isadora* in a sophisticated accent, which made me curious about why she paid more attention to her middle name than her first name. She wore a mint green dress, but upon closer inspection, I realized it was not just mint green. The layers of tulle made it look mint in the lighting, but in the shadowy parts, it was a more profound, almost grass green. I noticed how the tulle layered between greens, whites, and even a few hints of blacks to achieve the color effects that shimmered as the light danced off the sparkles sewn about. The top half of her dress was satin with crystals and pearls sewn in to create an elaborate swirl pattern up her front. She nodded her head before looking at the blonde to introduce herself.

"I am Princess Olivia Jade of Shediwark; nice to meet you," Olivia had the same fake smile as Regina, and I wondered if I had made a mistake by sitting here. She had a light pink dress on that complimented Regina's. It was not as elaborate, but it was still pretty. It lacked the pearls that created swirls on Regina's dress, nor did it have the multiple strategically placed layers of tulle to create colors to trick the eye, but it had sparkling rhinestones laced within it that caught when the light hit them.

"Nice to meet you both," I replied. I did not know what to say next and began to admire the porcelain teacups. There were small scenery images on each cup depicting what looked to be a story. My cup had a princess; she was dressed in a delicate blue and white gown. Each one of her hands had been claimed by a prince in a mask on each side of her. The three of them were walking down a stone path in the woods.

The cup on the table in the empty spot beside me depicted the same girl looking out the window with a candlelit next to an open book, but her eyes were not even reading the pages as she daydreamed out the window with her chin propped up on her hand. Personally, I would rather be reading the book and enjoying the breeze of the open window. I could not see the scene of the cup that accompanied the other empty chair, which was rather disappointing.

Regina must have taken notice of the teacup imagery as she lifted hers up. "Why does mine have a girl in a black dress like she's in mourning? How dreary!" Regina dramatically pouted. She reached over, grabbed the cup from the unclaimed chair, and swapped it out with her original one.

"Well, I think the mourning dress is more pretty than mine," chimed Olivia. She grabbed Regina's mourning teacup and swapped it. When Oliva set her original cup down, I could finally see the image the cup depicted. It showed a very battered woman with a man in the background and a jug of what looked to be ale in his hand. Definitely not the prettiest cup on the table, but it was hard to look away from.

"What does your cup image show now?" I asked Regina since I still had not seen it. She gave me an expression as if she could not believe someone would show interest in these cups, as if it was an inconvenience that I had asked. She rolled her eyes, and I tried not to slide down my chair.

"It is just a cup," she giggled but turned to show me anyway. On the porcelain sat the girl smiling on what looked to be her wedding day; she was wearing a giant white dress, and there were arches with white doves flying in the background. It was a stunning scene, probably the prettiest on this table.

"The artist did amazing work on these cups," I admiringly said as Regina quickly whirled the image back to her and set it on the table.

"Oh! Why thank you," chimed in a frilly voice as the chair with the cup of the daydreaming girl was pulled out. "My father is the artist behind them, and I helped on a few." Smiled a mousy brown-haired girl with flawless, gorgeous skin. She was beaming, which made it harder to look away from her beauty. Were all these girls just naturally knock-outs?

"They are quite gorgeous," I whispered in awe to meet the artist's daughter. She must have been a lady; I did not know of any kings that took on a skill like painting or pottery. I noted the absence of a tiara or crown on her head.

"Thank you. They were a very special request tea set by The Queen." She winked at me as she looked at her seat's cup image and chuckled to herself.

"Is something funny?" I inquired. Regina and Olivia were involved in their own conversation and completely ignored us. I was getting the feeling that those two were longtime friends.

"Oh, nothing really." The girl waved her hand to dismiss the thought. "By the way, I am Lady Rachelle Mortese of House Wandern," she supplied with a friendly smile still plastered on her face.

"I am Princess Persamina Rowena of Theorines," I responded. Her smile faltered a bit, and I wondered what I had said wrong.

"Oh." Her eyes scanned me up and down as her head cocked to the side, and her friendly smile turned into a sneer. "You are *that* princess," she snipped; her tone caught Regina and Olivia's attention as they turned back into our conversation.

"I beg your pardon?" I asked, unsure where this was going. Rachelle looked down her nose at me with complete disgust on her face.

"Your parents owe my father a great deal of money for his artwork," she spat out. All her ladylike pretenses had dropped. I recoiled back a bit in my seat. I had no idea what she was talking about.

"I am sorry, I am unaware of my parent's business ordeals," I tried to reply in the most diplomatic tone that my mother had taught me when it came to their business transactions.

"No?" she scoffed, unbelieving of me. "Sure is a pretty dress you have on; I wonder if the dressmaker was even paid."

"Oh! That is right, you are from the *poor* kingdom." Regina laughed.

"Think she will steal the teacups to sell?" chimed Olivia. Now, I really wanted to sink into my chair until I disappeared. Unfortunately, I knew that would be unladylike and highly unlikely to happen, but I could not just change tables. I glanced around the room, and all the other chairs were spoken for aside from the last empty chair beside me. I was going to be trapped until the tea ceremony was over.

"Oh, I do not think she would resort to theft. That is direct treason to the kingdom," giggled Regina. It was going to be a very, very long hour.

In my lap, under the table, I began to twist around the rings on my fingers I wore. I did not have a handkerchief to fiddle with, and I did not want to wrinkle my dress for all to see when I finally stood up to escape.

"So, what does a poor princess do for fun? Play the role of

servant to her parents?" chortled Regina, causing the other two to laugh as well. I am sure from the surrounding tables, it looked like our table was having a fun time, but it was anything but. I also hoped the surrounding tables could not hear what was being said.

"Oh, do you think she wears an apron to serve them tea?" added Olivia as the current servants came out and began to pour our tea. Rachelle did not add anything as the other two kept piggybacking off of each other, the jabs continuing to pile on me more and more. Rachelle sat there throwing me hateful glares as if I was the reason my parents had not paid her father. I had no involvement with their financial deals, but yet I was being punished for it.

The tables surrounding us were tittering with laughter and warmth. Oh, how I wish I could be at a different table, but then again, maybe this was my fate. Perhaps regardless of which table I went to, I would receive similar treatment. There were more lords and merchant daughters here than there were princesses. How many people could my parents possibly have not paid that were in this very room? Had I been sent to enemy territory? What did Princess Iryse Skyvien call them? Vicious Vipers? Did she know something I did not? I began to feel uncomfortably warm.

Sighing to myself, I let go of the hope for friendship in this new environment. I sat there quietly, my hands becoming raw from the constant fiddling as I began to eavesdrop on the surrounding tables. I began to hear about the outstanding tutors that certain princesses had and how some ladies had gone to certain locations for a family vacation. All the things I have always dreamed of doing but was never allowed to do. Their happiness and smiles caused an ache in my chest.

I tried to soothe the ache while giving my fiddling hands a break as I reached for my teacup. The three at my table had begun to talk amongst themselves, shutting me out. I wondered if the owner of the empty chair would have been just as cruel as them. I guess I will never know.

The green tea was sweet with hints of blueberry in it. I honestly did not mind it as I reached for a pastry from the platter to nibble on. Flavor burst onto my taste buds from the fresh fruit jam on top to the flake soft breading underneath. Was this kingdom magical to have their food be this delicious compared to what was served back home?

As the time dragged on, the three almost seemed to completely forget I was there. Every so often, they would work a jab into their conversation to throw at me, but otherwise, I enjoyed the tea and pastries to myself.

The tea ceremony was coming to an end as the others were beginning to leave their tables. I attempted to make a hasty escape, but in my clumsiness, I bumped my knee right into the table. Pain shot up my leg from impact; I tried to maintain my composure as my eyes found Rachelle. She quirked an eyebrow at me, and the other two princesses tried to hide their laugh behind their hands. I quickly looked back at the princesses and ladies leaving with the intent of following suit.

"Oh, Princess Persamina Rowena," came Regina's sing-songy voice. Cringing, I looked back reluctantly. "Seems you spilled your tea." She nodded down at my dress, and I followed her gaze to find the dark tea stain bleeding along the silk of the fabric. I could not believe I ruined this dress. It would take Eloise forever to remove the stain if she could.

I did not respond as I clenched my jaw. Tears pricked the back of my eyes as I tried to maintain my composure. I walked away from the table to join the group leaving. I tried blending in, hoping no one would look down and notice the stain. Simultaneously, I was trying to be mindful not to bump into another girl's dress and cause theirs to stain as well. Only one of us should be this misfortunate, and I did not want an innocent bystander to have their dress ruined on my account. Nor did I want another vicious viper after me.

By the time I reached the door to leave, the tears were fighting to spill. I just needed to escape back to my room. As I emerged into the hallway, I managed to slip out of the group, and as hastily as possible, I made my way to my corridor. I kept my head down to avoid making eye contact with anyone I passed in the hallway. My corridor was thankfully empty and quiet. I forgot all my princess manners as I took off in a run with tears streaming down my face towards my door.

The door to the room before mine opened; I did not have time to stop as I collided right into Prince Killien Knox.

"Oof!" I let out as I smacked right into his chest.

"My apologies, Prince Killien Knox!" I sobbed as I stepped back and tried to dart around him. But my attempts were futile as his hand wrapped around my arm. Gasping, I looked at his hand.

"Are you okay?" He quietly asked in a deep voice. His voice was not completely void of warmth but almost as if there was tenderness. It made it difficult to keep myself from sobbing harder as the tears streamed down my face. I shook my head as an indication for my answer. I tried to hide my face with my hands. I didn't want him to see the tears.

"Is there anything I can do to . . . help you?" He asked, uncertain. I slid my hands from my eyes to rest on my cheeks, looking up at his concerned face. Biting my lip, I shook my head. I was unsure if I should try to escape his grip or stay because he was a prince of this kingdom.

"You are Princess Persamina Rowena, right?" he asked uncomfortably, trying to make small talk as he shifted on his feet.

With a shaking voice, I nodded and replied, "Mina, call me Mina." All these formal titles had me worn out. I just wanted someone more than Eloise to call me Mina here. I just wanted some familiarity. Rarely did anyone ever utilize my full name while home. If Mother were around, they would address me as simply Princess Persamina. If Mother were not nearby, then they would call me Mina, the way I preferred it. Here, within a span of two days of hearing my full birth name come out of everyone's mouth, it was too formal, too cold, and too stiff. I would take just a smidge of someone else calling me Mina without all the formalities.

"Knox." I looked at him curiously as he supplied, "I like to be called Knox." He gave me a partial smile, and I returned it. My eyes were still slightly burning from the tears, but at least they had stopped falling. I did not understand why, but for some reason, I was not afraid of him. Despite the rumors that surrounded him, he was being friendly. A bubble of hope for friendship began to rise within me.

"Knox," I repeated.

"Mina," he responded. He still had a hold of my arm, and I glanced at it again. He took notice and let go of my arm instantly. "Ah, sorry. I will let you be." He bowed and then stepped around me towards the way I had just escaped from.

I watched him go until he was out of sight before hurrying to my room. I opened the door and slammed it shut behind me. I gave Eloise a fright as she jumped up from lying on the couch.

"Oh! Mina, you –" She took in my state. "– what happened?" she rushed to my side at once, wiping away the drying tears. New tears began to form as I recounted everything that had occurred and apologized profusely for the stain on my dress.

"Don't worry about the tea stain; I am sure I can get it out." She inspected it, turning the fabric this way and that. I could see her mind was already problem-solving how to remove it.

"Eloise?" I was afraid to ask the question, but I had to know the answers.

"Yes, Mina?" She was still inspecting the stain, and I could tell her attention was not entirely focused on our conversation.

"Was my wardrobe even paid for?" I asked, looking at the fabric bunched up in my lap, thinking back to the snide comment the girls had said. Was someone starving because of empty promises to pay the fee?

"In a sense, Mina, yes it was," Eloise's voice became quiet.

"What does that even mean?" I pushed.

"Many of the servants were sent to do labor for the seamstress in exchange."

"Were . . . you?" I was afraid to know the answer with how quiet her voice had become and how she was not looking at me. This was not her usual playful self.

"No need to worry about it. It-it's in the past." Eloise said with a sad smile on her face.

"Eloise, you need to tell me the truth." I leaned forward, taking both her hands in mine, forcing her to drop the stained fabric.

"Yes," her quiet voice became quite bitter.

"What happened?" I asked softly. Eloise turned her head, staring at the door, not saying a word. "Eloise," I pushed.

"If we made a mistake . . . no, just." I could tell she was struggling with her words. I was in a conundrum to push her to tell me or wait for her to be ready. I worried about what she was going to say; we have never had problems telling each other things prior. What could it be?

Eloise did not stop staring at the door as she whispered, "I always thought your mother was cruel with her abuse, but the seamstress . . . I had never seen a woman take joy in hitting another human being with a cane . . ." My heart tightened at what my friend was saying. " . .

. her eyes gleamed with happiness with every hit. Sometimes, she would draw blood from hitting us so hard." I sucked in a breath, wanting to interrupt but waiting for her to continue. The room began to swirl. "We were barely allowed to sleep, and I hope I never have to return to that woman's shop." When there was a long enough pause, and I felt that Eloise had finished telling me, I finally spoke up.

"When did this happen, Eloise?" She was always with me; I was confused about how this could have escaped my notice; tears were beginning to form in my eyes.

"Remember when I went to visit family?" She finally looked away from the door, giving me a partial smile with a slight shrug of her shoulder.

"No . . ." I squeezed her hands, and tears began rolling down my cheeks as the room started to spin more. She had come back happy and smiling; when I commented, she seemed a little off; she had told me it was just exhaustion from all the traveling and nothing more to be concerned about. "Why did you keep this a secret from me?" If I had known I would have done something about it, I would have . . . what could I have done against my mother? Mother had sent Eloise there; how could I have even protected my own friend?

"Because we need you to marry a wealthy prince," she replied, her eyes darting back to the door for a brief second. I felt she was not telling me the whole truth.

"What else, Eloise? What else are you not telling me?" My voice was barely more than a whisper, afraid to know what more there could be.

"My papa is weak, and we need more money to help him become better," she paused, looking back to the door before continuing, "and my mama can only do so much side work from the other servants and sometimes . . . at the local bar in the village nearby."

"Are my parents not paying your family enough?"

"In food and shelter, they are, without any real coins, we are all forced to stay. There is no chance of ever leaving without coins for passage." She had not stopped looking at the door when she said it with vehemence.

"Have you been forced all your life to be my maid and now to be here with me?" The pain started racing through me at the thought that Eloise, whom I had called my best friend, was actually doing it against her wishes. *Had my whole life been a lie? Did I truly not have any friends?*

Who would want to be my friend if they were forced to do it while their family and actual friends suffered because my parents refused to pay them? They were all trapped within the castle of Theorines, just like I was. The only difference was they were forced to serve their king and queen like slaves for food and shelter, while I was forced under the same people to be the perfect child, the perfect princess.

Eloise instantly locked eyes with me. "Absolutely not!" She squeezed my hands tightly. "You are my friend, and I am happy to be here to tell my family the stories I gleaned from our stay. Not to mention, you cannot be blamed when you were unaware of your parent's misgivings. You have always been so kind to all of us; we cannot blame you."

"We?" I prompted her, my curiosity growing as all my doubts about never having a true friend began to fade.

"All the servants at Castle Theorines," she supplied, "ask anyone there; they love you." She smiled. It was becoming difficult to breathe.

This mission was no longer as simple as it seemed. There was more that rode on me needing to marry Prince Rafael Baylor. My people needed me to fix my parent's mistakes. I needed to change my way of thinking; the people of Theorines were far more important than just me marrying a prince. If my kingdom had any chance of survival, I would need to secure the heir's hand in matrimony. This was not about wiping my parent's debts; this was to prevent a form of slavery amongst my people.

The next time I saw my parents, I would ask them about the current state of affairs that was happening in the Kingdom of Theorines. I needed to know what went wrong and why they left me in the dark this whole time. Bitterness filled me; they threw me into another kingdom to become surrounded by vicious vipers.

Maybe I could not fix it right away, and perhaps I had little right with only being the princess. But maybe, just maybe, if I could secure my hand in marriage to Prince Rafael Baylor, I could add stipulations to where some of the money went.

Chapter Four

"My precious Persamina, one day you will be queen of all the monarchies." My mother smiled as she brushed my hair in front of the mirror. Mother said only she could brush it because anyone else would ruin it, and fixing it would take a long time. Time that would encroach onto my princess lessons, and we could not allow that.

I looked at my mother's serene smile reflected in the mirror. Her silky fawn hair was braided up into an elegant style, while my plain black hair was straight without a single braid or even a curl. Since Mother had married Father, she had grown her hair out like the Theorines's way; while hers was not as long as anyone else her age, it still was long. I knew one day mine would be longer.

"You will be a beautiful queen, Mina." Smiled my best friend Eloise, and I smiled back at her before her head snapped to the left, and she fell backward from the crack of my mother's hand.

"That is Princess Persamina to you!" My mother had abandoned brushing my hair and was towering over Eloise with her hand raised in the air, ready to strike again.

"Mama! Tell me of your courtship with Daddy!" I rushed out, trying to put eagerness in my voice. I tried to divert her attention back to me. I watched her hand waver in the air before finally returning to her side, my panic subsiding. She stared down her nose at Eloise, who was holding her reddening cheek while fighting back tears. Mother turning back to me with brush in hand began to resume brushing my hair. She started to recount the story.

I glanced at Eloise, not paying attention to my mother's voice, I made eye contact with her. I gave a slight nod, that she returned. Her tears were now running down her cheeks, and her lip wobbled. She slowly rose and escaped out of my bedroom unnoticed by Mother.

I spent the rest of yesterday in my room with Eloise. This morning, I chose to have breakfast served in my room, not ready to interact with the other females. When it came time for tea, I decided to leave my room. While wandering the castle, I noticed even the cats here were more beautiful than the ones back home. Our castle cats were sleek and a tad flighty. They were more interested in finding their next meal than being in the company of humans. The ones here walked softly with dignity and had gorgeous shiny coats. They were found lounging around amongst many of the common areas and did not scurry away if you petted them.

I found myself having a hard time not petting them constantly. Rarely could I pet the ones back home due to how flighty they were, and Mother would reprimand me for how undignified it was for a princess to be chasing cats around. I grew up longingly staring at them, wishing one would befriend me.

Unfortunately, that never happened, and now I had a plethora, willingly to be petted, but I needed to be a princess in this foreign kingdom. That, however, did not stop me from petting them secretly when I knew no one was around. I could only hear the scolding my mother would be giving me if she was here and caught me.

I sat in the rose garden by myself with a beautiful, fluffy orange cat on my lap. I was elated even if I knew Eloise would have a time removing these orange hairs later from my dress.

I took in this gorgeous garden. There were rose paths everywhere, with a variety of white benches sprinkled about strategically for guests that sat on them to look like they were perfectly placed for a painting. The path was inlaid with a pinkish-red brick, making this place look all the more like a fairy tale. The tearoom had a terrace that led into the rose garden. Currently, all the outdoor tea tables were in view from where I was sitting. I could see a few of the other princesses, like Regina and Olivia, sipping tea on the terrace. I cast my gaze downward, hoping they did not notice me.

"Do you like the cats here?" A charming female voice asked. I looked up to see Queen Serenity standing before me with servants holding an umbrella over her as others fanned her. I panicked. Did I stand up to curtsey with the orange cat in my arms? Did I drop the cat as I stood? I wasn't practiced in this form of royal manners.

"Queen Serenity," I gasped.

"No, need to get up." She smiled sweetly, seeming to read my thoughts. She continued, "Pumpking will not enjoy it much,"

"Pump-king?" I became confused as my eyebrows furrowed. Queen Serenity dipped her head, indicating the orange cat on my lap.

"That is Pumpking, he is quite friendly and lazy, but he is one of my favorites." She looked fondly at the cat, who paid no mind to her.

"He is becoming one of my favorites as well," I replied, trying to form a bond or even some form of a relationship with Queen Serenity and, hopefully, my future mother-in-law.

"They say there is magic in cats, and if you are his favorite, he will grant you a wish," Queen Serenity continued onward. A children's story that one of the elderly maids would tell me in hushed secrets. Mother dismissed them as superstitions and did not want my head filled with them, but I desperately hoped they were not. I wanted a palace cat back home to befriend me and grant me a wish; as a child, it probably would have been wasted on me.

"I have heard similar things, Queen Serenity." I smiled. Queen Serenity paused.

"Just do not spoil him too much, or he will like you more than me, Princess Persamina Rowena." She laughed, winking at me before continuing her walk with her servants following close at her heel.

I watched her go while still absent-mindedly petting Pumpking. I never would have thought that Queen Serenity would know who I was. There were so many of us here, and aside from the initial entrance introductions from two days ago, I had not talked to Queen Serenity once since arriving. The only thing I had done thus far was that excruciating long and very embarrassing curtsey. Warmth flooded my face as I relived the memory.

I wondered if Queen Serenity took the time to learn all the princesses' names. Maybe even all the guests that were staying in her palace? But that would be quite an exhausting feat. I imagined she had more important tasks at hand than learning everyone's name, especially mine. My heart warmed that I was not just a nameless princess in her mind and that her favorite palace cat just happened to be on my lap when she was passing by.

Queen Serenity was not originally from T'lovoness. She had been born and raised in Grewt'en, like Princess Regina, where some still believed that names held weight. Regina may not have had a name like Queen Serenity regarding what traits a person should inherit, but it gave her a little more leeway on how she could act. *Oh! Maybe that is why she emphasized her middle name, Isadora; it sounded closer to sounding like she is adored with how she had said it. That made more sense.*

Regina's mother, Queen Fairness, ruled while surrounded by her consort of lovers. The Grewt'en Queen had many children, but the only three attending The Courting Seasons this year were Regina and then Regina's two brothers, Montgomery Victory and Percival Chivalry. The Queen did not need to marry as long as she produced heirs. She did not need to name her children's sire either, due to it being encouraged to have multiple partners.

Queendom Grewt'en had fascinated me as a child, but Mother was highly against me learning about it. She quite disdained the place, and I never understood why. They were the only current ruling queendom, and I often wondered what it would be like to live there? Women are in charge, and males have less power in the marriage. *Maybe that was why Regina had such a chip on her shoulder?*

Now that I thought back to Mother's lessons, Regina would be the next to rule for her queendom. Her brothers may be older, but since she was born a daughter that gave her the birthright to the throne. If Queen Fairness only had sons, then it would have come down to whoever her eldest son married to be the next queen.

That meant Regina could not be here for Prince Rafael Baylor because he had his own kingdom to rule when he inherited his throne. Regina was here for either a prince who was not an heir, a duke, or a lord. I could not think of any other plausible reason, and I highly doubted she wanted to give up her birthright to rule Queendom Grewt'en.

By all accounts, Regina would not be one of the competitors for me, and this made a weight off my shoulders disappear. I was already too afraid to go up against Regina, and I only had one occurrence with her. If I was not her competition, then I did not understand her decision to be cruel to me?

This made me wonder how many other guests in attendance were not actually here for Prince Rafael Baylor because they had another agenda on their plate. Maybe I did not have as much competition as I had thought initially.

Pumpking trilled in annoyance when I had stopped petting him while being deep within my own thoughts. To appease him, I resumed petting him. I wanted to stay on his good side for the minimal sake of Queen Serenity liking me.

An hour later, I was still in the rose garden even after Pumpking had left me for another grand adventure. I did not mind, though, as I took in the scenery and had a moment to myself. That was, until some girls walked by, looking at me and whispering. A few sneered at me, and I leaned back a bit on the bench. It was not like I could escape them by backing up.

I barely heard one of the girls whisper, "she's the one Regina told us about," before they giggled and glided past me. They were already spreading rumors about me from the tea event yesterday. *How much worse could it become?*

Chapter Five

Once again, I found myself standing in front of a mirror admiring my appearance in a sage green dress; while it was not my favorite, it was still pretty in its own way. Eloise flitted about fixing and tweaking various aspects of my hair and make-up. She had been adamant this would be the dress I needed to wear tonight. I chose not to voice my thoughts on the matter. I would have preferred to wear a different one, but Eloise had revealed she had been a part of creating this dress. Guilt washed over me as she continued to fix any imperfection she found. I wondered if she thought of a nasty seamstress whenever she looked at me wearing these dresses. Now, I needed to make sure I did not ruin another dress like I had the lilac one. While Eloise believed she could remove the stain, her attempts had been unsuccessful.

As I looked in the mirror, the only thing I could admire about the sage dress was the fact it made my long raven-black hair look magnificent. It reminded me of something like a cottage witch in the woods. Maybe I had been reading too many fantasy books with witches and cats granting magical wishes. After all, there was no such thing as magic in this realm.

For tonight's ball, I would need to capture Prince Rafael Baylor's attention. I just was not bold enough to push through the pack of ladies that always surrounded him. I sighed with a huff.

"What's the matter, Mina?" Eloise inquired, "You have been sighing a lot tonight."

"Oh, just thinking how I am never able to get within talking distance of The Prince." I sighed, again proving her point.

"I heard those close to him, just call him Prince Bay."

"Yeah, I have heard the same thing; definitely easier to say than the mouthful of Prince Rafael Baylor; unfortunately for the two of us, I am not on those kind of close terms." I rolled my eyes.

"Maybe you need to think outside the box from the other ladies," she replied nonchalantly, trying to hide a devious smile.

"What did you have in mind?" I smiled back. Eloise was always excellent at scheming and getting us into fun adventures back home.

I had been surprised my parents allowed Eloise to stay my handmaiden growing up, but then again, I never let her fall for the blame because I did not want my only friend to be taken away from me. I am pretty confident my father knew she was the brains of our adventures. He thankfully never let on to Mother about it.

"Well, what if you were walking by, and you just happened to trip into the masses, causing him to catch you." She pauses, tapping her chin. "Oh! No wait! No, that could be bad. If you ruin another girl's dress, he may take pity on her, and then you will also create more enemies within the ladies, and we do not need them planning against you."

I nodded in solemn agreement, watching the wheels turn in her brilliant mind. It was very endearing that she was more worried about ruining another girl's dress than the one she was currently mending. She kept tapping her chin.

"You could fall outside the circle, but I have a feeling you would just be ostracized. Go tonight, and I will need to keep pondering how to change things; thankfully, it is just the beginning of the season." She smoothed down my dress, stepping away and nodding appreciation at her work.

I nodded again more to myself than her, knowing I would not be talking to Prince Bay this evening. I may not even be able to come within a distance close enough to have a conversation with him. In my mind, though, I could pretend we were close enough for me to call him Prince Bay, but only in my mind would I allow that.

I purposely kept my next sigh to myself. I did not need Eloise to feel bad about not coming up with a plan right away. Eloise must have sensed my discouragement because she took my hand and met my eyes in the mirror, "Don't worry, Mina, we will figure something out. We always do." She smiled, and I gave a small smile in return. "Just go and enjoy yourself, and remember this is what would make past you jealous." She squeezed my hand, and I nodded. She always knew how to say the correct things to comfort me.

All the past years, my mother threw her grand balls, and I was not allowed to attend. I could hear the music and the laughter while I was locked away in my room, but that was the extent. Maybe Eloise was right; tonight would be my night to enjoy all the things I could not participate in when I was growing up.

The idea of the first ball had me overwhelmed with being focused on trying to make my way to Prince Bay as well as trying to not make a fool of myself. I already knew I did not quite fit in with the other girls. With what occurred earlier in the rose garden, it did not help how fast word spread from the first tea ceremony. Princess Regina and Princess Olivia were making it their personal vendetta to make me feel like an outsider amongst the other girls. I never heard any more whisperings since the initial group, but I definitely felt more eyes on me as they whispered to each other.

I desperately wished that Eloise could be more than just a handmaiden. Then, she could attend these events, and I would have a friend at each ball. At the very minimum, someone to talk to instead of staying out of everyone's way.

Leaving my bedroom, I began walking towards the ball. There were other princesses in clusters headed in the same direction. I tentatively smiled at them, but they just looked at me before looking at each other, giggling as they passed me. I paused, putting distance between myself and them before I began to slowly follow them down the corridor.

I had been walking slowly enough for the next group of girls gathering behind me to catch up. I tried to keep my head held high and in perfect posture, but my head dipped down at times as I chewed on the inside of my lip. I took deep, steadying breaths to concentrate as I walked and not make a fool of myself.

I arrived at the entrance of the ball and saw the three girls who had passed me join a group of other girls, all giggling together. I scanned the room and did not see any signs of Prince Bay anywhere. I tried to look on the bright side, which meant I did not have to see him surrounded by all the single females. Maybe I could rush to his side when he arrived. It was wishful and hopeful thinking on my part. I went to grab a goblet of wine to calm my nerves. The idea of beating the horde of females to Prince Bay's side versus actually pulling it off seemed quite risky. I downed the goblet of wine, setting it aside, and I reached for another to nurse.

While standing on the sidelines, I watched as the other guests danced. The prince still had yet to arrive as two more dances concluded. As much as I wanted to take Eloise's advice on enjoying the night that my past self would envy, I did not know which was more discouraging, to not have a chance of talking to the prince against my odds from the cluster of princesses or him not even attending the ball at all? I had been so focused on watching the attendees dance that I had not even noticed Princess Regina and Princess Olivia come up alongside me.

"Did you find that dress in the leftovers?" Giggled Regina, causing me to shift uncomfortably.

"The funny thing is she probably is delusional enough to believe she has a chance," chirped Olivia.

"Princesses, if you will excuse me." I bowed my head with a slight curtsy and clumsily tried to sidestep to get away from them and their cruel insults. They followed my sidesteps and smirked.

"We do not think so," Regina's voice became sugary sweet, and my stomach dropped. It was evident these two were bored, and I was going to be their current plaything. I needed to escape. My eyes darted about the room, knowing full well no one would come to my rescue. I had no allies, and Princess Regina had a far larger queendom than most of the attendees. I knew most would not go up against her for fear of ruining a future alliance.

I needed to think fast about how to get out of this, but I did not know how I would be able to do it. This would be a very long, horrible night if I did not come up with something. I tried to take another step back to escape them, but they followed suit again. If I kept this up, they would have me cornered against the wall, and all hope would be lost.

"Princess Regina, do you not come from a queendom? Why are you here if you are not here to pursue Prince Rafael Baylor?" I inquired, hoping to find some boldness come out through my voice like I tried to muster it. She scoffed at me, rolling her eyes.

"As if you understand anything." She took another step towards me, and I regretted even opening my mouth. But then both their faces turned to fear as they backed away. My brows furrowed, confused by this change.

"Please excuse us," they said in unison, dismissing themselves in a curtsy before practically running away. *What in the world was going on?* I stared, watching them leave. I became utterly puzzled but pleased with the change of events, hoping they did not change their minds and return. I began to notice everyone had cleared out from where I was standing. I felt a hand on my shoulder and whirled around to come face to face with Prince Killien Knox, suddenly realizing why everyone had left.

I instantly dropped into a curtsey, "Prince Killien Knox," I kept my gaze low, focusing on his shifting feet. I realized out of habit, I had addressed him formally despite our conversation.

"Rise," the soft, tender voice I knew was replaced with a stern tone. Taken aback, I looked up to see him sneering.

My heart dropped as I followed his order and rose. I gritted my teeth, bracing myself for what would come next. I glanced off to the side to see if there was an escape. I had not seen him since I had run headfirst into his chest. *Was this the habit I would fall into when it came to events in this room?*

He had been kind yesterday. Why was he sneering at me now? Did he hear the rumors? *Oh, no.* He had heard them, and now he knew why I was here, what my kingdom was like. He probably disliked me now.

The silence and awkwardness began to grow, and he did not seem like he was going to be making any attempts to break the silence.

"Can I help you, Prince Killien Knox?" I inquired nervously, afraid to know his response, as I noticed his clenched fist at his sides. His jaw was clenched as well. He was not even looking at me but at the floor.

"Knox," he replied with a scowl.

"What?" I almost stuttered.

"I told you to call me Knox." He did not take his gaze off the floor.

"Oh! I am so sorry; it was just habit." Relief flooded me as my body began to relax. "Knox," I remedied. He shifted his feet again.

"Would you . . ." He glanced at me and then back at the floor. "Would you like to dance?" I tried to contain the smile that was beginning to bubble to the surface. I wondered if he had ever asked a girl to dance. What I had interpreted as anger must have been nervousness, and I was misreading everything.

I curtsied and replied, "I would be honored, Knox." His head snapped up. His guarded expression was utterly startled as if he did not expect me to agree.

"I . . . I mean . . . You would? I . . ." He seemed to be uncertain about how to proceed. I tried to continue to stifle my giggle as I offered him my arm. He seemed grateful for my lead as he took my arm, straightening his posture.

I gave him a reassuring nod, causing his smile to turn genuine. He led me towards the dance floor, where the others lined up for the next dance.

The surrounding couples gave nervous glances our way. They were not very subtle about it either. Knox began to shift uncomfortably, his smile disappearing as he glanced at me and then back at the floor. For a prince feared by so many, he was awfully shy.

I leaned into him, causing him to take a slight step back with a surprised look. "Can I tell you a secret?" I partially whispered to him, and his eyebrows rose slightly as I continued my secret, "I have never been asked to dance before, so I may not be very good with a partner." I shrugged with a partial smile, and he slightly smiled as he leaned in to respond, "can I tell you a secret, too?" I nodded, giving up on containing my smile.

"I have never participated in a dance either." We both chuckled together with our shared secrets. I could already feel the hope that began growing from our last meeting.

The band started playing, and we stumbled over our first dance steps. We were a bit awkward and partially clumsy, but we giggled and smiled at each other as we corrected every mistake. The rest of the attendees melted away into the background when we fell into a rhythm. We continued through the song, and when the dance ended, we stepped back, with him bowing and me curtsying.

"Would you . . ." He scratched the back of his head. "Would you care for another dance with me?" He bit his lip as he smiled. I looked back and forth at his eyes before returning his smile.

"I would love that a lot."

His smile widened.

We danced two more dances, and I had never been happier and more out of breath than I was in this moment. We did not talk as we danced but laughed and smiled. With each dance, the room just faded away. I never noticed how the other people dancing gave us space on the floor or how they whispered as they looked at us. I was wrapped up in my attention to Knox. I was unaware that his brother had finally arrived at the ball.

If I had even paid remotely any bit of attention to what was going on around us, I would have noticed how his brother stared at us in a murderous way. Maybe if I were a bit more self-aware, I would have taken notice of how the other guests were whispering, with their glances going between Knox and myself to his brother and back.

After the fourth dance, we were both beyond out of breath. "Would you care for a drink?" Knox asked through a gasp, and I nodded eagerly with flushed and very sore cheeks. I had rarely laughed and smiled this much in my life, and my cheeks were beginning to feel the price from it. I never wanted this feeling to end. I started looking forward to the next ball and being able to do this again with Knox. We headed to the wine table with me on his arm, and people were parting out of our way.

"I'm sorry, you do not need to be associated with me if you do not want to be." Knox's smile disappeared from his face. I finally noticed the way the other guests were whispering to each other as they looked at us from a distance away. I pressed myself into Knox, trying to shrink away from the attention we were receiving.

He tried to drop my arm, but I would not let him as I tugged him to our final steps to the wine table. I wanted to attribute it to self-bravery, but somewhere, I fully believed deep down that if I did not make him stay and continue like this, I would never see him again. Maybe I was selfish, but I did not want to be left here alone in a room full of strangers whispering about us the way they were.

"Do not let them bother you. You hold the power here, not them," I murmured to Knox under my breath. His arm clenched tight against mine as his hand paused, reaching for a goblet. I watched as his hand shook. He clenched his hand into a fist and then unclenched it before grabbing the goblet. He let go of my arm to hand me my drink, giving me a forced smile this time.

"Thank you," he said quietly, and I nodded in response, accepting the wine as he grabbed one for himself.

"Are you enjoying yourself here?" He asked, attempting small talk.

"I was not until tonight." I took a sip of my wine to hide my embarrassment from my forwardness.

"Really?" He asked with a hopeful voice, and I made eye contact with him, taking my drink away from my lips and nodding.

We stood there in silence, enjoying each other's company. It felt nice accompanying the same space as someone else. Even though we both belonged here, I got the sense we were outsiders to the other guests in attendance. I found solace in my blooming relationship with Knox. I could not wait to tell Eloise about my night and how I finally had a protector from the other girls. Maybe protector was a strong word; he was not protecting me so much as his presence ensured no one else came close to us. She would be thrilled to hear I actually danced, though.

Oh, how exhilarating this all was; I stole small smiles back and forth with Knox. Butterflies were beginning to dance in my stomach. I was still utterly oblivious to the shadow standing over me until he spoke.

"You both look cozy together." We both straightened to find Knox's brother, Prince Bay, standing there before us. I gasped and instantly dropped into a curtsey, almost sloshing the wine onto my dress. I did not need to ruin another dress, even if I did not care for this one.

"Prince Rafael Baylor." I kept my head bowed low, looking down into the fabric of my dress as Knox stayed standing to his brother.

"Rise," crooned Prince Bay, and I did so while still not looking up at him. This was the closest I had been to him since the first night during that extremely long curtsy. Thankfully, he did not make me hold this one as long. My only hope was Knox would deal with this situation of his brother because, at the moment, I most definitely was tongue-tied.

"Bay," Knox said in response. There was not really tension, but I definitely felt the awkwardness. I tried to convince myself that I was imagining it due to my nervousness and nothing more.

"Princess Persamina Rowena of Theorines," Prince Bay stated, and I nodded slowly. "Have you been enjoying your stay with us?"

"Your kingdom is quite beautiful and very accommodating." What I did not add was how much I felt like an outsider until tonight. It was at that moment that Princess Regina and Princess Olivia found the courage to return now that the heir prince was here.

"Oh, I see you have met *The Locked Away Tower Princess*," quipped Regina. Both brothers looked at her before cocking their head to look at me.

"We thought for certain she must be *so* monstrous since her parents always kept her locked away during their balls," chimed in Olivia.

"I mean, their balls were not as extravagant as this," retorted Regina with a wave of her hand to motion to the surrounding decorations in T'Lovoness's ballroom. It was then that I realized they had been to my home and had partaken in events I was never allowed to. Were their laughs the ones I had heard through my bedroom door? I unconsciously took a step back, feeling the table against my back, my breath becoming shallower. The ballroom began to feel suffocating.

"Princess Persamina, The Tower Princess," tacked on Olivia.

"Come on, Bay, let us go somewhere more entertaining." Regina grabbed his arm to drag him away. It stung to know she was close enough to him to refer to him as Bay without using his full name or titles. But he did not budge. "Bay, come on," she pushed again, and I watched him shrug her off.

"It is Prince Bay to you," he replied coolly to her. Regina reacted as if she had been slapped. Shock flashed on her face before she shot me a glare as her face scrutinized mine. Everything about her energy now blamed me for how he had treated her.

It was clear Regina had not intended to be reprimanded. Nor have it been done with an audience close by to witness. At one point, she must have thought she was in a higher social standing with the T'Lovoness family to drop the titles. Unfortunately for her, Prince Bay just put her back in her place. I wondered, with Regina's claim to her throne, if she did not think she had to abide by all the rules. But now, to find out she was no better than anyone else in another kingdom. I would be lying if I did not find some small personal joy from this. I would have a lot more enjoyment if I knew she would not get revenge for this.

Prince Bay did not break eye contact with her as he added just as coldly, "Leave us and remember your place next time." Both princesses' hands instantly covered their mouths in complete shock as their pride became wounded for all to see and hear nearby. I knew the rumors were sure to spread very quickly. But would these rumors cover up the ones already spreading about me?

I wish I could say I kept fully feeling that self-enjoyment, but I knew they would find a way to get back at me for this. I knew they would take their self-inflicted mortification out on me, especially when it came to Regina. That girl was spiteful and bitter to the core.

They both walked away as briskly as possible without running. I heard Regina hiss to someone of lower status to move out of her way. I barely noticed Prince Bay's jaw tick ever so slightly when she said it.

Maybe if I were lucky, she would fall further and further from his good graces. If I became a bit more favored by him, it might give me the protection I needed to be safe from Regina and her little followers. Everyone surrounding us continued watching to see what would happen next.

"Would you care for a dance, Princess Persamina Rowena?"

Prince Bay extended his hand, offering it to me, and my heart leaped as it began to race at the unexpectedness. I gave him my hand as I glanced nervously at Knox, whose facial expression was glacier. Regret began to swallow my giddiness. I could not outright refuse the prince heir. This was everything my mother had been raising me for, but deep down, I hoped I would not lose Knox from this.

Prince Bay led me to the dance floor, and I heard whispering as we passed by. The few snippets I could hear were remarks about how I was the girl who held the ridiculously long, perfect curtsey that first night without complaint and that the Prince had smiled and called me pretty.

Their whispers extended that I was the first girl he had asked to dance in his Courting Season. I swore one mentioned marriage and future queen, but that could just be my excitement of being noticed by the prince heir.

Uneasiness coursed through me, lacing with the regret consuming me. I felt overly warm. This was happening, and I was not dreaming. If I was dreaming, I was uncertain if I would be disappointed or not.

He led us to a spot in the middle of the dance floor where he extravagantly semi-circled, ending with facing me. He took my other hand, giving me a confident, devious smile that caused my heart to flip. And then, before I could warn him of my poor dancing experience, the music began, and he started to lead me. I felt like I was floating for all three steps. Mortification flooded me as I stumbled into him. Looking up, I found his cocky grin with a raised eyebrow. He continued to guide me along without a word.

He said nothing with each mistake I made as he corrected it with the next step. He continued giving me that cocky grin as we danced. My mistakes became less and less over time as my confidence grew with him leading.

Dancing with Prince Bay was different than his brother. Where Knox and I were learning how to dance together, Bay led with confidence. Knox and I had fun; Prince Bay made me glide across the dance floor as we twirled and moved together. I was still conscious of the people watching us as I danced with Prince Bay. Knox and I had laughed. Prince and I did not speak during the dance; I mainly kept my gaze on his chest or down at the floor. Anytime I glanced up at his face, he had an amused expression watching me.

The dance, much to my dismay, ended. I curtsied as he bowed. My eyes were closed when I curtsied, or I would have seen his fingers come up under my chin. He Guided my head upwards to look at him.

"Your dress is beautiful, Princess Persamina Rowena," his voice was low. I flushed; Eloise apparently knew what she was doing when she had picked this color out. He let go of my chin with a wink.

"Thank you, Prince Rafael Baylor," I smiled, meeting his eyes.

"Please call me Bay." He grabbed my hand, bringing it up to his lips, and kissed the back of it. *Oh my.* He straightened back up. "Thank you for the dance, Princess Persamina Rowena." He winked and walked away, leaving me to gather my wits about myself. I turned back to the beverage table, but Knox was no longer standing there. I looked around the room and could not find him. My eyes found Bay across the room, and he raised his goblet to me as he tipped his head forward. Heat rushed into my cheeks as I smiled. He winked and then turned to talk to the gentlemen next to him.

I decided to leave the dance shortly after; I was a bit overwhelmed with the turn of events from the evening. As I walked, I brought my hands up to my cheeks, shaking my head in giddiness. I had danced, and not with just anyone, but the prince heir, and he told me to call him Bay. I squealed to myself.

"You seem to be enjoying yourself," a voice commented. The prince with no name emerged from behind the shadows of a pillar.

"You-you should have made your presence known," I yelped. The hallways had been deathly quiet. I did not think anyone else had been around to witness my bubble of delight.

"And miss seeing you be this giddy, Princess Persamina? I think not." He chuckled to himself.

"Who are you?" I blurted out, my eyebrows furrowing. I wanted to know who he was.

"Let's just say I am a friend and nothing more." He gave me that devilish smile with a wink.

"It's only polite you tell me your name," I countered.

"All in due time, Princess Persamina, all in due time." He chuckled, and turning, he walked away from me.

"That's not fair!" I shouted at his back.

"Life's not fair." He threw back over his shoulder. I watched him disappear through a door; I half debated chasing after him but decided against it. I did not want to be caught alone in a room with him; I did not need more rumors circulating about me. Instead, I chose to make my way towards my room. I could not wait to tell Eloise everything.

I turned the knob to my door, and Eloise immediately greeted me.

"How was he?!" She gushed, grabbing my hand and dragging me into the room.

"How did you know already?" I gasped, completely shocked. A little bit of my excitement deflated. I wanted to be the one to tell her.

"Oh, come now." She led me quickly to my chair in front of the mirror to start undoing my hair. "Handmaids and servants gossip, and you were the talk of the ball!" She gushed. "My Mina, *the* princess of the ball! They are already taking guesses of when the wedding will be!"

"The wedding?!" I gasped with my eyes widening.

"Oh yes! The prince hasn't taken an interest in any other female, so everyone is expecting it will be you," she mused as she teased my hair undone frantically. Her excitement had put her into quite a frenzy.

I turned to her, forcing her to pause on my hair. "Do you really believe so?" I wanted to believe what she said but did not want to be filled with too much excitement.

She knelt, grasping both of my hands with tears of happiness in her eyes. "I fully believe so. Your dreams are coming true!" I smiled back, knowing how pleased my mother would be with this turn of events.

"So, what was he like?" She pushed as she stood up to keep working on my hair.

"He was... He was truly a prince." I sighed, thinking back to his smiles and winks. "He told me to call him Bay."

Eloise gasped. "He did not!"

"He did! And that was shortly after he had told Regina to address him as Prince Bay when she had been calling him Bay."

"I did not hear this part of the story! I am going to yell at her when I see her next." Pursed Eloise's lips.

"Who?"

"Oh, no one. Just my source for the gossip," Eloise replied nonchalantly. "So why did the prince tell her that?"

"Well, I was at the beverage table with Knox and - -" Eloise's gasp and slight yank on my hair caused me to hiss.

"Apologies, but what were you doing with the prince's brother?"

"We had been dancing prior." From the look on Eloise's face, I knew that was not what she had been wanting to hear.

"You danced with him? *The Reclusive Prince*?"

"Yes, he was the reason Regina and Olivia stayed away from me, and prior to Bay asking me to dance, Knox was the only reason I was having fun tonight," I replied defensively. I would not let her take away my happiness.

"Wait, you're on a first-name basis with both brothers?" She asked, surprised.

"Yup, it seems so." I smiled big.

"Hmmm." She paused, thinking. "Makes me wonder if the prince did not ask you to dance because he was jealous of his brother?" She tapped her chin.

"Oh, I would hardly think so." I laughed.

"Well, you never know." She smiled before she finished the last bit of undoing my hair. I smiled to myself at the thought of the possibility that maybe Bay was jealous of his brother. Perhaps that was why he had come over and asked me to dance. But I did not think I could be that lucky.

Chapter Six

A few mornings later, I sat by myself at a table in the rose garden with a platter of pastries. I found contentment in watching the other guests mingle. I grabbed a raspberry tart, saving the lemon for the end as I watched the ladies shamelessly flirt with Bay. I never realized how shameless these girls were in their chasing until now. Ever since the dance from a couple of nights ago, these girls had become even more ruthless in their pursuit of him. I had a sneaking suspicion it had been due to the fact I was the only girl Bay had danced with. However, that had been the extent of my interaction with Bay, or even Knox, for that matter. Despite a few attempts, I had not talked to Bay since, nor had I seen Knox.

As I kept observing, I could now see why Bay seemed to keep everyone at a distance. They treated him like an object with the way they fawned all over him. It became evident they didn't want him; they wanted to claim his throne. I was aware that I needed to be right in there. I needed to be capturing more of his favor, but at this moment, I planned to enjoy myself and just take in the scenery.

"Is this seat taken?" A deep masculine voice asked, causing me to jump in my seat. I had been too busy watching Bay to have noticed that Knox had snuck up on me. He stood there wearing all black as usual, with the empty chair partially pulled out in his hand. He slightly fidgeted as he awaited my response. I could tell he was trying to appear confident, but I could see through his grand bravado. Being around this many people must set his nervousness on edge. He had not attended any of the events the past few days, and aside from the one interaction with his brother, I had yet to witness him talk to anyone else but myself. I began to believe he received his title, The Reclusive Prince, honestly, with his lack of attendance. There was a difference between Knox and me; he had a choice to not attend the events, a choice I never received growing up.

"No, it is taken," I replied and watched his shoulders slump slightly as he began to take a step away. I continued with, "by you." I smiled. His eyes widened a fraction in surprise, giving me a hesitant smile before pulling the chair all the way out and sitting down. I took a sip of my tea. I knew using my tea was an excuse not to make the first move in the conversation. That was until I saw him grab the lemon tart I had been saving.

"Ah! You took the lemon," I pouted without thinking. He paused with it midway to his mouth.

"Uh, did you want this?" He nodded toward the tart, looking at it before looking back at me.

"No, no, it is fine." I sighed, waving my hand. "You claimed it. I was the one not putting it on my plate. The lemon ones are my favorite." I finished by way of explanation. Upon seeing his apologetic, uncertain expression, I added, "I will just snag one from the kitchens or something later."

"Lemon is my favorite too," he quietly remarked before taking a bite. I smiled at him, and he once again smiled back shyly. Various rumors floated around him, but nothing was locked down as to why everyone feared him. With his lack of social skills and his always black apparel it probably exaggerated the fear and the rumors.

Like many parents with second-born children, I assumed Knox had been just an afterthought in the world. Typically, in royal families, the parents would focus all their attention on the eldest child and or heir. Knox was the spare prince. It made me wonder why, with powerful and influential parents, they never shut down the rumors. Was Knox such an afterthought in their mind that they simply did not care what people said about their youngest son?

"Knox," I say hesitantly. With the way things had ended between us at the ball, we had not done much talking. If I wanted this relationship to grow, I would need to get to know him better, even if it did make me nervous. "Aside from our love of sweet lemon tarts, what else do you enjoy?" I did not think bringing up our lack of dance skills would be appropriate.

He looked at me perplexed like he had never been asked the question or that maybe I should have already known the answers. I was not sure which it had been. However, if he did not want to converse, then he should have chosen to sit by himself instead of joining me. *What am I thinking?* He is a Prince of T'Lovoness; he can do whatever he wants without question. I was in his home, after all.

The silence began to stretch awkwardly, and I wondered if I had even asked the question in the first place. Regret and dread started replacing the feeling of happiness I felt moments prior. My eyes flitted back and forth between meeting his eyes and my teacup.

"I am sorry if that was inappropriate to ask." I blushed, feeling the heat creeping up to my cheeks, not meeting his eyes. I could still feel his gaze on me, and if I had to guess, he was still probably a bit startled that I had asked. My mother had trained me for everything except small talk; what was appropriate and what was not? Would she be scolding me right now? My stomach dropped at how much I was probably failing currently.

He softly asked, "would you want to take a stroll through the gardens?" I met his gaze, taking note of the slight flush on his cheeks that now matched my own. My heart stuttered at how shy he was. Despite the kindness he has shown me, I still expected him to be menacing and scary. The biasness Mother and everyone had of him was still ingrained in my mind. I questioned how long it would be until that version would be entirely replaced with the one before me —this shy, reclusive prince who always lingered in the shadowed sidelines.

I smiled softly as I dipped my chin. "I would like that very much." His uncertain smile grew with certainty until he showed all his teeth. I mirrored his smile back.

He stood up quickly and extended his hand to me as if he was afraid I would change my mind. He acted like he was not a prince with the ability to have anything he wanted. I felt like it was a few nights ago when he had first asked me to dance.

I placed my hand into his as he guided me to stand up. The warmth of his hand stirred something inside of me. When I stood before him, I slipped my hand out of his and entwined our arms, bringing them up for us to begin walking. It was after I realized what I had done out of habit that my stomach knotted as I felt heat flushing through my body.

"Oh! My apologies! I got ahead of myself." I gritted my teeth to bite back some of the embarrassment.

"No, no, it is okay." He reassured me as we began to walk towards the maze in the rose garden. We passed many of the guests, and the other girls started whispering behind their fans and then giggling to each other. My gaze drifted to Bay, and his gaze locked with mine. He gave me a smirk. My heart skipped a bit as I gritted my teeth harder. I was the first to look away.

I felt Knox's arm tighten on mine. "You do not have to walk with me. I know they are gossiping already," his voice strained. I looked up at his face and saw the tightness in his jaw, a reaction I knew was the result from everyone around us.

His eyes were staring straight ahead to the maze garden. He was probably anticipating for me to take this opportunity to run away from him, and my heart splintered just a bit from the thought of how utterly lonely he probably felt. I knew what that loneliness felt like. Days that faded into months and months that finally turned into years of isolation.

"Take me to your favorite place in the garden," I replied, before adding, "besides, we danced multiple times, let the rumors fly." I smiled, stomping my internal emotions down as I continued looking straight ahead. Out of my peripheral vision, I had seen his head turn towards me. His arm relaxed on mine. "Okay, follow me."

I glanced at him, and the strain in his face dissipated. His shoulders did not appear as tense as he walked us through the entrance of the maze.

I had yet to venture inside the rose maze. Fear of being lost in it was at the top of my list of reasons. The maze was giant, with high rose bush walls that one could not see over. We passed a few couples who gave us a wide berth each time, causing him to flush a bit.

"Please do not leave me in here alone. I fear I will never find the way out," I joked, breaking the silence. He chuckled.

"I promise to never leave you behind, Mina." My heart flipped again. His shy, quiet voice with that undertone of masculinity made me want to hold and protect him. "Do you miss home, Mina?" He asked, trying to continue the conversation.

"Sometimes, but I am enjoying my time here, Knox." I had to

bite out, guilt lacing through me of how much I did not miss home. He squeezed my arm in response as he led us deeper into the rose maze. At this point, we were no longer running into anyone.

We fell back into an easy silence. I assumed it was from his nervousness since he continuously glanced at me. I kept pretending not to notice. I thought with how we had just broken the ice, we would be past this. It seemed, however, that he put up walls after they were torn down. I questioned if it was a defense mechanism from past experiences.

"We are here," he announced. We entered an open circle in the garden with what looked like a forgotten fountain, but that made no sense since this was the royal garden, and everything surrounding it was well taken care of. How could it be the only thing neglected? It did not add up to the rest of the royal family's aesthetic.

"I asked the gardeners not to maintain it." It was as if he read my thoughts on the matter. "As a kid, I loved to come here to play, and with the fountain not looking pristine, I could pretend to have more heroic adventures." He must have realized he was talking rather passionately because he instantly withdrew within himself again. "Sorry, you probably are not interested in hearing things like this."

"I like seeing you smile," I blurted out, covering my mouth instantly.

"Oh." He flushed, scratching the back of his head as he shifted uncomfortably.

"You are not what I expected," I added. It must have been the wrong thing to say because he began to pull away from me.

"Yeah, I know I am The Reclusive Prince. I'm a tyrant, and to stay away from me because I may kill you like my name implies." He growled in frustration, not looking at me. I reached up and turned his face back to me.

"No, what I meant was I did not expect you to be so much fun to be around. I am enjoying myself." I tried to give a reassuring smile, but I was unsure if it helped. His eyes searched mine as his scowl slowly melted away.

"You are . . . enjoying your time with me?" He breathed.

"Yes," I whispered back. My eyes looked back and forth between his, my heart beating faster. We said nothing for a moment too long, and then he took a step back, clearing his throat.

"We should head back," he said.

"Okay," I responded half-heartedly. I offered Knox my arm lamely, and he took it. Maybe I overstepped my boundaries by touching his face. I forgot myself and my place.

We walked in silence for five minutes until he finally broke the tension, "May . . . May I see you again?"

I stumbled, and he caught me before I fell. "Thank you," I straightened out of his arms, smoothing my dress down. His finger caught under my chin as he guided my face up to look into his green eyes. "May I see you again, Mina?" He repeated his question to me.

"Yes," I breathed, my stomach fluttering at the thought. He smiled and nodded before taking my arm. We turned the corner and made our way to exit the garden. The whole time, I was trying to keep my facial emotions in check.

As we emerged, cliques of guests in the rose garden paths began to take notice. They whispered to each other, drawing more attention to us from others. The way they responded, their eyes roving up and down us. It was as if we had done something wrong. I felt like I had been caught red-handed but did not know by what. My gaze fell onto the prince heir.

Bay's back was to us, but it did not take long for the other princesses swarming him to begin whispering in his ear. He turned around, his gaze falling on us. He watched as Knox led us back to the table we had been occupying prior to our walk.

I felt the heat of everybody's stare on us, and I was trying desperately not to squirm under it. Bay was drinking out of his goblet. His eyes never strayed from us from over the rim. I did not think he was a jealous individual like Eloise had hinted at, but if he were, would what I was doing tip him in favor of picking me? A small voice said I did not want that, but I brushed it aside, attempting to ignore it. I became conflicted. I had enjoyed my walk with Knox, and I did not do it to make Bay jealous. Mother would have been proud of me, but for some reason, I was not proud of myself.

Knox released my arm to pull out my chair, and I politely sat back down in the same chair from earlier. He bowed. "Have a great day, Princess Persamina Rowena," he said stiffly before walking away.

What had just happened? I watched him dumbstruck as he headed towards the castle doors. Guests stepped out of his path as he made his retreat. I could hear the people whispering all around me. I could not distinguish their words, only that between their looks and giggles, it was about me and what they speculated had occurred. I felt my body warm as I tried not to squirm in my seat. I did not have time to filter my thoughts. Regina and Olivia were bee-lining toward my table.

"It is only *fitting* that The Tower Princess and The Reclusive Prince end up together." Sneered Regina. They both towered over me. Standing up from my chair was not an option due to their close proximity. I was trapped by them. I could not escape, and with Knox recently departed, no one was coming to my rescue. The small bit of happiness I felt was being replaced with dread.

"Do *not* say that!" I defended myself. I hated the titles being associated with me.

"Oh! *So* smitten to defend." Giggled Olivia.

"Two reclusive creatures," chimed Regina. "I guess love can even befall the likes of you." Regina and Olivia smiled at each other before simultaneously turning around and walking away from me.

I made the quick split decision to stand up. Turning around, I stumbled back into the rose garden maze, my vision blurring. They ruin everything. I did not want to be seen and already knew there were not many guests within the maze. How long would Regina's vendetta against me hold? I was never going to be strong enough to stand up against her. She was going to rule her queendom. Why would someone like me matter to her? Yes, I knew Bay had humiliated her a few nights ago, but why must she be so cruel?

Mother would be disappointed in my weakness. She would never tolerate it or allow others to treat her this way, but then again, Mother would be a Regina. She would have been the bully. After all, that's all Mother had been in my life, a bully I bitterly thought.

After a few twists and turns, I found a secluded alcove with a bench and sat down on it. I would worry later about figuring out how to exit the maze. I wrung my hands in the handkerchief I pulled out of my bosom. I tried to keep my sobs down. I did not need anyone to find me like this. It was bad enough I would even be attempting to rejoin the festivities after this. My face was probably already blotchy, my eyes puffy from the tears.

Mother taught me not to cry with her scoldings, and yet Regina knew all the right things to say to get under my skin. My only saving grace was while rushing into the garden, I had not seen Prince Bay. Knox had already entered the castle and most likely had not witnessed what had occurred. It's not like I expected either of them to do anything. I would be mortified for either of them to find me in this state.

I stared down at the handkerchief, taking in the embroidered flower pattern. It was the first stitch pattern I had done perfectly, and the little flowers bordered the edge in a rainbow of colors. When I proudly showed Mother my accomplishment, she scrutinized it. I stood there nervously at twelve years old. When she could not find any mistakes, she tossed it to me, claiming it to be "adequate at best." The pride I felt with my accomplishment had been stripped away with just those three words. I rarely stitched after that day.

"Oh, here you are," a voice said as my gaze snapped from my handkerchief to find Bay's face.

"Oh!" I squeaked in return, trying to dab my tears away frantically. I did not want him to see that I had been crying.

"Not that I am one to pry, but what happened?" He asked me casually. He came a couple of steps closer to me. I wanted to flee, but unfortunately, he blocked the only exit.

"It - it was nothing," I stumbled over my words. My gaze flitted from him to my lap, to the rose hedge, back at him, and then to the ground.

He closed the distance between us and sat beside me on the bench. My body stiffened in response as he positioned himself to face me. I felt the warmth of his body next to me.

"Look at me, Princess Persamina Rowena." I followed his order to look at his face, riddled with concern. My heart thrilled at the thought he possibly cared about me.

"Are you lying to your prince?" He asked with an edge of amusement in his tone. The amusement tone bothered me. He may be the wealthiest prince in all the lands, but that did not make him my prince... yet. I was still a princess to a kingdom of my own.

"I, Princess Persamina Rowena, am not lying to you, Prince Bay." I squared my gaze at him with this sudden amount of boldness and familiarity. "I was crying over a trivial matter." I tried to sound nonchalant with a small shrug.

He stared at me a moment longer before nodding. His hand

came up to tuck a strand of hair behind my ear. My breathing slowed, uncertain of what he would do next. He smiled, and I could hear my heartbeat in my ears.

"Very well, Princess Persamina Rowena." He cocked his head to the side, studying my face. I began to flush, knowing how a mess I probably looked in my current state and his complete focus on it. "I believe I told you that you could call me Bay."

"You are right, you did," I agreed. "You can call me Mina, by the way. . . All my friends do." All of the two friends I have in this palace, at least. Maybe it was presumptuous to be labeling Knox as a friend, but two sounded a lot less pathetic than one.

"Mina," he said slowly, testing it out before continuing, "that is a cute nickname." His smile grew, causing me to dip my head from the compliment. "So, would that make us friends then?"

"I would like that a lot, Bay." I could feel new tears wanting to form, this time from the swell of happiness and hope I began feeling.

"I would too, Mina." I looked up at him, his deep blue eyes holding warmth in them. I began to feel better about myself with him here. He chuckled to himself, shaking his head. "I have to head back, Mina. Will you be alright?"

"Yeah, I just need a moment. . . But I will be fine," I assured him. I wondered if he was this friendly with the other females.

He stood up and took a couple of steps before glancing over his shoulder. "Crying over Regina's snide marks *is* indeed trivial." He smirked with a wink before disappearing around the hedge. My heart stuttered a beat. He knew Regina had said something horrendous to me. He had come to check on me, and with that, we had become friends. Despite Regina trying to tear me down, she actually had just given me a gift. She gave me Bay's friendship. I smiled a little to myself. I had another friend.

After a few wrong guesses of which path to take, I finally figured out the way to the exit. When I emerged, I saw Princess Iyrse Skyvien and her older twin sister, Princess Tearani Ryver, sitting at the same table I had sat at before Regina and Olivia showed up. They were both watching me as I emerged and waved me over to them. I walked cautiously towards them as Iyrse motioned for me to sit in the empty chair. I listened to her silent command and sat.

"Princess Tearani, Princess Iyrse." I dipped my head in acknowledgment of the two twins. Both princesses wore matching golden tiaras with amethyst stones in them. Their hair was straight, and that was where their similarities ended. They were polar opposites of each other in every other way.

Iyrse with her platinum blonde hair, icy blue eyes, freckles dancing across her nose, and pale skin. She wore another light blue to almost white summer dress with crystal beads woven within. She adorned a sapphire white teardrop necklace with matching teardrop earrings. Iyrse had a very warm, bubbly, and friendly personality.

Tearani had dark brown hair that was almost black. Her violet eyes were darker than mine, and her eyes pierced right through anyone she looked at. Her skin was dark and very sun-kissed. While I had heard her talk a few times, she predominantly had a very monotone voice, void of any warmth. She was wearing an exquisite satin emerald two-piece dress. Unlike Iyrse's, which was adorned in enough crystals that it began to look like ice droplets, Tearani's dress did not have a single jewel on it. Instead, there were two very long slits up both sides of her legs to her hips. The top piece was strapless and woven tightly over her large bosom. She wore a necklace that reminded me of the sun. It was an open three-quarters of a circle filled with diamonds. Each ray of light being filled in with diamonds all the way to their golden-capped ends. She also had two long golden teardrop earrings that swayed when her head turned.

"Just Iyrse, you are amongst friends." Iyrse smiled with a roll of her eyes. I had barely talked to these two, and yet she was calling us friends. I glanced at Tearani, who was staring at me. She did one nod of her head to acknowledge she was agreeing with her sister.

"Then call me Mina," I replied.

"Cool! So, Mina, we were wondering if you would want to join us later on?" Iyrse was practically bouncing in her seat at the idea.

"What did you have in mind?" I asked curiously. No one had invited me to do anything with them outside of the daily itinerary list.

"You are invited to come back to our rooms to hang out," Tearani was the one to respond in her gravely monotone voice.

"Sure . . . I would like that a lot." I gave them both a smile.

"Good!" Iyrse grabbed a strawberry tart pastry from the tray. "There's a lemon one for you." She nodded her head at the platter.

"How did you know I liked lemon?" I blanched, a tad surprised.

"I watch you; you always save them for last," Tearani replied before adding on, "and you watch them like a hawk as people grab for a pastry."

"Oh." I had not realized how obvious I was.

"Most people would not notice, but Tearani notices everything." Iyrse laughed. I tried to relax a bit at this statement.

"Everything?" I questioned.

"Everything." Tearani blinked before looking out at the other guests. I followed her gaze to the group talking amongst each other. Regina and Olivia were in the center of it. I did not see Bay or Knox amongst the grounds.

"Olivia is sleeping with Prince Voltaire Edric of Kingdom T'Cudter, while Regina is sleeping with his brother Prince Devereux Theox," Tearani said nonchalantly. Astounded and shocked, I followed her gaze down at the couples she had mentioned standing in very close proximity to each other. I looked back up at Tearani in complete awe at somehow knowing these things.

"If you pay attention," Iyrse chirped, "Regina puts her hand on Devereux a lot, which causes him to smile. We have not quite figured out their code yet, but they have some type of communication pattern with their touches." I looked back at them, watching Regina put her hand on Devereux's shoulder as she squeezed it twice before dropping her hand again.

"I believe two squeezes means I want you, but I am not quite certain," supplied Tearani.

"How do you guess that?" I questioned.

"He gets a boner rather quickly," Iyrse giggled, and I flushed at the idea before noticing the bulge in his pants grow.

"Oh my," I giggled, looking at the twins. Tearani gave me a small smile, her eyes only slightly crinkling before she returned back to her neutral facial expression.

"It is either that or they are preparing to leave for a quick fuck," continued Tearani. "I have not quite figured it out since they do not leave right away or together for obvious reasons."

"So, what about Olivia? How did you figure that one out?" I asked, becoming even more inquisitive.

"I walked in on them," Tearani replied, and I gasped.

"Yeah, so have I," chimed in Iyrse. "They chose the dumbest and most obvious spots to do it."

"Stay out of the music room after 6 pm," added Tearani.

"Had no plans on going there anyways, but alrighty then. I definitely will not now," I said with wide eyes at the thought.

"Olivia is hoping Voltaire will ask her to marry him and become his queen, but he is just using her because he knows she is an easy lay," Tearani continued to add on.

"Does he have someone in mind?"

"Me," Iyrse replied with a roll of her eyes.

"You are not interested in becoming his queen?" I may have been pushing it with asking Iryse that.

"Not to someone who probably will cheat on me my whole marriage. Besides, I have different plans for my future." She gave me a sly smile.

"Regina," Tearani interjected, "is currently deciding whether Devereux would make a good consort for her queendom or not. He is trying very hard to prove to her that he will. He does not just aspire to be a consort but also to receive the honorary title of king as well. He does not want to be a random prince in some dusty history books with land to reside on with a wife and children that will all be forgotten about."

"I did not think queendoms granted the title of kings?" I questioned slowly.

"They tend not to. It is a very rare honor and would definitely make it more popular in history," chirped Iryse.

"Would Regina do such a thing?"

"Who's to say?" Iryse shrugged her shoulders.

"What is preventing her from choosing him as a permanent consort?"

"Nothing really, she just has not decided if she wants to commit to him for eternity, is all," Iryse said in exaggeration.

"Then why is she so mean to me?" If they were this observant, then, of course, they must have the answer.

"She is jealous of you," they replied in unison.

"Jealous of me?" I blinked, taken aback.

"You're gorgeous," began Iyrse.

"You are fawned over," added on Tearani.

"You have caught the favor of both T'Lovoness Princes."

"Her brothers cannot stop talking about you."

"Need we go on?" They ended in unison again. My mind was in a whirl of everything they had just thrown at me.

"Wait, her brothers?" That is what my mind decided to focus on.

"Regina's two brothers, Montgomery Victory and Percival Righteous, they both are hoping to win your favor to become king." Iyrse twiddled her hair.

"They have never even talked to me." I shook my head, not believing what they said for one bit.

"How could they." Tearani blinked at me. "When you have Knox showing up at your side at every given chance they could attempt."

"That has only been twice I have been by Knox?" My eyebrows furrowed in confusion. There had been plenty of times in the last few days when I was alone.

"And both times, the two brothers had been making their way towards you," Iryse replied flippantly, playing with her hair.

"I never seen any princes' doing so?" I tried to argue.

"Does not matter, we witnessed it," Tearani replied.

"And now Bay wants what Knox has," Iyrse continued to twiddle with her hair.

"What Knox has?" My confusion growing.

"You," they replied in unison.

Chapter Seven

Later in the evening, I made my way toward the twin's bedroom. Hours later, I was still confused by the information they had dropped upon me. Eloise had not been in my room when I returned to decompress a bit. She had not returned either before I made my way to the twin's room, which was fine. I did not need Eloise to help me, but I did want to talk to her about what the twins had said earlier. Eloise always had a good mind to put things into a new perspective for me.

I followed the twins' directions to their door, knocking. I did not have to wait very long. A very bouncy Iryse opened the door.

"You came!" She squealed, dragging me inside the room and closing the door shut behind us. Tearani sat in an oversized chair, looking out the window at the rising moon. She turned her head towards us. Blinking, she nodded once in acknowledgment.

"You did invite me," I supplied in answer, a little confused about whether she thought I would not come at all.

"Yes, we did, but after our conversation in the rose garden, we were not quite certain if we scared you off or not." Iyrse beamed, dragging me to the two empty oversized chairs residing by Tearani. I sat down in one as Iyrse took the other.

"You did not scare me off. My head is still swimming from all the information that you hurled at me, but I am well," I answered honestly.

"Don't you worry. We will fill you in on everything there is to know about everyone," chirped Iyrse confidently.

"If you look out the window, you will see Regina and Devereux sneaking into the rose garden," Tearani's monotone voice drawled. I shot out of my chair to race to the window. Looking down, the two in question were darting off into the rose maze. Once they passed through the arch, they disappeared from sight. The rose hedges were too tall to see which way they went. If we had been in one of the castle's towers, I was confident we could see into the whole rose maze and what they were doing.

"Would someone in the towers be able to see them?" I questioned.

"Most definitely, but we are assuming since no rumors have flown, that no one has seen them yet. Or if someone has seen them, they are of lower ranking and do not want to receive the punishment." I glanced back at Iyrse, who was focused on cleaning her nails. Glancing back out the window for a moment longer and not seeing any other movement, I decided to head back to my chair to resume my spot.

"We are the second wealthiest monarchy," Tearani began, "if anyone could spread the rumor and not receive backlash, it would have to be us." She blinked.

"But we don't like drama, so we just observe," added Iyrse. These two twins probably had more knowledge and dirt on everyone in this castle than they knew what to do with. They probably could destroy people's reputations with a blink of Tearani's eyes. I was beginning to feel relief that I was on their good side.

"We should sit together from here on out," Iyrse said randomly.

"Yes, that would be nice," Tearani replied, gazing out the window.

"I will not be attending tomorrow's tea ceremony, but I would like that a lot." I gave a half smile. Trying to navigate these two twins might be both fun and exhausting, but at least I would no longer be alone during the events.

"Because of your birthday?" Tearani turned her head slowly to me, blinking as she awaited my answer.

"Yes." I blushed, not anticipating they would have known that.

"We got you a present," Iyrse said before bounding out of her chair into the other room. She returned with a small black box tied with a pretty purple bow.

"I was not expecting this," I replied, startled as both twins watched me.

"We know, now open it!" Squealed Iyrse in delight. I undid the bow, lifting the lid, and gazed upon a simple gold chain bracelet with blue sapphire stones inlaid in it.

"It is gorgeous," I said as I picked up the bracelet from the box.

"It is a matching ankle bracelet to ours," Tearani replied as she lifted her leg up to show off an ankle bracelet identical to mine but with diamond stones instead.

"Mine has white sapphires," Iyrse lifted her leg, waving it about to show off the final matching piece. I began to blink back tears very quickly from the sudden burst of emotions I just received.

"Put it on, put it on!" Demanded Iyrse. Her bossiness caused me to laugh as I bent over to clasp it to my ankle. I inhaled deeply to push down the tears and emotions swirling within me.

"There! Now you are one of us!" Declared Iyrse. I sat back up and cocked my head at her quizzically.

"They are friendship bracelets; only the three of us have them," Tearani said with her way of a smile before looking back out the window.

"They were my idea," Iyrse exclaimed, giving herself credit for the idea. I was not going to question how the twins came to the idea that we were just magically friends after one day of conversation. This was probably one of the best birthday gifts I had received.

Chapter Eight

I aimlessly wandered the castle corridors. I knew I should be attending the tea ceremony with the rest of the princesses and ladies, but quite frankly, it was my birthday. I did not want to deal with Regina. I did not want her, Olivia, or anyone else to ruin my day. Even with the new profound knowledge I had gleaned from the twins, I just wanted a day to myself.

When I was younger and had eavesdropped on conversations from visiting guests at home, I would hear there was a library on the second floor of the castle. From the moment Mother and Father announced my departure from Kingdom Theorines, I had been anticipating on finding the library. I wanted to see it at least once in my life because if I left here and never took an opportunity, I would be forever disappointed in myself.

Kingdom Theorines had something you could potentially call a library. That is, if you did not have the faintest idea of what a library actually looked like. Granted, who was I to judge and make assumptions? My only experience and ideas of a library came from the books I read describing them. Even then, my knowledge was limited. Mother was not too keen on my love of reading.

"Reading is for people who hate their lives. You are not a bore, are you? No, you are meant to be queen of the wealthiest and largest monarchy." Her voice played in my mind as I thought back to that day. She had found me reading and ripped the book from my hands. She did not even think as she threw the book into the crackling fireplace, ignoring my pleas. To this day, I still do not know how the story ended or even what the title was. The only thing I could remember is it was about a Princess who did not want to be in an arranged marriage. She ran away to the Fae kingdom and begged their king to protect her from her future fate.

After that day, I ensured never to pick up another book again if my mother was nearby. Even during her parties, I was hesitant while locked up in my room. She had a habit upon occasion where she would come to check on me. She claimed it was because she wanted to make sure no one had attempted to harm me. I would just nod in agreement, feigning slight fear. I knew she did not want me sneaking out to be seen by anyone. Either way, I wanted another book to avoid suffering the same fate as the first one.

I came upon two beautiful gilded French doors. All the doors were extravagant here, but these were even more ornate with their golds inlaid into the rich dark red mahogany wood that was the staple color in the castle. Taking a chance, I pushed open to happily see I had found the library.

Joy filled me at my accomplishment. I took a tentative step in. It was deathly quiet here. Despite the quietness, it must have been regularly cleaned. There was not a speck of dust to the visible eye. But then again, King Regalius and Queen Serenity could afford regular cleanings of their whole castle, including the unused rooms. I dismissed the thought, not wanting to dwell on it, as I took another step in.

Where do I even begin? Books surrounded me everywhere with oversized chairs. How could I even begin to pick what to read? I guess I could just browse and hope something jumped out at me. It was a bit overwhelming. Rarely did my hands have an opportunity to receive new books, and now I had a plethora of them at my whims. I ran my fingers over the spines of the ones closest to me. Taking a deep breath, I began to lock this memory into place for later. When I had my own home, I would have a library. Then again, if things went according to Mother's plan, this would become my library.

I came to the end of the bookcase and was ready to delve into the next row when a hand fell on my shoulder. I jumped as I whirled around to find myself face-to-face with Knox.

"Knox!" I gasped. I did not know what I would tell him about my reason for being here.

"Mina." He nodded in greeting as we both stood there awkwardly. I counted down from five. If he did not say anything, I would break the silence.

Five . . . four . . . three . . . two . . . one . . .

"Do you come–"

"Would you care–"

We both started to say something at the same time, causing us to break out in laughter.

"Go ahead, Knox." I nodded, and he shook his head as he shuffled his feet before locking them into place, a nervous tick he must be correcting.

"No, I insist, Mina."

"Are you sure?" I was trying to fight back my embarrassment. Gritting my teeth, I hoped my face had not turned red. I wondered why he was here.

"Yes, please." He half-smiled encouragingly. I had a feeling we would just keep going around and around until I finally caved, which is what I decided to do now. Letting out a quick sigh, I curtsied.

"Alright, thank you. Do you come here often, Knox?"

"Well, I never leave since I live here," he joked, and at first, it took me a moment to catch on to what he meant.

"Oh! No! I meant the library!" I rushed out, causing him to laugh. My face scrunching up in confusion.

"I knew what you meant, and I am just teasing you, Mina." He chuckled light-heartedly. My face flushed at my mistake, as my skin became hot from embarrassment.

"Oh! My mistake." I looked at the floor, not wanting to meet his eye at my daftness. I mumbled under my breath, "I like it when you call me Mina."

"I beg your pardon?" His low voice asked as he leaned in closer to me.

"I like it when you call me Mina, no princess, no titles," I replied louder while still looking at the floor.

"It would be nice if you looked at me when we talked," he said instead, and I trailed my gaze from his boots up his black trousers, his overly detailed black jacket that was embroidered with smoke gray thread, and finally up to his face and his beautiful green eyes.

"Yes, Sir, I mean!" My hands came up to my face, covering my mouth at my constant blundering. "Knox! Yes, Knox!" His eyes widened in startelement at my outburst before he began full-on laughing. I realized the silliness of my reaction and joined him in laughter. The laughter died down, and he smiled as he said, "I come to the library regularly... Do you like to read?"

That was a loaded question. The simple answer was yes, but I did not know if I should tell him that. What if he told someone and it got back to Mother? What if he laughed at me for enjoying reading? I was hoping to come here in solitude with everyone busy today. Which would be the correct answer to give? Be true to myself or be the princess my mother had raised?

"I can tell you are in some sort of internal dilemma in your mind," Knox said, breaking my thoughts. "Just tell me."

I leaned in. "Want to hear a secret?" He nodded, leaning into me, feeling the sense of common ground from the first time I told him a secret about myself on the dance floor.

I whisper in his ear with my hand cupped. "Promise not to tell anyone?"

He nodded again.

"I love reading." I smiled. It felt nice telling him my secret.

He pulled back. "Can I tell you a secret?"

I nodded back.

"Promise not to tell anyone?" I giggled at him, repeating what I had said, and nodded again. He leaned in to whisper in my ear, "I like you."

I stilled, my heart stuttered a beat as my smile faltered, shocked at his confession. I had expected him to tell me he loved reading as well, not confess his feelings. He pulled away to study my face, and I did not know how to react or respond as my heart began to thunder in my chest. My mind immediately went to what had happened with Bay in the maze.

My hands began to sweat as my mind was spinning. The bookcases around us began to enclose in on us. I was conflicted. I knew feelings for Knox had been bubbling within me, but I brushed them off as feelings of friendship. My feelings were not a part of the plan. His eyes were searching mine for a response.

"Knox," I said softly, watching his lighthearted expression turn serious. I reached my hand up to touch his cheek, but he stepped back. His face became guarded with that well-known blank expression.

"Mina, calm down. I did not mean it like that," he replied casually, but I could hear the quick upticks at the end of his words. His blank expression remained in place, telling me he was lying.

"Are you sure?" I asked, biting the inside of my cheek. I wanted to look anywhere but him, but I was afraid of how he would interpret that.

"I get it. I am The Reclusive Prince." He scratched the back of his head. "I know all the females are here just for my brother. No one wants me." He ended with a sad smile.

"That is not true!" I nearly shouted to override his emotions, my hands gripping the fabric on his sleeves in my fist. His eyes widened in shock.

"Mina, you do not need to tell me otherwise; I know the truth." He shifted on his feet, glancing towards the doorway. I knew he wanted to flee.

"Stay with me. We are friends, right?" I was tugging at every string I had to make him stay. My hands squeezing the fabric tighter.

"Yeah . . . I guess we are." He began to relax a bit in his stance. I did not think he would leave, but I was not confident in my thoughts either. I relaxed my grip on his sleeves and then dropped my hands back to infront of me as I fiddled with my fingers.

"Okay, then let us go sit down and talk about books." I smiled at him, hoping this would put us back on even ground. He hesitantly returned the smile with a nod before taking a step toward the chairs. I went to turn to follow him but tripped over my own two feet, causing me to crash into him. I squeezed my eyes shut as we both went down, my back hitting the floor with him on top of me. His hand was underneath my head, preventing me from cracking it against the ground.

He was breathing hard against me. I peeked my eyes open to see his face mere inches away from mine. He was watching me. I reached my hand up between us to touch the side of his face. My heart began to beat faster from the molten look in his eyes.

"Knox," I whispered and then Knox's lips crashed down on mine, kissing me with desperation and a need of hunger. It took my brain a second to catch up before I was kissing him back, running my fingers through his long, luscious black hair. He moaned into my mouth, his fingers entangling into my hair, gripping me tightly. I wrapped my arms around his neck, bringing him closer to me. He broke the kiss, making me begin to protest.

"Mina, if I do not stop now . . ." he trailed off. I blushed, understanding what he alluded to.

"Well, this is a sight to see," stated a snotty voice behind us. We both jumped as Knox rolled off of me and away. I leaned up on my elbows. There stood Regina. My stomach dropped with dread. Why was she here? She was supposed to be at the tea ceremony. Why would someone like her be coming to the library? Was she here to hook up with Devereux?

I was at a loss for words of how to respond. Knox began to help me up; I did not take my eyes off Regina as she watched every single move. Knox tucked me into his side, and I fisted my hands into his jacket to keep me steady. He had his body partially in between Regina and me.

"Princess Regina Isadora," Knox greeted coolly.

"Prince Killien Knox." She dipped in a quick, messy curtsey. She did not even show him remotely the same level of respect as she did Bay. I wondered if she was annoyed that she was forced to dignify herself to give Knox any form of respect. That even though he was not the heir, he was the younger brother and still held more authority and power over her.

"Why are you not at the tea ceremony?" He asked. This caused Regina to blink at being questioned about her whereabouts. She most likely did not grow up like I did, always needing an alibi for her whereabouts. With next in line for her queendom, she probably was rarely questioned to begin with.

"Oh, well, I decided to take a stroll instead." She was lying, and we all knew it.

"Is that so?" Knox raised his eyebrow at her.

"Yes." With a vicious smile on her lips, my stomach began to form knots. "Imagine my surprise to find you with The Tower Princess." It was as if she dumped ice water on me. I glanced at Knox. His puzzled expression tried to work out what she meant. Surely, he had to have heard the rumors about me. This was not the first time Regina had called me a tower princess in front of him. Why did he look confused?

"Excuse me." I pushed out of his arms, running past Regina and out of the library. I needed air. I made a beeline back to my rooms. I would find sanctuary, knowing Eloise would not be there currently. Tears were already forming in my eyes as I stumbled. Regina was probably already turning Knox against me with how pathetic I was, just like my kingdom.

Chapter Nine

Eloise helped me dress for another ball, but in my mind, it was another chance to be potentially humiliated. After Regina ruined everything in the library, I skipped the rest of the events on the itinerary. Eloise sensed something was wrong, and despite her pressuring, I refused to tell her what had happened. I knew she would scold me if I admitted the truth. She had not been in my rooms when I bursted through the doors bawling. By the time Eloise showed up, I had my makeup already fixed and just pretended I needed a nap.

"This soft pink dress will look lovely on you," Eloise commented while holding up the gown. The dress was not as glamorous as my other dresses, but its abundance of tulle made it pretty on its own.

"Mmh, okay," I replied dully. Eloise tilted her head slightly to the side. I could tell she was mulling over whether she should ask me again what had happened or not. I braced myself, but the question never came. Instead, she began grabbing the dress to pull over my head. I raised my arms to accommodate.

"I think simple white pearls will compliment the dress."

"Mmh."

"How about I coil multiple sections of your hair to hang down your back and over your shoulder?"

"Mmh."

"Mina . . . What happened?" Eloise walked around to stand in front of me. "Please tell me."

I looked away from her, not wanting to answer.

"Mina, we don't keep secrets from each other. What are you not telling me?" She begged. I gritted my teeth, willing myself not to tell her. My skin felt tight, and I felt the burn in my eyes from trying not to allow the tears to form. She sighed and continued to help me get ready in silence.

Heading straight to the wine table, I grabbed a goblet. Tonight, it would be just me, the wall, and wine. I scanned the room and came up empty of finding Knox anywhere. Bay was in the middle of a group of girls, and unless I shoved my way through, there would be no way of reaching him. My back thumped against the wall as I used it as support, dejected. I let out a long sigh from my nose. If Knox did not show up, I would not have anyone to talk to or dance with. Then again, he probably did not want anything to do with me, depending on what Regina had told him after I ran out.

I grabbed my second goblet of wine, and Knox still had yet to arrive. I lost track of where Bay had wandered off to as well. Even the twins had yet to make an appearance; maybe they were not serious about being friends. I looked down into my goblet, swirling the wine around. My face began to feel the warmth from the wine.

"Do you enjoy drinking wine that has already been paid for?" Jabbed Regina. I glanced up. I was too consumed in my thoughts to notice her and Olivia. Thankfully, I did not think any of the other guests were close enough to hear Regina's comment.

"If you will excuse me." I rolled my eyes, shoving off the wall as I tried to slip away, but Olivia blocked me in. It was my fault for becoming lazy and using the wall for support in the first place.

"Not so fast." She smiled. "We want to know something."

"What is it this time?" I asked, mentally exhausted.

"You are here to manipulate Bay into marrying you," stated Regina.

"Is that not why everyone else is here?" I sipped from my goblet. I was bored and irritated, not wanting to play her game. Regina curled her lip at me.

"You sure do hang out with The Reclusive Prince a lot," Regina mused. I stayed quiet, not knowing where she was going with this.

"One would almost think you favored him over Bay. I hear the reason no one gets too close to him is because of a curse. Maybe curses are contagious and attract one another," she drawled on. "You must have some curse placed upon you, Tower Princess."

"No! No, I do not!" I defended myself. It always came back to my upbringing. I could not control or change how I was raised, but why did I need to be punished for it relentlessly? Did these people have nothing better to do? All because of my parent's poor choices in the past? I did not need another nickname attached to my name, either.

"Hmm, are you so sure? You were kissing Knox in the library," Regina countered. I was hoping she would conveniently forget that. Or, at the very minimum, I hoped she would never bring it up.

"You kissed my brother?" Bay's voice came accusingly from my side. I gasped, whirling to look at him, completely petrified. He glowered at me. Regina had set me up. I had been wholly focused on her and Olivia, that I had not been paying attention to my surroundings.

"No! I mean, yes, but- -," I tried to argue to preserve Bay's thoughts on me. I saw his disgusted face and Regina's cocky smile. She had set a trap for me to fall into at the right time. She waited for Bay to be nearby to hear.

"You know she is only here for your riches," chimed in Olivia. If I could, I would push Olivia off a cliff right now. Bay glanced at Olivia, and his hardened expression did not change as he glanced back at me. Regina trailed her hand up his arm and draped herself against him as she added, "I hear she has been spreading her legs for anyone who will pay her."

"No!" I gasped at the audacity of her lie.

"Oh really?" asked Regina. "Then why did I hear a duke say how mediocre you were the other night?"

"I do not even know what you are talking about!?" This was becoming ridiculous.

"You kissed my brother?" Bay repeated, the end of his sentence being a bit higher, his question sounding more like an accusation.

"Yes." I did not break eye contact with him, hoping that was the only thing he would believe from Regina and Olivia's vicious mouths. He stared at me, and I stared back at him.

He broke eye contact as he looked at Regina. "Come along, Gina." I did not miss how he called her a nickname similar to mine. He offered his arm to her, to which she took it, and the two walked away from me with Olivia in tow. Regina looked over her shoulder and gave me a smirk. Olivia, seeing her do it, mimicked the gesture.

I leaned back heavily against the wall. I had no idea how I was going to repair this damage. How did I even get myself into this whole mess? I was being punished for having feelings for Knox and having something special with him that Regina ended up spoiling and ruining everything. I just lost my chances of marrying Bay, and if those dreadful rumors got back to Knox, I would undoubtedly lose him too.

"Hey, you look miserable, everything okay?" I looked to my left to find Knox approaching. *Oh no.*

"No, it is not," I said, defeated. Concern washed over his face as he tucked some strands of hair behind my ear.

"What is wrong? What happened?" He demanded.

"Regina told your brother about our kiss- -"

"And you are ashamed?" He interrupted, accusing me as he pulled back.

"No! She continued that I have been sleeping around for money and- -"

"Wait, she what?" He interrupted again, confused. I relayed everything that had occurred seconds prior to him showing up. The part of me that had been nervous he would not want anything to do with me after Regina talked to him yesterday began to fade away.

"I will fix this all with Bay; do not fret about that," Knox assured me.

"Thank you," I said quietly. Hopefully, Knox could undo everything Regina just did to my reputation. I could only hope Bay would be more inclined to listen to his brother's words over Regina's.

"Now, come on, let us not ruin the night." Knox smiled, offering me his hand. I hesitantly smiled back, taking his hand in mine. He led us out to the dance floor, placing us alongside a few other couples. I noticed the nameless prince a few feet from us, but he had not looked our way.

"Someone catch your eye?" Knox asked, bringing my attention back to him.

"No, just looking to see who else was on the dance floor," I commented. I wanted to avoid upsetting him by bringing up another prince. The music started, and we fell into step with the melody.

Knox twirled me around the dance floor. Each spin made my uneasiness melt away. When he turned me back to face him, I looked up to find him smiling down at me. I gave him a shy smile back.

Between the two goblets of wine and the twirls he had me doing, the room became a bit out of focus. I tilted my head as I studied his face. I noted how his emerald green eyes had flecks of yellow and blue within them. Tilting my head to the other side, I realized he had very light freckles on his cheeks and nose—something I probably would never have seen if I had not been staring at him intently.

"You are staring awfully hard. Something the matter?" Knox asked. I tilted my head back to the other side, trying to understand what he had just said. Something about 'staring hard' and 'the matter.' My mind tried to work out the sentences as I squinted my eyes, trying to make it make sense.

"Mina?" He prompted.

"I've never noticed your freckles before," I commented the first thing that sprung to my mind.

"My freckles?" He questioned, raising an eyebrow, confused,

"Yeah, they're barely noticeable. If I had not been looking, I would have missed them."

"I was unaware freckles were something of interest to you?" Knox gave me an amused expression.

"You also have yellow and blue flakes in your eyes. I had thought they were only green, but now I see yellow and blue reside in you, too." I stated, ignoring his previous comment.

"And your violet eyes have pink and blue specks," Knox replied.

"Yeah, they do. Most people don't ever notice that about me, though. Then again, most people never see me, so how would they know?" I gave a sad shrug as I looked past Knox down at the floor. I realized we had stopped dancing and were just standing in the middle of the room as other couples twirled around us.

"Do you want to get out of here?" Knox asked. I nodded, not even looking at him as I continued to stare at the same spot on the floor.

He led me out of the ballroom and towards the library. The zoning out I had felt while in the ballroom was beginning to recede away with the cool air.

He opened the library door. The room was completely dark and quiet, just like earlier today. I highly doubted anyone else was in here. Knox turned on a few lights until we were to the comfy reading chairs where we settled in.

"Mina, tell me about a book you think about often," Knox began the discussion. I loved that he instantly wanted to distract me from my current life problems.

"Well," I started, knowing this was a long stretch, "there was this book I read a few years ago that I *absolutely* loved."

"What was the title?"

"Well, that is the thing, I do not know the title or the author or how it ended..." I twisted my fingers.

"Then how do you know you love it?" He chuckled at all the missing information. I propped myself up, excited to finally talk about this book.

"Well, see, my mother was against me reading, but I did not know that until she caught me reading, and well." This was where I began to worry about telling this part of the story. "She caught me reading and grabbed the book, and she threw it into the burning fireplace."

Knox gasped.

"And after that, I made sure to never read when she could possibly catch me," I finished.

"So, you were like a sneaky book reader, stealthy," he teased, causing me to smile to myself.

"Yeah, I was. This one time, I thought she was too busy to check on me during one of her parties. Well, I heard her footsteps approaching my door. I had to hide my book under my pillow and grab my needlework so fast so she would not suspect a thing. My heart raced while talking to her and continued to race minutes after she left," I laughed. It felt good to tell someone this story that was not Eloise.

"I could only believe how fast your heart was racing, so what was the book about? What do you remember?"

I began to tell him the bits and pieces I could remember of the book I had loved so much and thought of often just because I wanted to know how it ended. I had assumed it was a love story, but there were no guarantees.

"I know that book!" Knox jumped up, shaking his pointer finger, trying to think of the book. "It is around here somewhere." He ran to a bookcase with me following in tow. He began rifling through books as I stood to the side watching him. I was not confident I would even recognize it if I did put my hands on it.

"Not here, not here," he mumbled as he kept rifling and moving through the bookcases. He was in a frenzy looking for this book, and I was finding entertainment and endearment from how devoted he was.

"Aha! Here it is!" He pulled a book out from the shelf, "*A Court of Smoke and Mirrors*. I think you will enjoy the ending. It is a trilogy." He winked as he handed me the book. I took it, staring at the beautiful cover I had long forgotten about all those years ago. I brought the book to my chest, cradling it as I rocked, swaying back and forth, smiling at my gifted treasure.

"Thank you," I said, my heart warming from his kindness.

Knox took a step closer to me and another step. He brought his right hand up to my face as he caressed my cheek. Leaning in, he kissed me. I kissed him back, deciding not to hold back and resume from where we had left off earlier. He wrapped his arms around me, bringing me and the book still clutched to my chest closer to him. He took another step forward, making me take a step back. Another step forward and another step back until the back of my knees hit the settee.

Slowly, he guided me down. Without breaking the kiss, he took the book I had been so desperately clutching and placed it on the table beside us. He lightly rested his body weight on me as we continued to kiss. His hands trailed my body as my hands ran through his hair and down his back. I yearned for Knox. I needed him. His hand came up to cup my right breast, and I pushed my hips against his as he grinded back on mine. I could feel his hard cock pressed into me, and it made me giddy to know that I was the cause of it. I could make him physically feel this way.

"Mina," he moaned through our kisses.

"Mmh, Knox," I moaned back. Trailing my hands from his back to in between us as I began to play with the buttons on his shirt. I was nervous to make the next move, but I wanted to. He growled at my fingers, undoing a button of his. I knew what we were doing was scandalous, but I could not stop. I partly blamed the wine mixed in with the sadness I had felt. I just wanted to feel something with someone. The small part of me that I tried to ignore just wanted to feel needed.

"I take it there is no way to get you out of this dress," he said in a husky voice.

I giggled. "Not in a timely manner, no."

"Maybe we will just have to work around that." He gave me a devilish grin as his other hand trailed down my side and hip. I felt him grab my dress and work it up in between us. I abandoned undoing his button to help him as the fabric from my dress began to bunch up. I felt his hand brush against the skin of my inner thigh, causing me to tremble. His fingers glided up higher.

"Knox."

"Hmm?" His kisses trailed from my lips to my chin and down my neck, and I shivered.

"Can I tell you a secret?"

He nodded.

"I have never done this before." In my vulnerability, I had to tell him so he would understand my inexperience.

"Mina, can I tell you a secret?"

I nodded as he continued to kiss down my neck.

"Nor have I." He kissed my collarbone, and his fingers began to play at the edge of my panties. I tilted my hips up into his hand, wanting more.

"You do not think anyone will come in here, do you?" I asked nervously with worry.

"No, this is my lair," he growled as he stopped kissing his way down to my breast. His fingers slipped into my panties. His eyes caught mine as he said, "people do not come where they know I will be."

"What about me?" I whispered.

"You are mine now, Persamina," he growled, his eyes darkening as he plunged a finger into me; I gasped. He silenced my gasp instantly, his lips finding mine again. I moaned into his mouth, pushing my hips up into his hand.

I heard a noise at the entrance of the library, causing us both to freeze.

"What was that?" I whispered as quietly as possible.

"Maybe a cat?" He whispered back, not moving. We waited five seconds and did not hear anything, both of us holding our breath. Another five seconds and Knox began to push his finger in deeper as he kissed me again. I returned the kiss, running my fingers down his chest to resume undoing his shirt buttons.

"So, it is true," crooned Bay's voice from towards the library entrance. Knox and I froze as we looked at Bay leaning against a bookcase. He was not looking at Knox; his eyes were locked on mine, and I felt as if time had froze.

Distantly, I heard Knox tell Bay to get out of here, but Bay just kept staring at me, unmoving. I felt Knox withdraw his finger from me as he got off of me. Out of my peripheral vision, I watched him making his way to Bay, but Bay never broke his gaze from mine. Knox shoved him and began yelling to get out, but even then, Bay did not break.

It was the second shove that caused Bay to break our connection as he caught himself against a bookcase. Suddenly, Knox's yelling became louder as he was repeatedly telling Bay to get out. I realized the state I had been in and started smoothing my dress down over my legs before fixing my rumpled hair strands back into place as best as possible. I stood up when Knox started threatening to physically remove Bay from the room.

"Knox! Enough!" I commanded as I marched up to him. Both brothers looked at me in shock, either from someone giving an order to a prince or they had not expected me to speak up at all.

"Knox, just let him go," I added as my eyes caught Bay's, and our connection locked into place again. Knox was saying something, but I had no idea what it was. Bay must have heard him, though, because he nodded as he took a step backward.

"Good night, Mina," Bay said to me before breaking our connection again as he turned and left. I focused on Knox as he stood sideways from me, glaring where Bay had been standing moments prior, his fist clenched tight at his sides. His jaw worked back and forth as he ground his teeth.

"Knox." I reached my hand out towards him.

"No," he ordered. "Do *not* touch me."

"Knox," I repeated, worried this time.

"I need you to leave now." He continued to glare at the same spot.

"But Knox." I panicked, not understanding what was going on. It was like a switch had flipped in Knox. This was not the same man I had come to know. This man was cold without any ounce of affection. Pure hatred and loathing rolled off of him, and it scared me.

"Leave!" He roared. Whirling to where stacks of books sat on a table, he shoved them all off. The books went flying every which way. One of them hit me in the face before I had time to react and protect myself. My eyes widened as I took a step back, cupping my cheek from his rage. "Get out of my sight, now!" He bellowed. He did not even seem to care if I was okay. I did not think twice as I ran past him to make my escape out of the library and away from him.

I slammed the library doors behind me, resting my back against them. Not enough time had elapsed since Bay's departure because he was only a few steps away. From the loud banging of the doors closing, he turned to see the commotion I had made behind him. I watched as his eyes widened before taking a few steps towards me. I was breathing hard and shaking, letting the doors support my full weight. He stopped in front of me, neither of us speaking. I looked up at him, our gazes locking. Out of my peripheral vision, I watched his hand come up to touch my cheek. I flinched from the stinging sensation it caused. His eyes darkened as his thumb smoothed over it. He flicked his focus to glare at the closed library door and then glanced back to me.

He leaned in; our lips were close to touching. I held my breath, not knowing where this was going to go. My heart was hammering in my ears. His eyes did not reveal anything, as mine held so many questions for him. He pulled away and, taking a step back, turned and walked in the opposite direction of my room. I took a couple of steps forward, thinking I would follow him. However, I ended up leaning against the wall. Finding support, I tried to figure out what just passed between Bay and me. What just happened with Knox? My head swam with a dozen questions and came up with zero answers. I gave myself another few seconds before slowly making my way back to my room.

Chapter Ten

Two days had passed since that night, and I had seen neither Knox nor Bay around the castle. I was hoping I would see them tonight at the ball. Maybe try.... It never ceased to amaze me with all these balls they were throwing that it had been two days since that night and I had seen neither Knox or Bay around the castle. I was hoping tonight at the ball I would finally see either of the brothers.

Eloise had been a bit absent as well as she was spending more and more time with the other servants. Though I had a budding friendship with the twins, I was unsure if I could trust to tell them everything that had occurred. I believed I had come close to losing my virginity on my birthday to Knox, but the electric sparks I felt with Bay kept me confused. Bay was who I needed for a future husband, not Knox. I knew Eloise would scold me for allowing it to go that far with the younger brother. I believed she would keep my secret from Mother, but if she told another servant from home and if they told Mother... Not that Eloise has ever led me to believe that she would betray my trust, nor has she in the past, but I just could not take that risk in my life.

Eloise should be hurrying back any moment to help me prepare for the ball. Tonight, I wanted to wear the beautiful A-line dress that reminded me of a sunset. It started as a golden yellow at the top and slowly faded into a peachy orange until it settled at the bottom as a hot magenta pink. Various gemstones were inlaid throughout the dress, blending with the colors as they transitioned. It would not matter which way I moved; I knew the gems would sparkle against the light.

I would ask Eloise to style my hair up in a bun with two long curled coils of hair to drape over my shoulder. I went to the jewelry box in search of two thin, elongated teardrop imperial flame topaz stone earrings and the matching necklace. The jewelry would match the dress splendidly. All the other balls, I felt like a little girl playing dress up amongst the princesses. Tonight, I was done playing. Tonight, I will be the one to take the reins.

I arrived at the ball and immediately took notice the lack of either prince brother. I would not let this damper my mood, though. In my perusing, I caught sight of the twins and began to make my way across the room to them.

I did not get even halfway there before a group of princes blockaded me. One of the princes was the nameless one whom I kept running into. He gave me a wink. Prince Voltaire Edric, the one Olivia was sleeping with, smiled at me, and then there was a third prince with golden blonde hair and blue eyes that I did not recognize.

"Hello, Princess Persamina," began the nameless Prince. "Allow me to officially introduce myself. I am Prince Montgomery Victory of Queendom Grewt'en." His body swept into a gracious low bow. This was one of Regina's brothers. My eyes widened as I took a step back. He looked up as if sensing me putting the two pieces together and smiled.

"My brother is terrible at remembering to introduce me, his younger brother," The golden-haired one humorously said, "I am Prince Percival Chivarly." He bowed in turn, but not before he gave me a warm smile. Were these two truly Regina's brothers? I did not want to be deceived. This could be a trap to humiliate me as well.

"Princess Persamina Rowena," Prince Voltaire Edric said in a way to catch my attention. I locked eyes with his blue ones, and he grinned. "I am Prince Voltaire Edric." He swept into an even more gracious bow than the other two. His shoulder-length black hair fell forward over his face.

"It is an honor to meet all three of you," I replied uneasily with a curtsy. I caught sight of Iryse smirking at me over the three bowing princes while Tearani blinked before looking elsewhere in the room. I was sure there would be comments made when I was finally free of the trio.

Prince Montgomery Victory was the first to rise from his bow, with each prince following suit behind him. I found their synchronization quite comical.

"May I have your first dance, Princess?" Prince Montgomery Victory offered me his hand. I vaguely heard the band readying to start the first dance of the evening. I knew I could not outright refuse, and without either T'Lovoness brother here to save me, I was at these three princes' mercy; so *much for taking tonight by the reins.*

I gave a shy smile as I put my hand within his. "I would be quite honored, Prince Montgomery Victory."

"Please, call me Montgomery. Titles can be a little *too* stuffy." He flashed a brilliant smile that I am certain made the other girls swoon around him. He may not be heir to the throne, but I doubted his charmingly good looks would stop the girls from chasing after him.

Montgomery led us to the dance floor. He positioned us a few couples down from Regina and Devereoux. Regina had not noticed us entering the dance floor, which was probably a good thing. Scanning the room, I did not find Olivia, which explained why Voltaire Edric had been talking to me. I partially wondered where she was at but really did not want to dwell on it too much. There is no sense in fretting over it.

The music began, and Montgomery started to lead.

"Tell me about yourself, Princess," Montgomery began the small talk that seemed to accompany dances.

"Why didn't you tell me who you were all this time?" I asked instead.

"Where would the fun in that be? If you knew I was Regina's brother, you would have run away from me . . . and for good reason." He laughed.

"What do you want with me?" I remained guarded.

"To be your friend," he offered.

"Why?"

"Does it matter?" He countered my question with his own, and I stumbled. He caught me and corrected our steps to keep in sync with the couples around us.

"Thank you, and I suppose not."

"Excellent, now tell me about yourself," he tried again.

"Well, I am from Theorines and . . ." Montgomery cut me off.

"No, no, I know the basics. What makes you, *you*, Mina?" He gave that charming smile again. I was startled that he called me by my nickname.

"I love lemon pastries and being outside," I replied, trying again.

"I am a fan of cherry pastries," he commented.

"Guess we will not be stealing each other's desserts then," I teased. He slightly chuckled back.

"I suppose not." I had become a lot better at dancing than the first night and made it through the first dance with only three mistakes. Montgomery did not even blink when I made the mistake, just correcting me so we stayed in step with the rest.

The dance ended and I was ready to make my exit off the dance floor when the younger brother, Prince Percival Victory, claimed my hand for the next dance. At this trade-off, I caught Regina glaring at her two brothers. I tried to hide out of sight by being blocked by Montgomery's frame. Then, her glare landed on me. Prince Percival Victory led us to dance, breaking Regina's view of us.

What I gleaned from the second dance with the younger brother is he definitely preferred titles. It seemed being born into a queendom bothered him quite a bit. He most likely would never be a king and would have to settle. He was not rude or cruel like Regina; he just had a bit of a chip on his shoulder. The only thing he seemed fond of talking about was their baby sister, Princess Grace Lily. I got the distinct impression she had him wrapped around all of her fingers.

By the end of the second dance, I was already prepared for Prince Voltaire Edric to claim the third dance. I walked out to the dance floor with confidence as he took my hand in his. Prince Percival Victory bowed a little ruffled, most likely from the lack of respect that Prince Voltaire Edric gave him.

"Mina, Mina, you look quite splendid tonight," he began, starting off as if we were good friends. It took me a bit off guard that I almost messed up the first step of the dance.

"Thank you, Voltaire," I replied sweetly. His eyes glinted wickedly at this.

"You came in, took this place by storm, and now I have the most beautiful princess in my arms." He showered me with compliments. I blushed, not anticipating this.

"I thought you were with Princess Olivia?" I questioned. I barely caught his quick roll of the eyes.

"Nah, not really. She is not the final prize," he replied nonchalantly.

"Then who is?" I asked before I could stop myself.

"Why, you." He gave me a wicked smile that matched his wickedly delightful blue eyes. My breath hitched; not prepared to be in a predicament like this. I had been anticipating for him to tell me Iryse.

"Me? But w-why me?" I stammered out.

"Let me see, both T'Lovoness brothers see something in you, meaning you must be something special," he replied matter-of-factly.

"Both brothers?" I asked, pretending to be uncertain. I knew I was fishing for knowledge I already was aware of, thanks to the twins.

"Knox only talks to you, and you are the only princess Bay has complimented and danced with this whole courting season." Voltaire raised an eyebrow at me, seeing if I would challenge his statement.

"I do not know if that would make me special," I replied with a shrug, thankfully not missing a step in the dance. Voltaire chuckled, shaking his head at me.

"What?" I asked out of curiosity, not liking being left out of a joke.

"Not to be rude, but you are quite oblivious to what everyone else is witnessing and whispering to each other." He still had his eyebrow raised, expecting me to challenge it. He had fallen for my act.

"I just do not see what you and everyone else sees." I tried not to sound snippy with my reply. When Voltaire raised his eyebrow higher, giving me a knowing smile, I knew instantly that it had been harsh.

When the dance ended, I was ready to exit the dance floor. Voltaire caught my hand before I could head towards the twins.

"Mina, if we become nothing more than friends . . ." he paused to add emphasis, ". . . Then I would be very grateful for your friendship." He brought my hand up to his lips as he kissed the back of it.

"I will take the next dance," Knox's cold, stern voice came from behind me. I caught Voltaire's eyes dancing with delight as he winked at me, confirming what he already knew. He nodded his head to Knox, leaving the dance floor. Knox grabbed my right hand as my left came to rest on his shoulder.

"Why were you dancing with the likes of him?" He gritted out, glaring at me with icy, cold rage. I could not escape him once the music began. We fell into step with the rest of the dance floor.

"He asked me to?" I replied uneasily. After the way things had ended with us last, I was not sure how I should act around Knox. My cheek had a slight bruise that I had to cover with makeup to conceal the mark he had given me.

"You could have said no," he spat.

"I do not believe I did anything wrong, Knox," I replied, tacking his name on to emphasize my point. I really had done nothing wrong. I was asked to dance, and I simply said yes. Well, I really did not have a choice in the matter. How could I refuse three princes with larger kingdoms that were not poor? Even if Mother did not think that way, I did. I now understood more about what was at stake than just the kingdom.

Knox's grip on my hand tightened. I shot him a glare from the slight pain.

"You are hurting me, Knox," I said in a way, hoping to get him to loosen the grip he had on my hand. He was still glaring as he ever so slightly relaxed his grip. We did not speak anymore of the dance.

When it ended, he bowed as I curtsied. I caught sight of Bay, who had finally deigned to show up with narrowed eyes upon us. I turned away from him, rolling my eyes as I stalked towards the twins. They somehow managed to not move from their spot during all four of my dances.

Tonight, Iryse had her platinum blonde hair swept up into a bun with strands waved down along her face. She wore a powdery blue dress with a slit up her right leg. I saw her friendship ankle bracelet in its place. She wore a very chunky diamond necklace with matching diamond earrings. The only thing simple about her tonight was her silver tiara with small diamond gemstones.

Tearani wore a red body-fitted satin dress. It had matching leg slits that went up past the hips to her ribs. It was corseted with red ribbon from her ribs down to her hips. This was the first dress I had seen of Tearani's that was not strapless. It had a silk red sash around her neck that held up the mesh that connected to the very deep v-neck. She wore matching red silk arm sleeves that turned into lace with an eyelet around her middle fingers. Tearani's dark brown hair was done in a half updo with a golden tiara nestled on top. Her lips were painted red to match the dress, and she wore simple diamond earrings. She completely mesmerized me.

"You collecting princes there, Mina?" Iryse joked, breaking my trance of Tearani. Tearani said nothing as she continued to stare out at the dance floor.

"Something like that, it seems," I huffed.

"Wish you could have seen the way Bay looked like he wanted to burn everything to the ground with each dance," she continued on.

"Wait, when did he arrive?" I asked abruptly.

"He has been here the whole time," Tearani replied, not looking my way. "You just did not notice him. He never stopped watching you. When Voltaire kissed your hand, I thought he might have imploded."

"Yeah, it was quite fun to watch Bay with each passing dance," chimed in Iryse. "Especially when Knox took your hand. Did something happen between the three of you?" The images of that night flashed quickly through my mind.

"Something did happen, but do not push Iryse," Tearani scolded.

"How did you know?!" I gasped. Tearani turned her head slowly to me. Blinking, she replied, "I know everything." She blinked again before slowly turning her head back to watch the dance floor. I shivered.

"So, you know what happened?" I pushed with my question.

"No, but I know something happened," was her only reply. It gave me a little comfort to relax. I fiddled with my hands, debating whether I should tell the twins what happened or not. I barely came to a decision before Iryse interrupted my thoughts.

"Wait until we are alone together. Too many prying ears here." She smiled sweetly. She had a point as I looked around at the surrounding guests. There was no telling how many here were eavesdropping in on our conversation. If I had to guess, though? Probably quite a few, but it would not be just our conversation they were listening to. It would be every surrounding conversation, anywhere they possibly could obtain a snippet of gossip to spread amongst anyone who would listen. It was like a popularity contest of who knew the juiciest gossip. I was glad I was not a part of that. It just seemed like too much negative energy.

"Tearani, why do you choose not to dance with anyone?" I asked, changing the subject.

"No one has asked," she replied in her monotone voice.

"Anyone of interest?" I pushed.

"One." Her facial expression gave no indication of who, nor

would she probably reveal who it was either.

"Well, alrighty then," I replied awkwardly. I did not know how to move forward from there.

"Let's grab wine." Iryse looped her arm with mine. We left Tearani where she stood as we ventured to the wine table.

"She will not tell you who it is here, but when we are in our rooms together, you should ask her," Iryse chattered.

"I will try to remember to do that. I do not want to invade her privacy, though," I added on.

"You won't. Tearani likes you. You are a part of our tribe. One of us, you know, and all that," Iryse assured. At the wine table, she dropped my arm to grab two goblets, one for herself and one for Tearani. I grabbed my own goblet. As we turned back around, we noticed Deveoux chatting up Tearani.

"Well, that should be interesting," hummed Iryse to herself.

"Why is that?" I asked.

"Oh, nothing." Iryse led us back towards them. When Deveoux caught sight of us, he bowed to Tearani before walking away.

"What did he want?" Iryse asked, handing Tearani her wine.

"Nothing of sorts to repeat here." Tearani took a sip from her goblet. That ended that conversation. While the dances continued, no one asked the three of us to dance the rest of the evening. Instead, we found a table to sit at as we people-watched the guests. The twins continued to fill me in on every single guest's secrets.

By the end of the evening, I still could not understand why the three princes asked me to dance. Why Knox had been cruel or Bay's narrowing eyes. Knox had been nowhere to be found after our dance, and Bay never once looked in my direction the rest of the evening. I left the ball more confused than I had arrived. My only saving grace for having a good time was the twins. I promised them I would come over to their bedroom the following evening.

Chapter Eleven

I had been tossing and turning in bed for what felt like forever. In the middle of the night, I finally decided to give up on sleep. I could not get out of my head everything that had occurred at the ball. Maybe a snack from the kitchen would help clear my mind. If nothing else, then the walk to and from the kitchen should hopefully do the trick.

I did not want to wake Eloise, so I grabbed a simple pale blue dress to wear. It was simple enough that I could easily put it on without any help. I quickly tidied my hair in a low bun, even though I highly doubted I would run into anyone. On the off chance that I did, at the very least, they could say I was presentable.

I quietly opened my door to sneak out and hastily made my way to the kitchen. There was just something welcoming and homey about the kitchens. Back home, I had befriended our cook at a young age, and many times, she would have pastries amongst many other treats set out for me. How I did not ruin my appetite for meals was beyond me. I know princesses should not overindulge in food, but I just could not help myself. If it tasted amazing, then I just had to have another bite.

I had not had the time to make friends with this cook. I would need to change that. I knew there were benefits to being on good terms with the cook. Benefits such as not being scolded if I came into the kitchen randomly or maybe the benefit of the cook always having my favorite pastries made in case I did come for a visit. I liked being welcomed in a kitchen, truly being welcomed. And the only way that could happen is if I was on a friendly basis with the head cook.

I was aware of how protective and territorial cooks were of their areas. The King and Queen may rule their kingdom, but an intelligent royal would not mess with their kitchen staff, not to say all royals were wise. From the history books I had read, many royal cooks or cooks of higher households would have secrets to their recipes. If the royals fired them then the secret recipes would leave with them. The kitchen staff were also the first line of defense for safeguarding against being poisoned.

The head cook still respected the royals and probably even feared them, but I witnessed firsthand that even my parents respected the head cook in return. In this big of a kingdom, I wondered if The King and Queen even knew their head cook's name. I was far too lost within my own thoughts to realize I was already at the kitchen's entrance.

The fireplace was still burning with a kettle on it, as were a bunch of randomly placed candles. This kitchen put the one back home to shame. Everything was pristine white marble with gold emblems and filigree throughout for decoration. I was certain our royal cook would be on cloud nine if she saw this one, but she probably would also be overwhelmed. I asked her once if she would ever want to work in a kitchen like this, and she said she would love to see one operate and the system, but the stress was not for her.

There were multiple fireplaces of varying sizes with cast iron pots ready to be put on at a moment's notice. Brick ovens were lined along the wall, while varieties of herbs hung on another wall of what looked like the entrance to a pantry.

"Oh! Princess Persamina Rowena," a young woman squeaked, coming out of the pantry. I did not recognize her. She must be a maid or a part of the kitchen staff based on her attire. "I was not expecting you. Was there something you needed?" I was a bit confused. Expecting me? Did people make appointments for a random snack late at night? That was absurd sounding. *Who pre-planned that?*

"I came down for a snack; I could not sleep. I was hoping this would help." She blinked and nodded at me but did not move.

"Um, is it incorrect that I came here?" I asked, uneasy from the awkwardness that was beginning to fill the room.

"Forgive me, Your Highness." She bowed her head. "Generally, the other princesses send their handmaids to fetch them something. This just took me by surprise."

"Oh, I just did not want to wake Eloise up, and it is no trouble for me," I replied sweetly, but it still must have been wrong because her face became alarmed. "Is something the matter . . .?" I asked, waiting for her to supply her name.

"Stella," she answered. "And no, nothing is wrong." She paused to think, but whatever she contemplated saying, she must have thought better of it because she closed her eyes and subtly shook her head before taking a calming breath. Opening her eyes, Stella continued, "what are you hungry for, Princess Persamina Rowena?"

"Um, are there any pastries?" Why not just go straight to my love of sweets.

"There should be some leftovers from earlier today." She turned to reach for a serving platter, removing the lid to reveal dozens upon dozens of delicious pastries stacked on top of one another.

I walked the distance to where she stood to take a few. She did not comment on the amount I grabbed.

"Do you mind fetching me a glass of water?" I asked. It was awkward with her standing there watching me grab pastries and eat them. I was able to take care of myself. I did not need to be constantly monitored. It was not something I was used to back home with our small staff. Only Mother would stand over me, watching my every move, to point out every flaw.

"Yes, Your Highness, I will go fetch you some water." She curtsied and scurried off to another room. To eat in peace, or so I had hoped. She was back within the next second.

"Here you go, Your Highness." She placed the glass down in front of me.

"Thank you, Stella," I took the glass to take a sip; finishing, I set it down and looked at her. "What do you do here?"

"Oh! I am a scullery maid," she replied with flushed cheeks.

"Why are you still up then?"

"I just finished before you arrived." She cleaned her hands on her apron, and I nodded. I decided it was time to head back to my room. I grabbed a few more pastries and my glass of water. I gave a parting farewell to Stella as I left. She was not much of a conversationalist, and I wondered if she was not used to talking to people beyond the kitchen staff, let alone a royal. Maybe on my next trip to the kitchens, I could ask her if I could see her again. Maybe bring Eloise with me too.

I turned down a corridor and almost bumped head-first into Bay.

"Oh! I am sorry, Bay!"

"Apologies are all mine." He gave me an amused smile with a quirk of his raised eyebrow. "Doing a little kitchen late-night snacking?" He nodded at the pastries in my hands, causing me to blush. I had been caught red-handed in the act even though there was nothing wrong with me going to the kitchens. I knew it was not proper to be seen eating like a glutton while walking back to my room in the middle of the night.

"You caught me," I joked. "Want one?" I gestured my pastry hand slightly to him, thinking he would refuse. I decided to go with his joking mood and not question the change since the ball earlier.

"Only if you feed it to me." His silver eyes glinted deviously. My heart skipped a beat, and I inhaled sharply through my nose. I raised my hand, holding the pastry up to his mouth, trying to make sure my hand did not shake. He gently grabbed my hand in his, and without breaking eye contact, he took a bite. I watched him chew and swallow. He brought my hand back to his mouth. I assumed he was going to take the last bite. Instead, he sucked my pointer finger into his mouth. He sucked all of the powdered sugar ever so slightly off my finger. I inhaled a sharp breath from surprise. He just as quickly released my finger, smiling.

"Delicious." He licked his lips, causing me to bite my bottom lip. There was powder sugar still on his lips and some on his cheek that had come off from my hand.

"You have some powder sugar on your face," I commented as I used a pastry-filled hand to indicate at my cheek and corner lip to the location of where it was on his face.

"Kiss it away." His eyes darkened.

I about dropped the pastries and glass of water in my hands at his request. He gave me a challenging look, not breaking eye contact as he waited to see what I would do. I lowered my hand with the leftover pastries in it to my side and took a step forward. I was not going to back down from his challenge.

His eyes danced with delight from my braveness. I took one more step forward until my breasts were pushed up against his chest. I was not wearing a brassiere or corset. The fabric of my dress did nothing to hide my now-hardening nipples against his chest. Neither one of us spoke as my breathing became shallow. I searched both his eyes as I leaned in on my tiptoes. He sucked in a sharp breath as my hard nipples raised up on his chest. I kissed the powdered sugar from his left cheek, pulling back slightly to confirm. I still had permission to do so. He ever so slightly nodded. My heart was thundering in my ears. I leaned into his right side and gently pressed my lips to him again. My lips lingered at the corner of his right lip.

I pulled back, still searching both of his eyes. His devious eyes turned into molten desire. I gave a shy smile.

"There, you are clean of powdered sugar," I quietly responded. Coming back down onto flat feet, my breasts dragged back down his chest. Bay's hands came up to rest firmly on my hips as he yanked me closer to him.

"Do it again," he breathed. I went back up on tiptoes, and being bold, I set the glass of water down on the corner of a stand and circled my arms around his neck, careful of the pastries still in my other hand to not dirty him. I kissed his left cheek again before moving to kiss the corner of his right lip again. I had barely pulled back from kissing the corner of his right lip before his right hand trailed up my body, grazing my left breast, to come around to the back of my head. Smashing his lips against mine, he kissed me deeply, keeping my head firmly in place.

I tightened the grip of my arms on his neck as he dipped me backward, his tongue playing with mine. I felt the sparks flying from my first kiss with Bay. His left hand slid from my hips to my ass as he squeezed it. I felt his hardening cock press into me as he grinded against my body.

I began to kiss him back just as hard as he was kissing me. I kissed him as if he was the air I had been so desperately needing to breathe. He did not break the kiss as he brought me up from the dip and walked me backward until my back was pinned against the wall. He grinded his hips deeper into mine. His hand left the back of my head and came down to cup my left breast. I felt him roll and lightly pinch my nipple in between his fingers, causing me to moan into his mouth.

He ran his hand from my ass down to the back of my thigh as he hiked it up to his hip, giving himself more access to grind his very hard and very enlarged cock into my pelvis.

He broke the kiss. "Touch me," he demanded.

"I still have pastries in my hand. I-I-I will dirty you, and anyone could stumble upon us so close to the kitchen."

"Drop them," he growled. "I do not care, you'll come to find it's more exciting at the idea of being caught in the dead of the night." I instantly obeyed, dropping them to fall to the ground. I kept my left arm wrapped around his neck, digging my fingers into his hair. I dragged my right hand down the front of his chest, feeling his muscles through his shirt. I slightly hesitated, continuing my touch between our bodies until my fingers found his hard cock straining against his pants.

"Stroke it," he ordered. I squeezed slightly, as best as I possibly could, through the fabric and began to stroke his cock up and down. He moaned, his head falling backward as he grinded into my hand. Bringing his head back up, he captured my lips again in a deep kiss.

I continued to stroke his cock through the fabric of his pants as I felt his hand leave my left breast, trailing down my side until he reached the bunched fabric at my hips. He still held my right leg up on his hips as he raised it higher, grinding my back harder into the wall. His fingers skimmed the top of my left thigh, moving inward towards my panties. My heart raced as butterflies went crazy in my stomach. His fingers trailed from my inner thigh to across my now wet panties. His fingers began long, slow strokes. The feeling shot pleasure straight up my core as I silently begged for him not to stop. His long strokes were driving me crazy as his fingers would repeatedly drag from my clit back toward my entrance.

He began to pick up the pace as I returned the favor, our kiss deepening. When I felt his hand leave, I began to protest, but he deepened the kiss in response. I felt him fumble with his pants, then grab my hand that was stroking him. He guided it back downward, and I gasped into his mouth at the feel of his bare fleshed cock in my palm. I never imagined the skin on a cock would be so smooth. His hand had not yet released mine as he began to clench my fingers tighter, allowing me to squeeze his cock with more strength. He moaned in my mouth and picked up the pace, showing me how he wanted to be stroked. It was far easier without fabric being a barrier.

He released my hand as I kept up the same firmness and motion to his liking. I felt his fingers brush the top of my pantyline before slipping in, causing my breath to hitch. His tongue tangled more with mine as he began to thrust slightly into my hand.

His fingers began to rub over my clit and delve into my folds. I moaned again into his mouth. I grinded into his fingers as one slipped into me, his thumb circling and rubbing my clit. He hitched my right leg up higher onto his hip, grinding his cock into my hand, and I could feel the head of his cock rubbing into my inner thigh where my panties met.

He slipped a second finger into me, eliciting a gasp into his mouth. His thumb still rubbed against my clit as I felt the pressure begin to build toward my climax. I picked up the pace of stroking his cock, feeling his precum seep in between my legs as it rubbed back and forth. We moaned into each other's mouths as I rode his hand harder, chasing my climax. His fingers stroked faster within me until I let loose a cry into his kiss. My left arm tightened around his neck as my orgasm ricocheted through me. He continued to stroke his fingers with me as his thumb kept rhythm, keeping my orgasm pulsing. He lightly nipped my bottom lip as I continued to moan from pleasure.

Finally, as my orgasm subsided, he withdrew his hand from my panties. He brought his fingers up to his mouth, tasting my cum. "You taste delicious." Those three little words stirred something within me.

He brought his hand to the back of my head to tangle his fingers in what was left of my low bun. His other hand remained on my right leg. He jerked me forward, sliding his cock against my now sensitive clit through my panties.

"Let go of my cock," he growled through his teeth, and I obeyed. Letting go of him, I slid my hand around to his lower back to rest. His free cock began to slide faster over my sensitive clit as he picked up pace. I whimpered from the pleasure it was giving me with the friction of the fabric. I began to dig my nails into his back. He growled, thrusting harder against me. He bucked against me, slowing down his thrusts as I felt hot wetness against my inner thighs. He groaned as he put all his weight onto my body, his head resting in the crook of my neck.

He kissed my neck, causing a shiver to run through me before he pulled back to look me in the eyes. His hand released my right leg so that I was able to bring it down from his hip and stand back on both feet. I felt a little off-center with both feet back to firmly being on the ground. His left hand moved, coming up between my inner thighs where his warm, sticky seed was beginning to run down my legs. His fingers slid upwards through his cum until his knuckles hit my clit. He rubbed his knuckles back and forth over the sensitive bud, causing me to moan slightly. His eyes darkened from my reaction.

His hand left from between my legs, making me almost protest as my dress fell back into place. He brought his cum covered fingers up to my lips. I slightly opened my mouth as he gently pushed his fingers inside. Instantly, I tasted his warm, salty seed. I twirled my tongue around his fingers, cleaning his cum off. I watched him slightly bite the corner of his lip, smiling.

"Good girl," he purred, withdrawing his fingers. He dipped his head, giving me a once over as he winked and walked away from me without a word. I watched him go as I tried to process everything that had just happened. When he was out of sight, I let go of my breath. I realized at some point, I would have to unglue myself from the wall and walk back to my room.

I looked down to see the damaged pastries on the ground. My fingers were still sticky from the powdered sugar. I picked them off the ground lest anyone see them. That was when it hit me that we had done this in the open corridor where, at any moment, we could have been caught, and the risk had been worth it. My stomach dropped at the thought while my heart simultaneously raced. *What kind of hold did Bay have on me?*

I rushed back to my room to dispose of the pastries. I desperately needed to wash my hands and my inner thighs. I honestly despised having sticky fingers and hands. Scratch that I absolutely abhorred any part of my body being sticky from sugar. Once something on my body became sticky, I would need to continue to touch it. I would touch it repeatedly until I became utterly disgusted with it all. Opening my bedroom door, I tainted the handle to stickiness as well. I would need to let Eloise know it was dirty. I did not want to touch it again and soil another hand accidentally.

Quietly, I closed the door behind me, hoping I did not awaken Eloise. Scurrying over to the garbage can, I quickly disposed of the ruined pastries and immediately began to wash my hands, removing all stickiness. Blushing, I took a washcloth and wetted it. I bunched up the front of my dress to run it in between my inner thighs to clean off Bay's seed. Closing my eyes, I imagined instead, we were back in the corridor, and it was his hand between my thighs.

"Where did you sneak off to?" Eloise's voice made me jump, and I instantly dropped my dress. I whirled to face her, clutching my bodice to feel my racing heart.

"Eloise!" I gasped. "You gave me a fright!" She raised an eyebrow as if to say cut to the chase.

"I went to the royal kitchens for a snack because I had been tossing and turning." It was at this moment that I realized I had left the glass behind. I cursed myself out at my carelessness.

Her eyebrow did not lower as her eyes looked at the wet washcloth in my hand and back to meet my eye. I bit my lip, my body heating from being caught. I was not sure how much I should tell her.

"I ran into Prince Bay," I decided to settle on. "And we . . . kissed." Both her eyebrows shot up even further as her eyes widened. She gasped.

"The prince let you kiss him?"

"Well, not quite like a kiss-kiss but on the cheek and the corner of his lips." I decided that was all I would tell her. She did not need to know the rest of the details. Tonight's special moment was mine.

"Then why is your hair a mess?" Eloise challenged me.

"Because it was the middle of the night," I said in the way of explanation. She cocked her head to the side, waiting for me to elaborate more. I did not give in. She pursed her lips, slightly narrowing her eyes before shrugging and letting it go.

"I am certain if someone saw it, I will hear all about it later today." I did not let my expression change as my heart dropped, once again worried that someone may have seen what just occurred.

"Guess you will," I replied nonchalantly. We did not say another word to each other as we both headed to our respective bedrooms to attempt to sleep once again.

While lying on my back, I squished my cheeks between both my hands, smiling. My mind kept replaying what had happened with Bay over and over. The kisses, his fingers, his cock in my hand, our orgasms. I wanted him so badly. Guilt flashed through me as I thought of Knox, and I began to shove that thought deep down within me, locking it away to hinder it from ruining this moment. I pushed away the thought of Bay's physical reaction to me due to our limited interactions together. I decided I would not let logic get in the way of my happiness. I had half a mind that if I knew precisely where Bay's bedroom was, I would go to it right now. I knew what I did tonight was scandalous, but I would do it again if the opportunity presented itself. I desperately hoped that would be the case as I finally drifted off to sleep.

~

"Mina, you will do whatever is necessary to win Prince Rafael Baylor over." Mother repeated to me for the millionth time as I practiced my calligraphy.

"Yes, mama," I replied out of habit.

"Mother," she corrected me.

"Yes, Mother." I usually did not let that mistake happen anymore, but every now and then, it slipped when I was not thinking.

"I do not care if you have to seduce the heir. Make it happen," she tacked on.

Mother had just made a substantial and expensive purchase. Every time this occurred, she had become blunter and adamant with my lessons on the importance of what was at stake. I had begun to pick up on the routine of my lessons. When money flow was coming in, Mother focused on how a princess was to be prim and proper. But when significant expenses were incurred, and Mother could not buy a new dress or trinket she so desperately wanted, then it did not matter how I ensnared the heir as long as I did it.

My virginity was meant only for the heir. If I allowed anyone else, who was not the heir, to do anything sexual with me, it would ruin everything my mother had planned. She made a point to let every male in the castle know if they tried to take my virginity, their life was at stake. She had no issue ending anyone's life who crossed her. That mere threat kept me from ever acting on my curiosity with anyone. I bided my time with the romance books I snuck into my room to fantasize about what it would be like.

I often wondered if this was why I would be locked away and not allowed to attend Mother's balls. If I found a connection with another royal heir at the ball, my mother certainly could not kill another king and queen's child. I never asked Mother if that was the reason.

For the few times I cried, begging to be able to attend, all I ever was told was they were locking me away to keep my beauty a secret. After a few more balls had come to pass when Mother's patience finally wore thin, she screamed at me while throwing stuff to stop asking and that it would never happen. After that day, I stopped asking her for anything, too afraid to incur her wrath again.

Chapter Twelve

The following morning, I found it quite tedious to keep to myself what had happened the previous evening between Bay and me. As I walked into the tearoom, I headed towards an unoccupied table when I did not see either twin present. I made it only a quarter of the way as I was caught off guard by Tearani's monotone voice simply commanding me to "sit with her." An almost full table of princesses surrounded her. I paused momentarily, surprised I had not initially noticed her among the guests.

Today, she wore a vibrant yellow two-piece outfit that made the rest of the princess dresses look drab. Her top only covered her bosom, and then a long skirt accompanied it, with her bare leg showing through a slit. Her midriff was exposed entirely, showing off her pierced navel. She blinked at me expectantly. I glanced at the only empty chair at the table, surrounded by other females, and back at her. She dipped her head once in a nod, and that was that. I was sitting next to her, listening to the other girls.

As I sat there, the other princesses chatting, all I could think about was Bay. I could not tell Tearani about it with these vicious vipers about that, or I would be raked across the coals on multiple fronts. Instead, I sat there quietly, sipping my tea and listening to them chatter. Sparks of guilt coursed through me with the thought of Knox. I kept pushing the guilt away, reminding myself I needed Bay for my kingdom.

Iryse was not present, and I must have looked a bit distraught due to her absence. Tearani, reading my thoughts, simply said, "playing hooky." It was evident that these girls were sitting with Tearani because she had the second wealthiest kingdom. There had been rumors Eloise had heard that were beginning to make their rounds in hushed whispers that her parents may turn their kingdom into a queendom. They wanted Tearani to reign over it. I believed Tearani would make an excellent queen, fearful and downright deadly but nonetheless a wonderful queen. I would need to ask the twins about the rumor later.

"I heard from a servant that Bay was kissing someone in the hallway last night," gossiped a merchant's daughter whose name I did not know. My stomach dropped as I attempted to keep my face in a neutral expression. It did not prevent me from fiddling with my fingers in my lap as I tried to keep my leg from bouncing.

"Wonder who she is?" Regina venomously spat.

"Probably just a servant herself." Olivia rolled her eyes, chiming in. I began to lean in towards Tearani a bit for protection. It made me uneasy to be sitting at the same table as the two. I was still waiting for Regina to bring up my dancing with her brothers. It was evident Olivia knew about my dancing with Voltaire. She kept throwing me daggers.

"What do you think, Mina?" Tearani asked me. I was startled as I looked at her. She gave me a slow blink, awaiting my response.

"P-pardon?" I stuttered. I had not anticipated being brought into the conversation with these girls. I saw a reflection of knowing warmth in Tearani's eyes before it disappeared. Of course, she probably already knew the truth. Miss hawk eyes missed nothing.

"Do you think it was a guest or a servant, Mina?" Tearani pushed forward with her question. I had never witnessed her like this before. Granted, I had never been around her when she was with other royals, so maybe this was how she obtained her information.

The thought of someone having seen it occur made me both exhilarated and terrified. At the very minimum, they had seen a kiss, but what if they had seen more? Images flashed in my mind. My back pressed against the wall, and my leg hiked up over his hip. My dress bunched up in between our bodies, with his fingers inside me while my hand stroked his cock. My face began to flame.

Tearani never stopped watching my reaction. This cat had her canary. I would need to tell her and Iryse everything when we were alone. I realized I would be trusting to tell twins I had just become acquainted with but was not trusting enough to tell Eloise, with whom I had grown up with. How would I answer this question with a table full of vipers? I could not outright tell them the truth. I already received enough venom from them.

"Oh, um well- -," I twisted my finger faster in my lap out of sight.

"Like she would know," Regina rudely interrupted before I had a chance to weave my story. I began to shrink back into my seat. "Princess Persamina Rowena is a good little girl and stays in her room with her maid like *The Tower Princess* that she has always been," she added on smoothly, giving me a challenging look. I just nodded, afraid to speak.

"See, she saw nothing and would know nothing."

"Yes, however, I asked if she thought the rumors were true. I never asked her if she saw," countered Tearani. She gave Regina a leveled gaze, almost daring to be challenged.

If Tearani's Kingdom Hayverton became a queendom, it would overrule Regina's Queendom Grewt'en on two fronts. Hayverton was already wealthier and more prominent than Grewt'en. The only bragging right Grewt'en's heir currently had was being the only queendom in the lands, but now that could all change, and it was evident Tearani challenged it against Regina. More than a few times, I heard Regina make remarks dismissing the girls who would have to follow in their husband's footsteps. Regina would never have to abide by that. I thought back to a page I had read on Queendom's rules regarding their relationships.

Queendom Queen's Personal Relationship Rules

A Queen may marry and bestow a title to their spouse. The spouse would become the highest rank lover in The Queen's entourage

-'Queen Second' would be the title granted if The Queen married a female.

-'King' would be the title granted if The Queen married a male.

-All involved would continue to have an open relationship, regardless of marriage/titles.

All heirs produced by The Queen would be legitimate.

-All children produced by The King or Queen Second would be bastards.

-Compensation would be provided to the mothers of The King's children.

-There would be no compensation for the sires of The Queen Second.

-Children of The King or Queen Second would be sent to higher privileged

apprenticeships and scholarly schools of their choice.

-The King is required to keep a record of every female he slept with to

prevent random people from claiming he sired their child.

-The Queen Second record keeping was optional.

It is encouraged for The Queen to have multiple lovers and multiple children

-There is no limit on how many lovers The Queen takes.

-Sires do not need to be named for The Queen's children.

-The Queen's lovers are at the mercy of what The Queen allows for their own personal side lovers.

-Any lovers of The Queen who do not have the title of King or Queen Second will not be granted the special privileges if they produce a child unless deemed so by The Queen.

If The Queen has relations with another monarchy and they sire a child together, it will depend upon the circumstances

-If the child's sire is a king or Lord and is eligible to be his heir, he will have first rights to the child, as long as The Queen already has an heir. If the Queen has no heir, she will have first rights to the child if it is a daughter.

-If the sire has heirs, The Queen and the sire can come to an agreement on custody of the child. This may be shared custody or sole custody to one parent.

-If there is questionable debate on the legitimacy of the child's sire, it will be at the digression of the sire to claim the child as his own or not.

-It is highly discouraged that The Queen has relationships with other monarchy males if they do not already have heirs in place for the above reasons

CONSIDERING Regina and her brothers looked nothing alike, I garnered the impression that they probably did not share the same father. I did not know what the two younger siblings looked like. I became curious if any of the royal Grewt'en's siblings shared the same father. I wondered what kind of upbringing that would be like considering I was an only child.

Tearani and Regina continued to stare each other down. I knew they had grown up together, and I questioned how much the twins had spent in Regina's company in the past. Were the princesses all more civil around each other in front of the parents?

Regina finally broke her stare with a huff. She excused herself and left with Oliva in tow. Tearani watched the two leave, blinking before she turned her head to look back at me. She was awaiting my response. I was not entirely certain why she was pushing on the matter. She had never been like this when it was just her, Iryse, and myself. She barely spoke when it was the three of us.

I took a quick breath, "Well, I think that would be an awfully bold rumor for a maid to make up. If it got back to King Regalius and Queen Serenity, would that not potentially put said maid in danger of being punished? Surely they would have ways to find out who was spreading the rumors?"

Tearani blinked with a nod before she looked at the remaining two at our table; I followed her gaze. The other two girls, whose names I still did not know, must have decided my answer was boring. Maybe it brought too much political logic to the table because they changed the conversation. They chatted amongst themselves about their travels, leaving Tearani and me out of the conversation. Out of my peripheral vision, I watched Tearani turn her head towards me. I looked at her with a raised eyebrow. She winked before looking back at the other two girls. I about fell out of my chair.

When teatime ended, I chose to head to the outdoor terrace. The other girls headed to the needlework room. I knew Tearani would not be attending needlework, and with Iryse absent from teatime, I highly doubted she would be in attendance either. The idea of sitting alone in a room full of those vicious vipers with sharp little weapons in their hands, without the twins in attendance to sit by, did not sound appealing to me. I decided I was going to stroll through the gardens instead.

As I walked out the French terrace doors, I took a deep breath, smelling the scent of hundreds of roses and feeling at peace. I was not brave enough to walk in the rose maze alone, not just yet. I knew I would end up lost, and they would need to send a rescue team in to find me. Hopefully, it would be before nightfall.

I left the terrace and began to stroll along the path surrounded by rose bushes. They smelled beyond heavenly. I was in the pink rose section, making my way over to the peach area. It intrigued me that the rose bushes were all sectioned by color. I knew this worked in favor of princesses and the dresses they chose to wear. A few times, I would catch a princess being painted in a section of the rose garden that complimented her dress color.

"Mind if I join you on this stroll?" I looked to my right to see Knox walking through the maze towards me. I hesitantly smiled. Thinking back to the previous evening of Bay and myself and then to the ball and how Knox had acted, I was not entirely certain where we stood. To be fair, our last two interactions together had not been left on the best of terms.

"I would enjoy that," I replied evenly. While I was uncertain of everything, I was still too nosey and wanted to see where this conversation would take us. I changed course so our paths could meet up. He was clad in his typical black attire with dark smoke gray threading, creating elaborate whirling designs.

"You look beautiful today, Mina," he complimented. I had not anticipated him to be this friendly. He talked as if the two previous occurrences had never happened. A twinge of guilt zinged through me as a flashback of last night entered my thoughts again. I mentally shook the memories away as I was doing nothing wrong. I was not solely Knox's, and with how he had recently treated me, I did not know if I wanted to pursue that path anymore.

"You look rather dashing yourself," I replied stiffly. He smiled, giving me a wink, not even noticing how uncomfortable I was with him there. He acted like nothing had occurred. He led us to a bench, indicating for me to sit down as he followed suit to sit next to me.

"I want to apologize for the way I have recently acted." He broke the tension. I looked at him, waiting for him to continue. I was not sure I was ready to forgive him. After all, in his rage, I did have a book hit my face, and then he danced with me roughly. "Sometimes, I let my jealousy get the best of me."

"Go on," I needed more explanation than just that. I knew I was fishing a bit to hear more about this so-called jealousy.

"I like you, Mina. . . A lot," he continued, scratching the back of his head. "And when I see anyone stealing your attention, I become worried that they will take you away from me."

"Take me away from you?" I did not dismiss him declaring his feelings for me, but I needed to know more about what he meant. I liked the idea of him claiming me as his, but on the other foot, I had never agreed for him to be this territorial. I could not dismiss the fact that agreeing to be his would eliminate my chances with Bay, and after last night, I did not want that.

"You are starting to mean the world to me, and I just do not want to lose you." His eyes held such vulnerability. He sat here laying out his fear. I swallowed, not knowing how to proceed. He leaned back, looking up at the sky. We barely even knew each other. We danced a few dances and had a moment on my birthday; how could I already mean this much to him? Then again, I had fewer interactions with Bay and willingly did more last night. However, I could argue with myself that Bay was the endgame. I could take those necessary risks, but Knox was not the same.

"Look, Mina, I understand that maybe I am not your first choice, but. . ." he paused, still looking at the sky. "You are mine."

I inhaled sharply, my eyes widening as I watched him. He did not take his gaze from the sky, as if he was hoping and wishing for the answer he wanted to hear and not the one Mother would have wanted me to give. No one else was around us when he made his confession out loud. The pause between us was growing incredibly awkward. He shifted a bit in his seat, and I clenched my teeth as the muscles in my stomach clenched.

"You do not have to give me an answer," Knox finally said, leaning back forward, he looked at the ground. "I just wanted you to know." He got up without looking at me, and I did not say a word as I watched him walk away.

Chapter 13

I did not linger long in the rose garden after Knox's departure. I decided to try to find him, and the library was my first place to look. With the other girls busy with needlework, the hallways to the castle were quite empty. This made travel to my destination far easier to achieve.

I was not entirely sure what I would say once I saw Knox. I just did not want it to end on that note. He had explained why he had reacted the way he did, and I believed I could forgive him for it. With everything that had occurred between Bay and me, I could not promise to give Knox my heart. I needed to see where my path would take me with Bay because my kingdom needed me to save it. However, I did not want to lose my friendship with Knox, but I did not want to give him false hope either. I needed to figure out what I would say once I saw him. With the way I was rushing in looking for him, I was running out of time to figure my speech out.

I arrived at the decorative library doors and pulled one open as I ducked inside. The room was dimly lit, meaning someone had to be here. As I walked further in, I began looking back and forth between the aisles, making my way toward the cushioned seating area. My thoughts danced at the memory of Bay catching Knox, and me interlocked on the ground. I blushed quickly, my stomach clenching. I shook my head to clear away the memory.

I rounded the corner of the library shelves, and on the couch, a book resting over his face laid Knox. My dress made a soft rustling sound. Lifting the book slightly off his face, he peeked from underneath the pages to see me standing there. He lifted the book off his face, putting it on the end table as he sat up straight.

"Mina? What brings you here?" He asked, confused. It was as if he had not just declared feelings for me in the last hour outside.

"Knox, I am not quite certain I can give you my heart just yet," I began, letting the words tumble from my mouth without overthinking them. "But I can give you my friendship. I want to get to know you better," I finished. I watched as he mulled over my words in his mind. I held my breath for the briefest of moments before he finally nodded.

"That is a fair thing to offer, and I accept," he replied, but he did not smile. "I hope though, with time . . . that I can win your heart over, too."

"Only time will tell, Knox. Only time will tell," I replied. He did not know that he already had pieces of it, something I had not realized until moments earlier. It was just a matter of not knowing what could possibly happen between Bay and myself. I decided to push past this lull in conversation and awkwardness. I went over and sat next to him on the couch. He regarded me warily, his eyebrow raised in question to my next move.

"Let us get to know each other better. Tell me about your friends, Knox." If there was even a chance of this blossoming into more than a friendship, I wanted to know everything I could about him. Even if it stayed as a friendship, if he became my brother-in-law, I still wanted to know things about him.

"My main friend growing up was my brother Bay," Knox said with a shrug. "No one wants to play with the cruel, reclusive spare brother that may kill them." My heart twinged a bit. I was uncertain if it was because of the isolation he felt or because of the guilt of knowing what Bay and I had done last night and how it could affect Knox if the stars aligned and I did marry his brother.

"But why did they call you cruel?" A quick image of the book flying and hitting me in the face came to mind. I tried to dismiss the idea, but then the memory of his death grip on my hand during that dance pushed its way forward. Did he have a temper as a kid? Was he a bit too rough?

"I was a bit too aggressive as a kid; my parents did not even try--," he cut himself off. "I mean, Bay was enough."

"I understand. I only had Eloise," I supplied.

"She your sister?"

"No. I am an only child, but she is the closest thing I have to one." I smile to myself at the thought of my best friend. The same best friend I was now keeping a scandalous secret from.

"Tell me about her." He broke my thoughts.

"Why?" I asked, uncertain of where he was going with this.

"Well." He smiled before rushing out, "You know my brother. I would like to hear about the girl who is practically your sister. Tell me a memory of you two."

"Oh! That makes sense; let me think," I twirled my hair, looking up to the ceiling for the answer.

"So, this one time Eloise dared me to steal apples and apple pie tarts from the kitchen and–" My mind became lost within the memory from fourteen years ago.

"Mina! Just do it!" pressed Eloise with her nasally eight-year-old voice, "Cook won't discipline you!" She added sweetly. I glanced at her cheek, which was forming a handprint bruise upon it. Feeling guilty, I nodded.

The plan was to grab some apples to feed the horses. We needed to butter them up to allow us to ride to the lake and eat the pies—just the two of us on a picnic together. We wanted to pretend to both be long-lost princesses unfound, venturing into the wildly ways of the world.

The kitchen was not bustling at this time of day. Many of the kitchen staff were gathering ingredients for the next meal. Cook would still be in there, as would the scullery maids, but they would not heed me. My heart still raced at the thought of this adventure Eloise and I would pull off. I walked to the kitchen and glancing in, it was surprisingly completely empty. I had worked up a whole plan for if I encountered someone, and now I was a little disappointed that I would not be able to set that plan into motion.

I spotted the apples and sweet pies in the middle of the table, and after making one last sweep of the room, I ran in to grab a basket and threw some apples in along with a few pies before hightailing it back to Eloise.

"You were fast!" She exclaimed as we ran to the stables.

"No one was in there!" I supplied, still shocked.

"That's crazy! Cook never leaves!"

"I know!" We were both running on a high and a bit winded as we made it to the stables and went straight to my mare's stall.

"Hey, Missy." I smiled as I petted her nose. "I brought you something." I procured an apple, and her ears pricked forward. Eloise stood nervously behind me. It may have been her plan, but she was ridiculously frightened of horses. I would understand if it was another mare. Mares were temperamental brats with the worst attitudes, but

thankfully, my Missy was one of the rarities. She had to be for a princess like myself to be able to ride her. If she had not been, Father would have sold her off in favor of another even-tempered horse.

"Why don't we just take Missy, and you can ride behind me?" I offered. I knew Mother would have scolded me for my poor speech, but it was just Eloise and me. What could it have harmed if I said 'don't' over 'do not'? The tight grip she had on my shoulder lessened.

"Okay," she mumbled, giving in to the idea.

"Princess, would you like me to saddle Missy for you?" The stable hand, Kip asked. This was the one part of the plan we could not sneakily do.

"Yes, please, Kip," I replied, "Eloise and I want to go on a picnic in the pasture by the lake." I gestured with my picnic basket. Kip nodded and started readying Missy for us.

Once she was ready, he helped us both into her saddle and Eloise put a death lock grip around my waist the whole way there, even though I kept us at a regular walking pace.

"Later, I learned Cook overheard our plans and purposely made my kitchen retrieval extremely easy," I laughed. Knox joined in, laughing as well.

"Sounds like you and Eloise caused a bunch of mischief."

"Oh, we most certainly did." My heart warmed at sharing a bit of myself with him.

"Unfortunately, due to the time, I have to be somewhere. I hope to see you soon, Mina." He stood up abruptly. He reached for my hand and lifted it to his lips, kissing the back of it. I felt the energy in the room lose its warmth. For the second time today, I watched as he walked away, uncertain if he genuinely had somewhere else to be or if he just wanted to get away from me with the way he dismissed himself. I decided to stay there and enjoy the silence and comfort the library could grant me. This was far better than needlework.

I spent a few more minutes in the library before heading towards the banquet hall for lunch. Knox had put me in a good enough mood that I decided not to have lunch in my room. I wanted to join with everyone, and I already knew the majority of the time, one of the twins frequented the banquet hall during meals.

Entering the banquet hall, I caught sight of Iryse, and I practically made a beeline towards her. Tearani was nowhere in sight. It was intriguing that now the other twin was playing hooky.

"Missed you at teatime," I said by way of greeting.

"Yeah, I wanted to sleep in this morning." She shrugged, leading us to two empty chairs. Iryse fluffed her very pale lilac dress that shimmered to almost white as she sat down in the chair. She always had this ethereal beauty about her. If I was being honest with myself, both twins did. It was when Iryse smiled she became exceptionally beautiful. I pulled out my chair beside her, similarly fluffing my simple emerald dress as Iyrse had.

"I think this is the first time I have seen you attend a meal that was optional," commented Iryse.

"Probably because it is." I laughed.

"I don't blame you, but it is nice to socialize." She grabbed her teacup to take a drink.

"We both know I have enemies, and the only two females that talk to me are you and Tearani." I picked up my teacup.

"Touché." she raised her teacup at me in salute, causing me to laugh again.

"Iryse, may I ask you a question?" I had been wondering about something for a while, and I just needed to know.

"Hmm?"

"You do not seem interested in either of the T'Lovoness brothers or anyone for that matter, so why are you here?"

"Same as you, Mommy dearest sent me." She rolled her eyes. "So here I am. I will flirt, I will party, but a T'Lovoness or anyone else is not for me," she sighed as she grabbed a finger sandwich. Iryse was definitely not like the other princesses. She helped herself and had no qualms if she lacked proper table manners.

"Why not?" She now had my curiosity piqued. She waved her hands, indicating towards the ballroom and guests.

"Do you see all this?" I nodded in response. "Not for me. I want to travel. I want to see the world. I do not want to be someone's decorative little queen or wife."

"But you are a princess, Iryse!" I gasped, completely shocked by her ambitions. She smiled, winking at me.

"But I am not the oldest princess, so like Knox, I am just a backup plan." She took a bite of her sandwich, looking off into the distance. "Someday, I will do great things as a mighty traveler."

"Are you looking for a merchant husband, then?" I inquired. She rolled her eyes.

"Pfft, as if. I will do this unmarried. I am not looking to be tied down." She took another bite of her sandwich without a care in the world. I blinked several times in complete shock.

I was raised my whole life to aspire to be queen one day and now to hear another princess aspire to be a world traveler. I never realized there could be another life option out there for royals. It made me wonder what I would want to do if I had a life like Iryse. I suppose potentially something to do with books because of my love for reading. Maybe something with horses? I did not believe I was brave enough to be an unmarried world traveler.

Iryse was breaking down every barrier in my mind while simultaneously rebuilding all the possibilities—places I never even dared to allow my mind to go. I watched as these other girls fought to be the next Queen of T'Lovoness, and yet Iryse's mind was elsewhere. I realized how much I truly admired her. Now, it made more sense of why she had been kind to me. She was not here vying for Bay's or anyone else's attention. She was simply here to play a role her mother expected before she could prepare her life to traveling.

"What about Tearani?" I prompted, curious since she was the eldest.

"She is here for her chance for Bay." I felt myself beginning to bristle as I became a bit territorial. I felt my cheeks flame instantly as I realized how quickly I reacted. Iryse took notice as well. She added, "she is not really interested in pushing it, so do not view her as competition. She already has come to terms with the fact that Mommy and Daddy will arrange her a marriage after this season if she does not secure her hand in marriage." Iyrse waved her hand in the air while looking down at her food. "She does not want to rule a kingdom this large, so it is why she is not attempting to compete. Plus, she has someone in mind as well. I doubt our parents will approve, but we shall see."

I mulled over this new information about the two twins. Iryse never mentioned anything about the rumors of Hayverton becoming a queendom. I wondered if it was because it was simply a rumor or because Iryse did not want to confirm it just yet. There were enough listening ears around us, even if they were involved in their own personal conversations. With the new information Iryse had given me about them, it explained why they were not blood-thirsty evil to me.

"Why are you both so nice to me?" The instant need to know had put me in a chokehold. Iryse had been the first evening we met, and Tearani had been every time after that. Iryse looked over at me with raised eyebrows.

"Never thought you would be bold enough to ask that," she stated. "You are not to be blamed for your parent's actions, is the way we view it." She shrugged. I about sagged in my chair; she was the first one to get it. Even though her twin was not here, they got it, and I found myself feeling relieved.

"Tonight, you will come to our room. We have much to discuss." Iryse ordered.

"What?" I had been hoping they would have conveniently forgotten.

"Do not give me that 'what'." She did air quotes to emphasize her point. "Nonsense. You know what, as do Tearani and I. We need to get this all out on the table on that rumor circulating from last night."

I felt like Tearani as I blinked at Iryse, gulping. My face flushed, and my stomach clenched. I lost my appetite.

"That confirms enough for me." Iryse nodded to herself. "Our room, after lunch." I instantly thought of the ball that would take place tonight.

"Don't fret. Worst comes to worst, you will get ready in our room." Iryse nodded again to herself and grabbed another finger sandwich, seemingly unbothered.

Iryse was leading me back to their room. I felt like she was dragging me there because she could not wait to hear all the details. As she threw open the doors, I saw Tearani sitting in the same chair as last time, gazing out the window.

Iryse slammed the door shut without a care in the world of how loud she was. We both made our way over to Tearani to sit in the surrounding empty chairs. Tearani had not stopped looking outside to acknowledge our presence.

"Alright. Dish! What happened last night?!" Squealed Iryse,

propping her elbows on her knees, she rested her head in her hands, leaning into me, waiting to hear the story.

"Um, more than just kissing," I awkwardly replied. Iryse gasped with glee.

"Tell me more!"

I began to recount the details from the beginning. I blushed and stumbled over the words during the more intimate parts of the story. The guilt that flashed through as I thought of Eloise, I tried to dismiss it, but it lingered. The two of us barely saw each other unless it was to prepare my outfits, and even then, we did not say much to each other. It felt like a crack was forming between us, and I blamed myself and my secrets for being the cause.

"Interesting that the only gossip we heard was a simple kiss," Iyrse said in complete awe.

"I think I am more embarrassed that someone saw and who knows how much," I commented.

"Well, considering they never name-dropped you, I am going to say they did not see much."

"I hope not!" My face flamed, and my hands made a clapping sound as they landed on my cheeks. The rumor was already scandalous. I did not want my name being attached to it. Those vipers would have a delightful field day.

"You were correct earlier," Tearani spoke for the first time. "If the rumors were to elaborate . . . whoever began them would most likely be dealing with serious consequences from Bay's parents." I peeked out from behind my fingers at her; it gave me time to ponder that statement and the potential protection I had from it.

"Tearani, you mentioned you are interested in someone . . . Who is it?" I asked, deciding it was time to change topics. I would prefer some of the focus to be off me for a bit.

"No one you know, just a lord's child," she replied nonchalantly.

"Are they in attendance?" I pushed.

"Yes." Tearani did not even stop looking out the window as she responded to my questions.

"It'll really depend on what our parents decide," chimed in Iryse, "if they choose to switch over to a queendom, then Tearani can have whomever. . . But if they stick with a kingdom, then she will need to marry Bay, or they will pick a spouse for her." There was the confirmation I had wanted on the rumor floating about.

"I do not want Bay, nor does he want me."

"Then it will be an arranged marriage," countered Iryse.

"Not if I can convince them to switch to a queendom." I had the distinct impression this was a conversation these two have had on multiple occasions.

"You two do not have a brother to take the throne?" I questioned.

"Nope, just the two of us. Mom couldn't conceive after giving birth to us, so they settled." Iryse paused momentarily, pondering before continuing, "if they don't make Tearani the ruler, then the throne will go to our father's baby brother, who wants nothing to do with it." She shrugged.

I looked back at Tearani. I began to get the impression a lot weighed on her shoulders with multiple future outcomes.

"If you become a queendom, then Tearani can marry whomever she chooses?" I pushed.

"More or less. It will be a lot like Grewt'en, where marriage can be for political gain or even for romance if it is chosen. Tearani could have multiple partners if she chose." Iryse waggled her eyebrows at me, causing me to giggle.

"I could not imagine juggling multiple partners," I responded.

"Isn't that what you are currently doing between Knox and Bay?" Iryse replied instantly before covering her mouth. I sobered up a bit. I had to admit to myself it was a bit like what I was doing.

"True, in a sense . . ." She was not wrong, but I would not say she was fully correct either. I was still trying to navigate through my own feelings.

"If you married Knox, you would be reigning Queen to Theorines. Technically, you could still have Bay as a secret side lover," Tearani commented. I blinked at her.

"Excuse me?" I was baffled by her statement.

"Your country is not locked down to only being a kingdom. Was it not your father's grandmother that ruled a queendom?" Iryse questioned. That was true; my country did flip back and forth. I just never had given it much thought with all the lessons Mother gave that it would flip back to being a queendom with my ruling it. I thought back to an earlier conversation with the twins, where they had commented about me ruling Theorines as a queendom. I had chosen not to feed into it at the time. I had completely ignored and dismissed the thought.

"I suppose so. I just never gave it much thought . . ." I trailed off.

"I probably would start giving it a lot more thought; you *are* an only child. Unless they find your father's missing brother to rule, there are no other heirs in the direct lineage. Who would be the next to take over Theorines? To our knowledge, you are the intended heir ruler. Everyone here knows that." Iryse raised her eyebrow at me, giving me a funny look.

"I was never raised that way. I was only raised to marry Bay," I became a bit defensive. What did she mean that everyone knew that? How did everyone but me know this? Why had I never come to think of ruling like my deceased great-grandmother did?

"Only so your mother can pay off her debts. She just wants more funds is all. . . to buy more things." Iryse leaned back in her chair, kicking her legs to prop on the coffee table. My head began to whirl at the possibilities.

"But I was never trained to rule a queendom," I tried as a way of explanation. Tearani slowly turned her head away from the window to look at me.

"Nor was I."

Chapter 14

I ended up getting ready with Iryse and Tearani in their room. I could not tell if Eloise was pleased by this change of location or not. She stayed mostly quiet as the twin's handmaids helped them assemble into their own dresses. While I only had Eloise, they had six total handmaids helping them prepare. Their handmaids were more lavishly dressed than Eloise, who wore a very simple second-hand dress that had once been mine. I thought it was quite extensive at six handmaids, but I did not want to comment on it.

I knew it had been a bit of a burden for Eloise to relocate all the necessary items needed to get ready for this evening. Last night, I had worn that gorgeous sunset dress, and tonight, Eloise prepared a dress that reminded me of a clear, starry night. Another A-line dress, although this one was strapless. It began at the top as a dark cerulean blue and blended its way down to black at the bottom. Diamonds had been sewn throughout the dress that reminded me of stars. My necklace was an upside-down diamond crescent moon, and the matching earrings dangled from my ears. Eloise coiled my hair into a very large and perfectly round bun on top of my head. She had left out a chunk of hair that she had expertly braided before wrapping it around the base of the bun. This was the first time I had my hair completely up and not showing off the proudness of my Theorinian hair length.

"Your Eloise sure is exceptional," complimented Iryse. I caught the hint of Eloise's blush in the mirror as she finalized the finishing touches of my hair.

"She sure is. I do not know what I would do without her." I smiled as I caught Eloise's eyes in the mirror. She smiled back at me. At that moment, I knew I would need to tell her the truth, or this guilt would consume me.

Iryse decided we should all wear similar dresses. She donned an A-line dress as well. Hers, however, started out white up top and slowly blended down from a powder blue that reminded me of snow on a full moon night to a darker cerulean blue that almost matched the top of my dress. Whereas mine had diamonds sewn throughout, hers had various shades of blue topazes sewn in a very elaborate design. She deigned a large ice blue topaz necklace that was oblong with matching earrings. She wore her hair down with little braids throughout.

Tearani wore another two-piece dress with her midriff showing. I caught sight of her navel ring again. She had ruby gems in it that matched her ruby pendant, circled by diamonds. A pair of matching earrings were in place. The top of her dress had loose shoulder straps draping over her arms. It was a dark midnight blue with blue sapphires sewn throughout. The bottom half was lightweight tulle. For half a second, I believed this dress may not have a split in either leg. Until she began to walk, and then I caught hints of both her thighs. Her friendship anklet still in place. Her maids had made her hair extra wavy. She looked like a goddess walking on earth as she graced us with her presence.

I walked with the twins down to the ball. Curiously sparked me at what the twins would comment on tonight. As we arrived, I noted Bay was already in attendance. He was not looking in my direction as he listened to a lady I didn't recognize talk. I did not know how he would respond to seeing me here after our rendezvous.

"Quit fiddling with your hands," scolded Iryse, and I instantly dropped them to my side, listening to her. It did not take Iryse long before she shoved a wine goblet into my hand.

"Can't have you standing like a statue. You're too ramrod straight, relax." She rolled her eyes at me. I took a big gulp of the wine to ease my nerves. Tearani did not say a word as she gazed out amongst the people.

"You know, Iryse, you should use proper speech as a princess," I commented quite boldly. She huffed and rolled her eyes.

"You sound just like my parents, tutors, and everyone else. Raise me with servants all my life, and I will speak like them, too." She did another eye roll. I decided not to push the subject.

I was drinking from my fourth goblet of wine, and the warm room swayed before me. Normally, I would have cut myself off at two, but Iryse kept pushing them into my hands the moment one became empty. I was uncertain what her tactic was, but I could not refuse her. None of us had left the wall, and it did not seem to bother either of the twins one bit. Knox still had not made an appearance. Bay had not looked over at me once from his entourage of females. Despite Iryse's attempts, I was beginning to feel down in the dumps.

Tearani glanced at Iryse before nodding in a direction. Iryse nodded back, and turning to me, she told me they would be right back. I leaned against the wall as I watched them both leave. My face was beginning to lose feeling; I already could not feel my teeth in my mouth, and my nose tickled. In the haze of my vision, I watched Regina and Olivia walking my way. It took a moment for my drunken mind to catch up to speed that I should probably make my escape. It was too late, though. Why was I always being cornered?

"Stay away from my brothers," warned Regina. She was seething mad about something I had no control over.

"Stay away from Prince Voltaire Edric as well!" Olivia practically shouted at me. Thank the goddess for this wall that was supporting me.

"Why? Afraid I'll steal your fuck buddy, Livvy?" I retorted before my brain could catch up to my slurring drunken mouth. Olivia sucked in a sharp breath, jerking back with her hand covering her mouth.

"How did you kn - - I mean," she caught herself as I lazily smiled at her, giving a knowing look. "You do not know what you are talking about, Tower Princess!"

"*Ohhhh*, so insulting," I drawled. "Is that a means to hurt my feelings, Livvy?" I had no idea why I was calling her Livvy, but my drunken mouth would not stop. Olivia's face scrunched up, turning as red as the wine in my goblet. I looked over at Regina as I continued on. "As for your brothers, they approached me with Voltaire." I flicked my gaze at Olivia. "Oh yes, we are on a first-name basis, no titles stringed along, Livvy." I smiled wickedly.

"Who do you think you are?" Regina accused. "You have no right to speak to us this way!" I stayed smiling at them, not responding to Regina's accusations.

"Just, just stay away from my brothers and Voltaire!" She threatened again. I pushed off the wall, minimally losing balance as I swayed.

"Your brothers came to me, Reggie, same as Voltaire. Who am I to refuse a dance with a prince of higher birth than me?" I batted my eyes innocently at her. Her face became completely disgusted by my act.

"You are drunk," she bluntly stated.

"And you're a bitch," I retorted in a syrupy sweet tone. Regina and Olivia both sucked in a breath as they glanced at each other. Regina jabbed her finger into my chest, causing me to fall back against the wall. Good, because standing was becoming exhausting, and leaning against this wall was a lot easier. Regina's face was mere inches from mine.

"I am warning you. Stay. Away. From. My. Brothers."

"Why? Afraid I could become your sister-in-law?" I taunted. Her eyes flashed with anger as her nostrils flared.

"Do not even for a second believe you are good enough for either," she gritted out.

"Just imagine being sisters-in-law as I ruled on my own queendom with one of your brothers by my side... Maybe both? I hear having multiple lovers is quite common in queendoms." I winked with the biggest Cheshire grin I could muster. Regina's eyes widened at the thought before she backed away from me.

"You took it too far, Tower Princess," she warned.

"I only speak the truth; apologies that you cannot handle hearing the truth, Reggie." I winked again just to get more under her skin. Olivia had been awfully quiet during all this, and that was when I realized she was no longer behind Regina. She must have run when Regina's face was inches apart from mine.

"Where did your lackey go?" I asked. I watched Regina's face as her mind began to work on what I meant before her head whipped behind her to find the missing Olivia. "Did she run away scared?" Regina's face whipped back to mine as she took a step closer again.

"I will say this one last time. Stay. Away. And. Do. Not. Touch. Things. That. Do. Not. Belong. To. You." She enunciated through gritted teeth. I chuckled at her.

"What I touch is none of your business."

"What is going on here?" Montgomery's deep voice came from behind Regina. Regina's eyes widened slightly before she turned to face her older brother.

"Nothing, Monty. Just be on your way," Regina deflected.

"Does not seem like nothing. You have Mina backed against the wall." He gave her a questioning look, seeing if she would deny it. Regina did not miss the beat of him calling me by my nickname as I watched her stiffen.

"She is just not feeling well. I was checking in on her," Regina lied.

"Bullshit. We both know you do not like her. While I do not understand why . . ." Montgomery's eyes roamed over my body. "She is a charming princess to talk to." Montgomery moved his sister out of the way to stand in front of me. He put his hand to my forehead. I knew from the wine that my face had to be very flushed by this point.

"No fever, probably just too much wine," he said as he grabbed my hand. "Come on, let's get you out of here." He began leading me to the double-door exit. I focused with all my might to put one foot in front of the other while stumbling as I walked in what I believed was a straight line behind him. In our haste to the door, my eyes briefly locked with Bay's scowling face. Montgomery pulled me, causing me to break eye contact and go back to focusing on walking. We were outside the ball in cooler, breathing air before I knew it.

"Where is your room?" He asked me, still tugging me along. I stumbled a bit over my feet. He paused and then scooped me up into his arms. "No sense in you breaking an ankle when we are heading the same way."

I blushed. I had never been carried like this before. Through my muddled thoughts, I attempted to give him directions. I think I told him to take too many rights because we ended up in an area I did not recognize. He chuckled as I continued to overcorrect the way I believed we needed to go.

He continued to carry me like this, up the stairs to what I believed was my floor, without a single complaint. The silence became a bit awkward, but I think I was more grateful for not having to walk all the way back to my room. I probably would have needed to crawl with how much the wall had been supporting me in the ballroom.

"What are you doing with Mina?" Bay's cold tone came from behind us. Montgomery stopped, turning to face Bay.

"She drank a bit too much. I rescued her from my sister and was just taking her back to her room to retire for the evening. No need to fret, Rafael." I felt Montgomery's grip tighten on me, pulling me closer to his chest. He was being a bit protective for a man I only had exchanged a few sentences with, predominantly during a dance. I wondered why Montgomery called the heir by his first name.

"I can take her from here," Bay replied in response. It was not quite an order but yet not quite an offer either.

"No need, we are almost there, and I have managed this far," countered Montgomery. I knew Montgomery was grasping for straws since I had already given him the wrong directions three times. They stared each other down. All I wanted was my bed. My head felt heavy, even with me already resting it against Montgomery's chest.

"My kingdom, I insist," Bay said, finally breaking the silence. Both Montgomery and I knew there was no argument against that statement. Bay had more power in the hierarchy at this very moment. Montgomery nodded his head. Bay closed the distance between us, and I was transferred over to his arms. Closing my eyes, I nestled my head in his chest, smelling warm cinnamon and fresh winter snow.

"Good night, and thank you for taking care of my Mina, Montgomery," dismissed Bay. I faintly heard Montgomery respond with a good night. Bay walked the remaining distance to my room without needing my directions and, upon opening the door, found the room to be cloaked in darkness. Eloise must still be with the other servants.

"Where is your handmaid?" Growled Bay.

"Probably with her servant friends," I yawned. "She spends a lot of time with them now." I shrugged in his arms.

"Very convenient with Montgomery bringing you up here alone, eh?" He accused. The alcohol was still swishing in my brain because I was not even phased by his comment as I nestled my head more into his chest.

"You smell really good," I commented, the first thing that popped into my head. Bay merely chuckled but did not respond.

"Mmmhh, Mont was just being a gentleman."

"Really? You do not think for a second he would have not tried anything?"

"Considering he saved me from his sister, no?" I yawned again. Bay was still carrying me in the dark, trying to avoid the furniture he could see by moonlight streaming in through the large windows. "What about you, all alone with me in the dark?"

"That is different. I know my intentions. What I do not know is his," growled Bay.

"And what are your intentions, Bay?" I asked boldly. He did not respond right away as he kept walking towards my bed in the dark.

"What are your intentions, Bay?" I asked again, demanding an answer.

"They are complicated," he finally replied, still growling.

"Tell me what is complicated." I pushed on as he walked through my bedroom. He placed me on top of my bed so that I was sitting with my legs dangling over the edge.

"Let me guess, you are going to need help getting out of this dress?" He avoided my question to ask his own. I nodded because I did not know when Eloise would be back.

"And you wonder why I do not believe he would not have tried anything," Bay grumbled to himself. Turning me so my back was to him, he began undoing the laces on my corset. Inch by inch, the dress loosened, and I was able to breathe more easily. The swimming in my head lessened up as well. When he undid the last one, I took in a full, deep breath.

"Feel better?"

I nodded. I looked over my shoulder, the moonlight cascading down on him. It made his silver hair remind me of starlight. I caught him watching me.

"Stand up so we can get this off you." He ordered.

I nodded again, listening to him as I stood up. I swayed and caught myself against him. Giggling to myself, I felt his hands skim my waist, making certain my corset was loose enough before he began to pull the dress over my head. He threw it on the chair by the window, and I now stood there in my light blue strapless slip dress.

The moonlight shining down on the both of us. I took a tentative step towards him. When he did not back away, I took another step. I reached up to touch his starlight-shining hair, running my fingers through it.

"Mina," he breathed. I went up on tiptoes and kissed him softly on the lips, leaning into him to help steady myself. He wrapped his arms around me. Deepening the kiss, he pulled me closer, and I wrapped my arms around his neck. He turned us ever so slightly, guiding me until I was sitting down on the bed again. He released his hold of me as he braced his arms on both sides of me. His knee came up between my thighs, and I pulled him deeper onto the bed with me.

He rolled us until I was lying on top of him, his hands skimming my sides. He began to harden beneath me, and I broke the kiss to look at him. He was watching me.

"Mina, you are so breathtakingly beautiful," he said as his fingers came up to brush the rogue strands of hair that had escaped my bun away from my face. I blushed. He continued, "what I would love to do with you right now." His eyes darkened at the thought as he looked down at my breasts, barely covered with the thin fabric.

"What *would* you love to do with me?" I asked. I desperately wanted to know what was going on in his mind. Was he feeling the same things I was? I hoped it was not all in my head. I just wanted and needed him right now. After last night in the corridor, I wanted to go all the way with Bay, not because of Mother's lessons pounding it into me, but because I felt something between us. The way I would catch him looking at me. The way he came to check on me after Regina in the rose garden. My heart began to surge from the emotions coursing through me. I adored and wanted this man.

"The real question is, what would I not want to do with you?" He growled. "I want to taste you and have you coming in ecstasy from my tongue. I want to fuck you so deeply until you are screaming my name loud enough for everyone to hear." I shivered at the thought of all that he was promising.

"Then do it," I dared him.

"Not tonight, sweet Mina," his growl became ragged.

"Why not?" I began to pout. He promised something that sounded deliciously inviting. What I desperately wanted and needed, he was telling me no.

"Because you are drunk, and when I fuck you for the first time, I want to make sure you remember it," he promised. I leaned down and kissed him tenderly. His concern and care for my sober state were endearing. Pulling back, I smiled at him.

"Thank you, Bay," I eased my body down to be tucked in between his arm and side. Nestling my head on his chest, I breathed in his scent again. Cinnamon and fresh winter snow.

I must have dozed off for a bit, because when I jerked awake, I felt Bay getting out of my bed. It was still nighttime, and the room was dark. I heard him walking towards my bedroom door. He opened the door, and just before he walked all the way through, I chose to speak up.

"Bay, I would never have trusted him to undo my corset." He lingered in my bedroom doorway before softly closing the door shut behind him.

Chapter 15

The next morning, Eloise was all a chatter about the latest gossip she heard from the other maids. I pretended to listen as she fiddled with braiding my hair. My mind was thinking back to the kindness that Bay had shown me. Montgomery was kind, too. I still did not think he would try anything like Bay had been concerned about. Montgomery reminded me of a caring brother. He looked out for me, even if it was against his blood-related sister. I wondered if I would be running into Bay today. *And what about his promise?* I shivered.

"Are you cold, Mina?" Eloise broke from her prattling to ask me.

"No, no. I am fine," I responded. She resumed braiding my hair while I resumed imagining all of the delightful things Bay had promised to do to me.

Arriving at teatime, I began to make my way towards the twins before I was interceded by one of The Queen's personal handmaids. The Queen was requesting an audience with me today for tea. I was a tad nervous. I had seen her regularly pull individual girls to chat with during teatime. That is, of course, when The Queen actually showed up. While teatime was on the itinerary at her request, she was a very infrequent guest to it.

I followed the maid to where Queen Serenity sat away from the other guests. This part of the tearoom was all creams and golds, with large white ostrich feathers being lazily fanned by the servants surrounding The Queen. There were dozens of cushions surrounding the whole area.

Queen Serenity wore a dress that matched the décor. Her dress was large enough that I was certain she could fit a small village beneath it. I was afraid to know how heavy it was, especially with all the additional lace, pearls, and beading upon it. Queen Serenity waved a fan that matched her dress in front of her face. I would catch glimpses of her usual friendly smile from behind it. Once I approached her, I curtsied.

"Queen Serenity." I smiled.

"You are Queen Lydia's daughter," Queen Serenity stated to me, and I was a bit taken aback by the blunt addressment to me in response.

"Yes, Queen Serenity, I am." I dipped my head, uncertain which way this was going to go.

"You can rise." She released me from my curtsey. She nodded her head to the empty chair before her. A servant pulled it out and pushed it in for me as I began to sit.

"Your mother and I were in the same season together," she added.

"Mother never told me," I replied, finding new information and wondering why she had never mentioned this to me prior. This seemed like important information that could have been utilized to my advantage.

"I suppose not. I was the one to win King Regalius's hand in matrimony." She smiled coyly. This made even less sense as to why Mother never mentioned it. Could it have been that Queen Serenity had humiliated her by becoming the queen of the wealthiest and largest monarchy?

"Oh, I see." I did not know what else to say as I tried not to shift in my seat.

"I do hope there were no hard feelings," Queen Serenity continued, taking a sip from her tea. "Because she and I were quite close during our time together."

"She has never said anything insulting. Only that you were quite beautiful." I omitted the part where she said that her son, Prince Rafael Baylor, must also be beautiful like his parents. My mother had assumed correctly because Bay, like his brother Knox, was very handsome.

"Hmm, she was quite a lovely lady as well." Queen Serenity seemed displeased by my response, but I did not have anything else to give. Even if my mother did bad mouth Queen Serenity, I still would not relay those words to her as I did not want my family or kingdom to fall into ill favor with Kingdom T'lovoness.

"Tis a shame she and I have lost such communication over the seasons," Queen Serenity continued, lest the conversation stalled.

"You mentioned you were close during your season?" I pushed. I wanted to know more about my mother and her past. I hoped asking was not too bold.

"Oh yes, quite. We were quite inseparable." She took another sip of her tea. "It was very uncommon to not see us together during that season."

"Were you friends prior to the season?" Aside from the story my mother would tell me of how Father fell in love with her, I did not have any other insight into her season. It was now that I realized I really did not know anything about my mother's past.

"No, we met because of it. She was a merchant's daughter from Theorines, and I was a High Lord's daughter from Grewt'en." This was the first time I had ever heard that Mother was a merchant's daughter. I never knew my grandparents or any other relatives on her side. I never had an idea of where she came from. I was very aware of my father's ancestry. Looking back, anytime I asked about her ancestry, she would always change topics.

"For how close we were, I was quite hurt when she would not bring you around," Queen Serenity continued. I did not know what to say to this. I had not expected The Queen to be so open about these things. Maybe it was because of her friendship with my mother that she was willing to share these feelings.

"I am sorry," I apologized for my mother's behavior.

"'Tis not your fault, Mina," Queen Serenity waved her fan as if she could just fan away those thoughts. "You were a mere child. You have turned out quite exceptionally well. I can see you have won my son's hearts as well." She raised both her eyebrows in a knowing look. It occurred to me that she had called me by my nickname and had not addressed me formally. One of her sons must have been talking to her.

"I am quite fond of both of your sons," I smiled. I hoped I had responded correctly. Her smile and friendly conversation were nice, but she left most of her sentences in a way that was difficult for me to respond to.

"Just do not go breaking both of their hearts. While I would not mind you as a future daughter-in-law . . ." Queen Serenity paused before continuing forward, ". . . a mother is very protective of her children and would hate to see them hurting," she concluded. I was not certain if she was threatening me or just expressing how she would feel. I certainly did not want to know where that threat would go. Let alone I should not have to worry since I definitely did not want to break both of their hearts. I was here for Bay.

"You should not have to worry about that, Queen Serenity," I replied. "If anyone were to leave here with a broken heart, it most likely would be mine."

Queen Serenity's smile faltered a moment from my response before she quickly recovered, fanning herself faster.

"Very well, I hope we have tea again sometime soon." She dipped her head, dismissing me. As calmly as I could, I stood up and made my way towards my original intended purpose to the table the twins occupied.

"Well, what was that all about?" Iryse questioned before I was able to even sit down. Tearani was watching the other guests as she sipped her tea.

"Apparently, she and my mother were best friends during their season here," I replied, taking a quick drink from the teacup before me.

"Really?! And you did not know that until now?" She asked, completely in awe like I had been.

"Nope. Mother never made mention of it once. I feel like if she had told me, I would have had a better edge up on things and would not have been so blindsided by that little tidbit of knowledge just now." There was some bitterness in my voice as I said it. All these years, I was locked up in my tower away from everyone, never able to attend any social events. My mother dared to have the audacity to keep this kind of information away from me. Sometimes, I feel she left me in the dark about so many matters that I would fail when I arrived here because my lack of knowledge was beginning to make me look foolish.

"You are thinking mighty hard over there," Iryse placed her hand on top of mine. I snapped out of my spiral, shaking my head as I looked at her. "Whatever it is, we are here." She smiled.

I made my way back to my room after teatime. Had I even attended a single needlework time since arriving? Thinking back, I do not believe so. Maybe I had on day one? Either way, I was not starting today. I did not feel like going to the rose garden and figured I could read a bit in my room before making my way to lunch. I had not had time to read the book 'The Court of Smoke and Mirrors' with everything going on, and I felt this would be a good time to escape from the world.

Eloise was tidying up my room when I arrived, which I found odd since she was rarely around anymore. I was not complaining; I just had come into the habit of having the space all to myself.

"Oh! Mina, you have a letter from your parents," Eloise informed me. I went over to the letter tray to pick up the letter and see what my parents had to say. I have not received a letter since my arrival. To be fair, I also had not sent any letters to them either.

Dearest Persamina Rowena,

Darling daughter, we plan on coming to visit Kingdom T'Lovoness. We simply miss you and would love to meet all your new friends along with seeing a few of our old friends. We have also sent letters to King Regalius and Queen Serenity. They are aware of our arrival.

Life has been quite dull in the castle without you and with everyone at T'Lovoness. We have not hosted any balls, so you can simply understand how I am currently feeling.

Much love,
Mommy and Daddy Dearest
King Gideon and Queen Lydia of Theorines

"My parents are coming," I said, holding the letter numbly. Eloise stopped tidying up and came to my side, wrapping her arms around my waist; she rested her head on my shoulder.

"Don't worry, it'll be fine," she tried to comfort. I glanced at her, raising an eyebrow, and she smiled with a shrug, pulling me tighter to her.

"This is going to be anything but a tea party," I placed the letter down on my vanity as I walked out of Eloise's arms, beginning to pace.

"When will they be arriving?"

"I am going to assume any day now," I began twisting the rings on my fingers.

"So, this is a very short notice . . ." Eloise sprang into action, making certain my dresses and accessories were in proper order, and I was right behind her helping out. We were in a cleaning, organizing, frenzied whirlwind. We both knew my mother would come to my room and critique everything. I had to protect Eloise at all costs.

There was a sharp knock at the door. We both looked at each other in fear. I gulped before nodding my head for Eloise to get the door as I rushed to the mirror and began to fix anything out of place. Eloise barely had the door open before my mother barged in wearing a bold magenta dress. Father followed in tow. That letter could have come a day sooner.

"Persamina, darling," Mother purred. She had her arms spread, walking towards me. Before I could respond, she instantly embraced me in a hug, but not tight enough to crush me and ruin either of our dresses.

"Mother, Father, I just got your letter mere moments ago," I informed them. Mother rolled her eyes, fanning her hand at the empty air. "We sent that letter weeks ago. I swear peasants become more and more lazy by the day." She turned towards my wardrobe. "Speaking of peasants. Eloise," she called. I had to hold my cringe internally.

Father wrapped me in a hug, not caring if he put creases in my dress. I heard Mother's hiss as I hugged him tightly back. He had shaved off his beard since I had left, and his long black hair was past his knees, tied in a loose braid down his back. He kissed the top of my forehead, telling me he loved and missed me. Letting me go, he began walking around the room, admiring the various details.

"Yes, Your Majesty?" Eloise walked to Mother. Her head downcasted, she dropped into a deep curtsey when she stood before Mother.

"Hmm." She looked Eloise over before pushing past her to begin perusing my wardrobe. She flicked my dresses with such disdain. Her eyes flicked to Eloise, who was still holding her curtsey. Mother raised an eyebrow at Eloise before turning back to survey the room.

"Mina," my father said, catching my attention. I turned to look at him. My father was a man of few words. He rarely spoke, and aside from family interactions such as dining together, he was absent in my life. I partially resented my mother for this, because she would shoo him away when he tried to make attempts.

"It is Persamina, stop calling her Mina!" Mother scolded him. He stared at her, but as I studied him, I realized emotion was brimming under his surface. His jaw was clenched, and he had actually been downright glaring at her with an emotion I could not put my finger on.

"Yes, Father?" I asked nervously, feeling the tension in the room.

"Are you enjoying your time here?" He asked.

"Yes, Father, I am," I replied courteously. In my mind, I thought to myself, it really depends on which part of my time here he was asking about. I loved my time with the twins. My time with the other princesses, not so much. I was beginning to really enjoy the balls while attending them with the twins. While my heart was becoming increasingly confused between the two brothers, I was enjoying my time with them nonetheless.

Mother would unquestioningly accept whatever I said, and she would see what she wanted to see. Father, on the other hand, could see through the lies and bullshit that anyone fed him. He shifted his gaze back to me, losing the glare as he stared at me for a few seconds before finally responding, "Very well." I blinked a few times at his response, anticipating him to call me out on it. His eyes flickered to Mother again with that emotion showing in his eyes, and then back at me with a subtle nod. I nodded in return.

Mother kept inspecting various parts of the room. Eloise was still curtseying; my heart went out to her. At least, though it was not in a room full of strangers like I had endured on my first night here. However, being in front of your King and Queen could be very intimidating when you do not have a leg to stand upon. I stood trying not to fidget, lest I be disciplined by Mother. Father slowly made his final inspection at the door to leave my room. The quietness was becoming excruciating.

"Lydia, we need to go to our room, dear," my father's voice was void of all emotion as he finally broke the silence. I rarely heard him ever give her an order. Mother's gaze glanced at him, to us, back to the mantle she had just been inspecting, giving it a lingering look before finally turning to walk to my father. He extended his arm to her, and she slid her arm within his. I noticed they both leaned away from each other as if they were the last people each other had been wanting to touch. With her free hand, she reached out to touch my cheek, lightly patting it, "We will see you at supper, darling." Then, they both departed out of the room.

When the door closed behind them, I watched Eloise finally release herself from her curtsey. We both looked at each other with wide eyes. I slowly let my perfect straight posture relax as we both let out a huge breath of air. This was only the first day of their arrival. We had no idea how long they would stay here. My fun vacation was coming to a halting stop.

"Eloise..."

"Yeah?"

"It is time to bring out the showstoppers."

"Yup," she popped the 'p' when she said it. We had been selecting simple dresses this whole time, but now, with my mother here, we would have to hold nothing back. Everything was going to have to be perfect.

Chapter 16

Hours later, my hair felt like it was being ripped out of my skull. Eloise was throwing in various elaborate twists and braids. She called in reinforcements from the scullery maid, Stella. I was unsure how, but those two had met and became fast friends. I was not one to complain; Stella was definitely helping speed up the process of getting ready.

"If I have any feeling in my head after this, I will be shocked," I whined.

"Shush," Eloise chided, "Your mother won't be happy any other way." I rolled my eyes. We both knew she was right.

"This is a lot of fun," Stella chimed in. I watched her in the mirror. She was smiling as she twirled my hair into a curl. This was probably much better than being in the humid kitchens as a scullery maid.

"I can put in a request for you to be one of my maids while I am here, Stella," I suggested, watching her expression go from smile to complete shock. She started finessing with my hair even faster. "I am serious, Stella; I can do it." I smiled. I watched as Stella looked at Eloise, who gave her an encouraging smile.

"Okay," she said quite softly, smiling to herself. "I would like that a lot."

"Alright, I will put the request in immediately." I smiled. It would be good for Eloise to have someone here regularly to talk to and help her out. Not to mention, it could help move Stella up in her palace career.

Eloise walked away to my wardrobe to pull out a dress that looked like starlight, taking my breath away. I instantly thought of Bay's hair from last night.

"Oh, Eloise, I do not know if I could wear that." I blushed, taking in the gorgeous silver-white dress with white and blue sparkles sprinkled throughout it.

"You can, and you shall wear it at the next ball," she chirped back. "Your mother is here. We need to dress to impress her. . . or feel her wrath," she threatened. I shivered, knowing full well what that wrath was like.

"Okay, you have a point. Now to figure out the current dress," I relented with a sigh. I knew full well the corset would be tightened even more severely than it had been prior. I was going to be feeling the indents and the bruises later. With potential new scarring to add to the collection.

Breathing was horrendous. Each step was limited. Eloise and I selected a gauzy white dress with cherry blossom branches and flowers sewn throughout it. Everywhere there was a flower, pink morganite stones were sewn. Eloise had to put a hoop skirt with extra crinoline over the top of it to make the bottom an enormous bell shape. With each step, my bottom swayed dramatically. The dress was strapless with a deep v-neckline. Eloise had pulled the corset laces even tighter than prior. This caused my breasts to appear larger with the tiny waistline, and the cleavage line became quite revealing. It was the most exposed I had ever dressed while being here.

We agreed upon a round watermelon tourmaline gemstone surrounded by white quartz stones. Matching earrings were in place. My hair was styled in a chignon with multiple wavy locks framing my face to still show the pride of my length as the locks of hair flowed down past my knees. Eloise lastly placed the tiara with the biggest emeralds and black onyx stones on top of my head.

I made it to the banquet doors, gently placing a hand on the handle to steady myself. I desperately was ready to sit down from the extra weight of everything. I knew, though, that sitting down would not relieve anything as it would cut into my breathing. Mother would watch my every move out of the corner of her eye.

I slowly pushed open the door. My eyes skimmed the room until I finally found my parents sitting directly next to King Regalius, Queen Serenity and their two sons at the head of the table. There was a single empty chair next to Mother that was directly across from Knox. He wore an expression that translated to wanting to be anywhere but here.

Bay, on the other hand, looked like his respectable, corrigible self. Like a true prince heir as, he listened to Mother while she talked to him and Queen Serenity. Father was in deep conversation with King Regalius as his gaze flicked on and off to Queen Serenity. I took as deep of a breath as I could muster, but in reality, it was short, quick, shallow breaths before I began to make my way towards them.

I felt multiple pairs of eyes on me. I tried not to look anywhere but towards the empty chair meant for me. I had never sat this close to the front of the table. It never occurred to me how far this walk would be until now. I happened to glance to the right and locked eyes with Montgomery. He winked at me, and my breath hitched. I should not have looked. Regina's pinched red face sat beside him, her green eyes glaring at me.

I kept walking towards my chair. I did not recognize the person that would be sitting to the left of me. Currently, I was okay with not knowing who they were. I knew full well that Mother would make a point of bringing me into every conversation with Queen Serenity and her two sons.

"Ah, there she is, my darling daughter, Princess Persamina Rowena." Smiled my mother by way of greeting, introducing me to the table. I fell into a deep curtsy, thinking back to all the times Mother made me do it with this tight of a corset. I stood back up as a servant stepped forward to pull out my chair. I took my seat as they pushed it in underneath me. I could feel everyone further down the table looking blatantly at my family and me. Heat began to creep up my neck.

"Your mother was telling us how you were quite exceptional at needlework." Queen Serenity smiled at me. She and I both knew full well that I had never attended the needlework session with the other princesses and ladies.

"Ah, yes." I smiled in return. "I started at a very young age and picked up on it quite rather quickly."

"Honestly, back home, she almost always has a needle in her hand," my mother added with a laugh. She placed a hand on my arm that was to signify adoring affection. Mother must have been thinking of the time before I created my rainbow handkerchief. I caught Bay raising his eyebrow at me with a smirk.

"That is quite interesting to hear." Smiled Queen Serenity sweetly. She tilted her head ever so slightly, and I was certain she was going to tell Mother I had never attended a single needlework session. Queen Serenity looked back at Mother, "Lydia, remember how we used to skip needlework during our courting season?"

"Oh, I do not recall that." Mother smiled back, taking a quick sip from her drink.

"Oh, come now, Lydia, we both skipped needlework all the time," pushed Queen Serenity. It was odd hearing Mother being addressed informally. She would punish anyone of a lower ranking if they did not call her either 'Queen Lydia' or any other similar formal title.

"I highly doubt that." Waved Mother's hand, dismissing the notion.

"We were both atrocious with a needle and thread. Alas, thankfully, it has not trickled down to your daughter for bad habits. She is a delight in needlework hour." She smiled that syrupy, sweet smile to Mother, waiting to see if Mother would challenge her or not. Mother tightly smiled before looking down, trying to hide her pursed lips. Queen Serenity looked at me and winked. I did not know what to make of this turn of events. Queen Serenity had outright insulted Mother's skills and gotten away with it.

The servants brought out the first course, steamy potato soup. Now, it would be a battle of what was an appropriate amount to eat for Mother's approval and what would be enough so that I did not starve. I could attempt to sneak down to the kitchens later, but with Mother in the castle, I did not think that would be the wisest idea. With Stella now a part of my handmaidens, I could send her. Mother did not know her yet, meaning she would just blend in with all the other servants working in the castle.

I decided my best method would be to follow suit and eat when either Mother or Queen Serenity took a spoonful of soup. But I could not do both, and I obviously could not copy one of them. I just had to find the line where Mother would not chastise me.

I looked up to see Knox mouth to me. *Are you alright?*

I mouthed back, *No.*

Bay caught my eye and mouthed, *Can we help?*

I slightly shook my head while glancing at my mother. Thankfully, both parents were engaged in conversation, not to notice the silent words we exchanged. I decided to take a quick liberty with three spoonfuls of soup. The potato soup was filled with an unimaginable amount of flavor. I closed my eyes, savoring the taste. It saddened me that I would not be able to finish this bowl. I breathed in as slowly and deeply as possible to remember the soup's smell. I opened my eyes and noticed both Knox and Bay staring at me. I bit my bottom lip, glancing towards my mother, who was still in deep conversation, and then at the person to my left, who was also immersed in conversation.

I am starving, I mouthed to them.

Then eat, Knox mouthed back, giving me a weird look. Bay rolled his eyes as he smacked Knox's arm, mouthing to him, *She is not allowed to!* Knox looked at him, to me, and back to him, confused.

Why not? Knox mouthed to Bay, to which Bay motioned with his head to my parents. Knox still did not seem to get it. I was going to assume that is what happens when you are the reclusive prince. He did not attend enough events to know that females were expected to barely eat in public.

"Persamina, darling," Mother crooned, drawing my attention to her as I was mid-spoonful to my mouth. I looked at her, and she glanced at the spoon and back to me, cocking her head with a smile. I slowly set the spoon back down into my bowl, leaving it there as I rested my hands on my lap. I smiled at her. She watched me for a second longer before returning her attention back to what King Regalius was saying.

I stared at the soup, biting my lip, twisting my rings in my lap frantically. I took a breath as I watched the soup steam rise from the bowl. I could hear the surrounding spoons sometimes accidentally clack against their bowls as the others ate. I just stared at that bowl, pretending that I did not want it.

The bowls were soon cleared away from in front of us, and then the main course was placed down before us. I looked at the plate and truly wished my parents were not here. To be specific, I wish my mother were not here; Father would not care one bit.

"Princess Persamina Rowena, do you enjoy chicken?" Asked Queen Serenity as she took a bite from her fork. I took notice that she had once again addressed me formally. I was unsure if she had done so because Mother was here or if her one time of being informal earlier was to emphasize her point.

"Yes, Queen Serenity, it is one of my favorites." I smiled, mimicking her. I could feel Mother's eyes cutting right through me. Out of my peripheral vision, I could see both Bay and Knox watching me, as well. Father and King Regalius had been talking about hunting and planning a few outings during Father's visit. Father glanced at Serenity, taking a slight interest in our conversation, before returning his attention to Regalius.

I went to take a forkful of potatoes and heard my mother clear her throat. I changed direction to stab a forkful of salad and did not hear her clear her throat again. Right choice. I sighed through my nose, taking a bite of the salad.

I glanced up and saw Knox digging into his chicken while Bay stared at me, chewing his food very slowly. I stabbed another forkful of salad to shove into my mouth.

Queen Serenity was eating without remorse. Mother barely touched her plate. I stabbed some of my chicken and a swipe of potatoes with my next salad bite. It was not the greatest food combination for taste, but it at least had a bit more substance. Mother had not noticed either. I repeated the process, being a bit more daring in my swipe of potatoes. It was the third time that Mother cleared her throat that I put my fork down on the plate. Out of my peripheral vision, I noticed she looked back to Queen Serenity. Stella would definitely be making a kitchen run for me tonight.

The main course was cleared away as chocolate cake slices were placed down in front of us, and they smelled heavenly. I knew it was a rich dark chocolate with an extra good helping of frosting on it and molten chocolate lava oozing out of its layers. I picked up my fork and went to take a piece of the cake on my plate when I felt my ankle get kicked from my right. I gritted my teeth. My stomach rumbled loudly in protest. I placed my fork back down with as much willpower as I could muster without any frustration surfacing. Folding my hands, I placed them back in my lap.

"Do you not like cake, Princess Persamina Rowena?" I looked up to see Queen Serenity cock her head to the side. I knew she had seen me countless times eating sweets in her presence.

"I do, but I am just not hungry," I replied with a soft smile, hoping I was convincing. I tried hard not to let my eyes show how desperately I wanted this rich slice of delicious heaven in front of me.

"Oh, one bite will not hurt you," she prompted.

"You should definitely try it, Mina." Smiled Bay at me with a wink as he took a bite. Mother instantly heard how informal and friendly Bay was with me, and her whole disposition changed.

"Persamina, you should definitely try the cake. I am certain you can surely not be that full." Smiled my mother, joining in.

"Very well, I suppose you are right." I smiled, picking the fork back up and taking a bigger portion than Mother would have approved. I stuffed it in my mouth. The flavor bursting on my tastebuds. I held back the moan I so desperately wanted to release. It was even more heavenly than it smelled. It was not dry, and I wanted to devour this whole piece and maybe a second piece. Oh, what the hell, I wanted to devour the whole damn cake.

"It is quite delicious," I finally said, taking another bite. Both Queen Serenity and Bay smiled in response to me. They each took another bite of their own slice of cake.

I tried not to look at Mother as I took another bite. She was staring a hole right through me. I glanced over at her and watched her eyes flick from the fork to the cake, to me, and then back down to the plate. I held in the sigh as I placed the fork down on my plate gently.

Knox was practically scraping his plate clean from the cake. Bay was only halfway done. He was watching me. He did not even have to mouth it as his expression said *Are you okay?* I closed my eyes with a smile as if to say *No, but it would be fine. Do not worry about me.* When I opened my eyes, his response did not believe me. He put his fork down on his plate, signaling that he was also done eating.

"Let us retire, dear," said King Regalius as he rose, offering his hand to his wife. She took it, standing up next to him. The rest of the room, including myself, also stood up in honor of them. As they made their exit, I excused myself as well. I knew if I had not practically fled, Mother would have made me stay longer to talk to Bay. While I would not mind talking with Bay, I did not want it under the scrutinizing eyes of my mother.

I knew there was a chance Mother would be visiting me tonight. I had no choice but to head straight to my rooms. If Mother showed up later and I was not there, I knew the punishment would be severe. If she showed up and it was only Eloise, I was afraid of how far Mother would go. I did not want Eloise to receive the raw end of the deal due to me.

As I made my way to my rooms, the corridors were empty, with most of the guests still in the banquet hall. I would have run if my dress allowed it. The sooner I got to my rooms, the sooner Eloise could help me loosen this corset. With retiring to my room for the evening, I would even be able to put on a nightie. My hope for the nightie is mother would leave me alone upon seeing it. The palace had no big activities for tonight, meaning Mother would not expect me to attend anything to make appearances. I would curl up in my nightie to finally read my book.

I opened my door and stumbled upon Eloise and Stella kissing. *Oh! Ohhhhh!* Their friendliness made a lot more sense now.

"Mina!" Eloise jumped up, startled. Stella stood up as well with flushed cheeks. Looking down, she clasped her hands behind her back. "It is not what it looks like!" Eloise continued.

"Eloise, you do not need to hide anything from me. It is fine." I waved my hand. "Just please loosen this corset, then you can return to what you were doing. I will retire to my room." Eloise must have been expecting a far different reaction from me. She paused for a moment before jumping into action. She began loosening the corset strings and I finally took my first deep breath in. I lolled my head back in complete relief.

"How was it tonight?" Eloise asked nervously.

"I am starving. Mother and Father sat next to King Regalius and Queen Serenity, with both sons sitting there as well," I ranted.

"Oh no! I can run to the kitchens for you!" She rushed out, and I shook my head.

"No, it is fine. Mother will recognize you. . . I was going to send Stella, but I am not interrupting you two. I am just going to go to bed," I finished. My stomach disagreed as it let out a loud growl. I sighed, bracing my hands on the vanity with the full weight of my body.

There was a knock at my door, and my heart dropped. I did not think Mother would get back here this quickly. I hung my head, letting out a heavy breath.

One . . . two . . . three . . .

"Answer the door," I sighed, pushing off the vanity. I straightened up to perfect posture with my hands folded in front of me on top of one another to await Mother to come in and chastise me.

"Stella, go hide in the servant's wall," I said quietly over my shoulder. Mother did not need to see her just yet, and Stella did not need to see what might unfold next. I heard her quickly scurry across the room behind me, opening and closing the servant's entrance mirror.

Eloise opened the door. I braced myself, but it was not my mother on the other side. Bay stood there at the entrance of my room.

Chapter 17

Bay rushed into my room with a covered plate. His face was laced with concern. I had an inkling there was food underneath the covered dish, but I only dared to hope.

"Bay, what are you doing here?" I asked, completely surprised.

"You need to eat," he stated. He put the plate on my table and lifted the lid. It was the main course and dessert from earlier. "I would have grabbed the soup, but I did not have the confidence to travel with that without spilling it everywhere. There is also no salad," he added. I brought my hands up to cover my mouth as I began to laugh, and tears formed in my eyes. The concern he had for my well-being completely touched me. I bet it had been a sight to see the prince heir traveling down the corridors with a food platter in hand.

"Bay," I said, taking steps towards him as he stood there by the table with steaming hot food. He took a step towards me and, taking my hand, he led me the rest of the way to the chair. He pulled it out and pushed it in as I sat down.

"Please eat," he begged. "That was too painful to watch at dinner tonight, so please." His eyes filled with concern. I picked up the fork and delved into the food. I closed my eyes and threw my head back with the first bite while moaning at how delicious the potatoes were.

I brought my head forward and opened my eyes to see Bay standing there. His dark eyes drank me in with hunger. I could no longer taste the food as I stared back at him.

"I... should go," he said in a voice that neither of us believed. We both knew he was not serious. Instead of turning around to leave, he chose to stand there watching me. We stared at each other. *I wanted this man.* There was another knock at my door, and this time I knew it had to be my Mother.

I did not break eye contact with Bay as I told Eloise to let her in. Out of my peripheral vision, I watched Eloise hurry to my bedroom door for the second time. She barely had it open as my mother slammed it the rest of the way, barging in, already shrieking.

"How dare you! Persamina- -" she faltered as her gaze landed on Bay, "Prince Rafael Baylor," she gasped. Her gaze flicked at him, to me eating, and back at him. I watched as she regained her composure. "Certainly, it is utmost ill-mannered for my daughter to be eating in front of you. Eloise, clear this away," she barked. "Persamina, I thought you had enough to eat at supper," she threatened with her eyes.

Eloise was rushing over to follow Mother's orders with trembling hands, but Bay stepped forward and put his hand in front of the food platter, preventing her from clearing it away.

"No, I brought the meal to Mina, insisting she eat more than she did. It is under my order." Bay leveled a gaze at Mother, daring her to challenge him. The friction crackled between the two of them. I desperately wanted to take another bite of food but did not want to test the limits.

Mother, realizing she would not win, decided to accept her loss. She and I both knew my hand in matrimony to Bay all depended upon him and if she insulted him now, it could ruin her entire plans. She had no inkling what Bay and I shared between the two of us. She had no idea how close I had become with his brother. I would love for Bay to become my husband, but his friendship would mean a lot to me, too.

"Very well," she said to him, and looking at me, she added, "next time, make sure you eat more at supper." She pursed her lips before turning to leave. Eloise closed the door behind her. I sank into my chair with a sigh.

Bay pulled up the other chair to sit next to me. "She's that tough, huh?"

"You have no idea." I rolled my eyes, taking another bite.

"Oh, I think I am getting an idea." He looked at the door as he said it before looking back at me. "You are nothing like her."

This caused me to pause mid-bite. I felt something crack, flooding me with relief. I felt lighter and finally able to breathe more easily.

"Mina?" Bay questioned, and I looked at him, "Why are you crying?" I had not realized tears had formed from the rush of emotions I felt. I quickly wiped them away, giggling a bit.

"Apologies, I just always hoped I would never be like her, and your words just unlocked something. It feels freeing." I smiled. He stared at me a moment longer before he finally smiled back.

"Eat," he commanded, and I dug in with even more vigor.

When I had completely finished my plate, I looked up to see Bay smiling at me, and I smiled back. This was nice. I could see myself doing this for the rest of my life.

"I should go," he said, standing up. I instantly stood as well.

"Walk me out?" He asked, offering me his arm with a smile. I gave a small smile, dipping my head and giving him my arm. We did not say anything as we walked to the door leading to the hallway.

He stopped right before opening it, turning to me and unlooping our arms. He brushed my hair back, "I will be back if you are restricted from being able to eat again." He winked. He leaned down and gave me a soft kiss on my lips as a goodbye. Opening the door, he walked out. I watched as the door closed behind him. I instantly leaned against the door for support, my mind reeling.

Eloise gave me a knowing smile. "When you are ready, I will get you out of those clothes." I smiled back at her. I looked down at my hands as I twirled my rings. I had a knight in shining armor to protect me from my mother.

Chapter 18

With Mother here, it would be mandatory for me to attend every single event. I was already mentally exhausted thinking about it. Queen Serenity saved me last night, but would she still be on my side today? It was hard telling.

Normally, Eloise would dress me in simple dresses, but now we would have to be more elaborate in my style. We could only hope it appeased Mother in every sense. Otherwise, she would be reprimanding Eloise, and I would receive a tongue-lashing. This meant I had to start getting ready two hours earlier with Stella helping us.

"I look like a strawberry shortcake," I said, looking in the mirror.

"But a very delicious strawberry shortcake," giggled Eloise. I rolled my eyes. The soft pink dress skirting was even larger than last night's dress. There was another hoop skirt under this one with crinoline as well. The tulle made the dress skirt so large, and how it fell reminded me of whipped cream. It was not just one shade of pink but multiple variations of the color, with some lilacs and lavenders thrown in the mix. They layered on top of each other—the dress changing colors depending on how the lighting hit it. The top bodice was silk white with pink lace threaded through the open eyelets of the sweetheart neckline. I wore a white pearl necklace with matching earrings.

"I will let you know if it makes a prince hungry for me." I winked at her. She began to cackle, braiding my hair on one side as Stella went back and smoothed the areas already done. Stella did not speak much; it was understandable that she was probably still uncomfortable, and after last night with how Mother stormed in, she probably became a bit more withdrawn.

"Stella," I said. "You are quite skillful with hair. Have you done it before?" I asked, wanting her to feel included.

"No, Princess. Eloise is just a good teacher." She blushed.

"Mina, we are past formalities, I thought?" I corrected her.

"Yes, Mina." she smiled.

"Do not let what happened between my mother and me get in your way of how we act. I will try to do my best to protect you and Eloise, but it does not always work." I promised and warned all in the same breath. It was the truth, and Eloise knew how far I went to keep her safe, but sometimes, it just did not work in our favor. Mother was not entirely kind to anyone of a station rank below her. Now, she was in a kingdom with a king and queen with more money and land than her. She was not as high of rank, but she would still receive the same level of respect. She knew the Royals of T'Lovoness could destroy our kingdom if they so chose to. Past friendship or not, between Queen Serenity and Mother, the tides could easily change, and I suspected they already had. Mother keeping her past friendship with Queen Serenity a secret from me, made me believe there was more to the story than anyone was letting on.

Entering the breakfast hall, my gaze fell on my parents sitting at the head table, just like the night before. I knew if I attempted to have breakfast sent up to my rooms, Mother would scold me. Catching sight of Bay sitting next to his mother meant I would be able to eat. Mother would not dare challenge him. Sadly, there was no sign of Knox being present; a part of me became slightly saddened by this.

As I reached the table, I caught sight of Mother's overly extravagant dress. She wore our kingdom's colors with the deep, rich emerald green for the velvet dress, black lace sewn along the edges, and ran down her arms as sleeves. There were little slate gray ribbons sewn about and also weaved into her chignon. Her signature scalloped emerald necklace was fastened around her neck with matching earrings. I may look like a dessert, but she looked like a frog. Prior to coming here, I had always thought of her as serene and graceful, but now I found she looked tacky.

Meanwhile, Queen Serenity had been donned in creams and whites again. The dress was splattered with various shades of pink polka dots. It was not Queen Serenity's usual style. Her hair was in two long braids down the front. It was almost like she had done her look to be quite girlish.

I dropped into a quick curtsey as I greeted everyone at the table before sitting down in the same seat as I had the night prior. The servant stepped forward and took the lid off my plate. The smell of eggs and bacon filled my nose. I was going to enjoy every single bite. I began to dig in and could feel Mother watching me from the side of her eye. I looked up to smile at Bay, and he smiled back at me before looking at Mother. He smiled at her when she made eye contact with him. *Checkmate.*

"Princess Persamina Rowena," Queen Serenity said, by way of

getting my attention, Father and Mother turned their attention to her as well. "If you are free later, we should take a stroll through the rose garden to show your Mother. I am certain she would love to see how much it has grown since she was last here." She smiled sweetly. I did not know what game she was playing at, but I had a feeling it would end badly for myself one way or another.

"Yes, that would be quite lovely," Mother replied instantly. I tried not to grind my teeth.

"Shall we do it during needlework hour?" Queen Serenity supplied.

"That will be perfect." I smiled, instantly answering.

If she was going to give me an out of needlework while Mother was here, then I would take it without complaint.

"Mind if I join?" Bay asked. My heart leaped at the idea of him being there to buffer anything Mother did or said. However, Queen Serenity answered before I or Mother could accept his offer.

"Not this time, Rafael." Queen Serenity patted his cheek. I noticed she preferred to address both of her sons by their first names only. "Let us ladies spend some time together."

"Very Well." He smiled at his mother. Queen Serenity turned to say something to her husband, and Mother slightly turned, trying to eavesdrop. Bay mouthed, *Sorry.*

I walked down to the tearoom, dreading the next hour of my life. I knew I would be dreading all of today, but teatime just seemed a bit more stressful with Mother about. I was hoping I would be able to beat Mother to the tearoom so I could sit with the twins. I needed their companionship to help ease my mind for just a bit.

Unfortunately, Mother was already there when I arrived, seated next to Queen Serenity. I caught the twin's eyes, and Iryse waved me over. I shook my head. Tearani blinked before her head slowly turned towards where I was destined to sit. For the briefest moments, I swore I witnessed Tearani's lips pursed as her eyes narrowed, but in the next blink, she returned to wearing her regular observing expression.

I walked towards Mother and The Queen. Catching all the subtle dirty looks the other girls were throwing at me. *Trust me, girls, I would rather be sitting with my friends than where I am headed.*

"Persamina darling, did you become lost?" Mother chided with a warning look. "You are quite late."

"My apologies, Mother, Queen Serenity." I curtsied, bowing my head low to emphasize my supposed apology. I wondered how I could be late when I felt I had made a mad dash here after breakfast. They must have taken a shortcut to arrive before me. Straightening back up, I noticed Queen Serenity smile at me as she nodded her head. I took my seat as the awkward silence stretched out. We all took a sip of our tea at the same time.

Mother finally tried to break the silence. "Serenity, this does take me back to all our tea times during our season." Smiled Mother, trying to relive their season memories.

"Ah yes, we sure did enjoy teatime." Queen Serenity smiled back as she set her teacup back down. "If I recall, Queen Opal loved everything in strawberry flavor that year.

"Oh yes, every season was a berry flavor theme." Mother laughed at the memory.

"As her daughter-in-law, the year of blackberry was the worst." Queen Serenity shuttered. I noticed how Mother slightly shifted in her seat at what she lost.

"Because you do not like blackberries?" I asked.

"Despise them," she replied with pursed lips.

"Why did Queen Opal choose themes each season?" This was never a part of my history lessons, and it was quite intriguing.

"Well, from what she told me, once I was married to her son, it kept things interesting." She laughed. "None of the attending families who sent their children knew the season theme prior, so clothing clashed. Families would mad dash to the dressmakers to have whole new wardrobes to be made in honor of the theme." She paused to take a sip of her tea before continuing, "and it made the kitchen staff put their creativity and skill levels to the test. Many of the variety pastries you taste today came from her courting season themes."

"Like the lemon tarts?" I asked eagerly, forgetting Mother was there.

"Oh yes, that was an interesting season." Laughed Queen Serenity. Mother sat there stewing, unable to interject.

"Everyone wore yellow, white, and green attire once they realized the theme." She flourished her hand in a gesture to encompass the whole room. "The dishes were both sweet and tart depending. But oh, how the room was filled with yellow dresses and even some yellow suits." She chuckled, amused at the memory.

"Yellow is probably my least favorite color," chimed in Mother.

"Hmm, I do not believe I knew that about you," replied Queen Serenity dismissively.

"It is why there are no yellow dresses in Persamina's wardrobe." Mother smiled sweetly, ignoring the dismissal. *I guess I had never noticed the lack of yellow dresses.*

"Alas, I have not seen a yellow dress on her. However, her opening night dress was quite gorgeous. The same color as my son Rafael's eyes," commented Queen Serenity. *She noticed.*

"Oh, was it?" Mother responded nonchalantly.

"Yes, a perfect match to mine as well." Queen Serenity

continued. I began to feel a briskness in the air about us. "Since my eldest received my eyes."

"We were the blue-eyed beauties that season," Mother replied.

"I am sure there were other princesses with blue eyes, probably far lovelier than just a lord's daughter and a merchant's daughter's eyes," stated Queen Serenity. I sipped my tea.

"Persamina, unfortunately, did not receive my eyes." Mother replied in kind, ignoring Queen Serenity's insult.

"Definitely, her father's King Gideon's eyes, so lovely." The Queen reached her hand over to my face, lightly her fingers held my chin, turning my face to look at her as she inspected my violet eyes.

"Yes, yes, very lovely and rare with those violet eyes." Mother complimented, but I heard the rush tone to it. Queen Serenity let go of my face.

"Why did you do away with the season theme?" I asked, feeling their conversation was slowing down.

"For a time, I thought about having a theme to honor the late Queen Opal, but then I realized they were always her thing, never mine." She smiled sadly. I felt there was more to the story than that, but it was not my place to push it.

I was certain if Mother had married King Regalius, she would have taken the themes and made them more extreme than just food each season. She would thoroughly enjoy watching the other families scramble for her extravagant parties.

I wonder if I would even have a choice in the matter regarding who I married. Probably not, not that I had a choice now, but if Mother was running the show of the wealthiest monarchy, she would be arranging my marriage. I would not even be able to partake in the season since it was arranged. Instead, I and multiple other females fought for our hands in matrimony to one male.

A few hours later, I was standing outside the doors of the needlework room. Queen Serenity never specified on where we were to meet, but she had said during needle hour. A few of the princesses were situated on cushions in little alcoves along the corridor, not wanting to sit in the room with their needlework. I was curious about what the conversation would be like with Mother, Queen Serenity, and myself.

"I think it is time for our stroll," Queen Serenity stated, interrupting my thoughts as she breezed through the door from the needlework room. She had changed dresses and was now in a light blue airy dress; her lips were a little pinker, and her face had more color to it from being flushed. It was a smidge warm today, maybe too warm from the usual heavy dresses she wore. Mother was following her, and her lips puckered as she had still been wearing the same dress since breakfast.

Mother and I followed Queen Serenity. We walked past the other girls, and I caught Regina and Olivia sneering at me once Queen Serenity and Mother had passed them. I wished I could hurry up my steps, but I was at the mercy of their slow, graceful pace.

We made it outside, and I continued to follow behind the two queens and their glacier pace. I think I would pick two hours of needlework over however long this stroll would take. And that was the problem; I knew needlework was an hour long. This stroll could go far longer than that. I was beginning to regret my earlier thoughts at tea time, being thankful for Queen Serenity getting me out of needlework.

No one talked until we made it through the entrance of the rose garden maze.

"This was not here during our season," Mother stated.

"No, it was not. I put it in right after my wedding," chimed back

Queen Serenity. Part of me fully believed Queen Serenity stated things the way she did on purpose to rub it into Mother.

"Any particular reason?" I could hear the edge in Mother's tone as it went up an octave.

"I just simply loved mazes and wanted to put my mark on this castle," chirped back Queen Serenity.

"I love the rose maze," I chimed in, trying to contribute somehow and not be completely forgotten as they each pecked at each other.

"Oh, I know you do," Queen Serenity replied knowingly. *Shit,* I should not have said that. Mother turned her head back to look at me, and I wished I could crawl into a hole and die with the look I received.

"Really, you *love* the rose maze, Persamina? *Why is that?*" Mother inquired.

"Oh, Lydia, relax." I could practically hear Queen Serenity rolling her eyes. "I know she loves the rose maze because she often strolls in it with her handmaiden. Stop thinking ill of your beautiful daughter," she scolded. I froze mid-step as Mother also came to a halt like she had been backhanded. I had never once walked in the rose maze with Eloise. Why was Queen Serenity lying?

"I beg your pardon, Serenity?" Mother gasped. Queen Serenity turned around to square Mother up.

"You heard me. You have been here for two mere days and have been scrutinizing your daughter non-stop," she bluntly stated. "Your daughter has been a lovely guest. She has had it a bit difficult here due to your poor life choices." Her eyes flicked at Mother in accusation. "But aside from that, she is quite respectable, and both my sons are quite taken with her," she surmised.

She left Mother utterly speechless for a few seconds as she tried to regain her ground on a response. I mouthed to Queen Serenity

Thank you without Mother seeing since I was two steps behind her. Queen Serenity smiled in response not to let Mother know.

"Are we hearing wedding bells then?" Mother asked. That was all Mother seemed to have understood from Queen Serenity's tongue-lashing.

"That is up to Rafael or Killien."

"Does Prince Rafael Baylor have his eye on any other Princess?" I did not miss how Mother stayed with the formalities regarding Queen Serenity's children.

"I do not delve into the affairs of either of my sons. If one so chooses for her hand, then I will be delighted to have her as a daughter-in-law." Queen Serenity stared Mother down, awaiting her response.

"Yes, very well," Mother snapped. "If you will excuse us, Serenity. I would like to talk to my daughter alone." There was a tone of warning in her voice.

"I believe I asked you to attend this walk with me. However, if you would prefer to have time alone with your daughter, then fine." Queen Serenity's tone was a bit high-pitched, and I knew Mother had overstepped her bounds. She bowed her head to us and walked in the opposite direction back out of the rose maze.

Mother started walking down the maze, and not knowing what else to do, I followed behind her quietly. It was still early enough that I knew not a lot of people would be in the maze, but there may still be a few lingering about, and that was a chance Mother would have to be concerned to fret over.

After a few more turns, she finally stopped, with me stopping in tow behind her. "You are a complete disappointment," her voice shook, and I bit my lip, not saying a thing. "We had a goal, Persamina, a goal." I looked at the ground, bracing myself for the lecture. She whirled on me, her hand stopping inches from my face as I squeezed my eyes shut, biting my lip, embracing for impact.

"I cannot marr your face, you stupid girl," she seethed, and I gulped, looking at her.

"Why are you here?" She began, knowing how I was supposed to answer.

"To marry Prince Rafael Baylor."

"Are you allowed to fail?"

"No."

"What happens if you fail?"

"Not allowed."

"Is his brother an option for marriage?"

"No."

"If Prince Rafael Baylor chooses another female, you are to . . . ?"

"Eliminate her."

"By . . . ?"

"Any means possible."

"Good, you are dismissed." She stared at me. I returned her stare a moment longer before I turned and started walking toward the entrance of the maze. I made it to the entrance, and there was Bay standing with his back to me.

"Hey Bay." I smiled, feeling relief at seeing my knight in shining armor. He turned, and his expression was layered in ice. My stomach dropped.

"I heard everything," he said coldly.

"What?" My heart began to sink as I felt nauseous.

"The conversation between you and your mother."

"Bay, it is not true," I defended. "It's her, all her!" My legs shook as they gave out from below me, and I sank to the ground.

"And I thought you were special." Bay sneered coldly, looking down at me. "All you Princesses are the same; nothing stands out about you. You are all weeds."

"But . . . you said," I tried to argue.

"All sweet nothings," he spat, "You want my crown for my gold; you are the poorest princess here, and you thought I did not see through it," he continued, though there was no warmth held within his eyes. "What is even more pathetic is you were so desperate; you went against your Mother's wishes, and you went after my brother."

"No! That is not true!" *Why would he believe that?* I formed a friendship with Knox, and it was not about securing a place.

"Oh? It is not, is it?" He scowled. "So many lies amongst the castle. How will I ever believe you?"

Tears began to well in my eyes as I shook to hold them back. I looked down at my lap, admitting defeat. No matter what I said, he would not believe me. He would not believe that it was my mother's goal for me to marry him, not mine. I thought I found a friend in both brothers and, yes, maybe a love interest as well, but it was not because of my mother's goal. It was because it happened naturally, and now, because of my mother, I was losing everything.

"Already just accepting the truth and not going to deny your lie," he jabbed.

"Why bother," I mumbled numbly.

"What?"

I looked up at him, glaring through the tears, "I said, why bother? No matter what I say, you will never believe me, so I am not going to try to change your mind." I awkwardly rose from the ground so he was not towering over me. "Yes, I came here because of my parents needed money for their kingdom, but I ended up forming a friendship with both you and Knox." I jabbed my finger very unladylike into Bay's chest, "And all the romance that has occurred was natural, not a part of some scheme," I seethed.

"Do not touch me," he gritted. I withdrew my finger from his chest.

"I will not allow you to twist my actions against me." With that, I turned on my heel and walked to the castle doors, needing to escape to my room as I wiped the tears from my eyes. I had not anticipated Bay being cruel, not from a man who had been my savior last night and this morning.

Chapter 19

I had no desire to participate in any more events. Between Bay and my mother, it was exhausting. I really did not have a choice because Mother would drag me kicking and screaming. No, that was an exaggeration. In reality, she would punish Eloise in order to make me go.

I dragged my feet to the banquet hall for dinner, and my parents were sitting in the same spots as before. Unfortunately, next to Knox's empty seat sat Regina, and my heart sank—*no escape for the wicked.* I took note that her brothers were seated next to her as well.

No matter how much I tried to delay my walk to my seat, it came too quickly, and then the servant pulled out the chair, and I sat down. Neither of the T'Lovoness brothers was in attendance.

"You look lovely, Princess Persamina Rowena," complimented Percival.

"As do you, Prince Percival Chivalry," I replied.

"But not me, Mina?" Teased Montgomery with a pouted lip.

"You do too, Montgomery." I giggled with the roll of my eyes.

"Hello, Mina," Regina said all too sweetly. I did not miss her white knuckles or the tick in her jaw. I knew her friendliness was a front for Queen Serenity and my mother, Queen Lydia.

"Hello, Princess Regina Isadora," I replied formally to show we were not on informal terms. While her brother Percival preferred formalities and I would entertain it, I would not give into Regina's informalness.

"Oh, Mina, I thought we were past formalities." She laughed, waving her hand like she was clearing the air. I stared at her.

"Persamina, darling," Mother purred. "Surely you and Gina are friends?" Gina? *Gina*? How could Mother be on these friendly of terms with my nemesis? Montgomery snorted, and I caught Queen Serenity's eye. She gave me a half smile, already knowing this was not the case.

"No worries, Lydia, I will just invite Mina out to more events." Regina winked at my mother, and I watched as they shared a knowing smile together. I think I am going to be sick.

"Don't trouble yourself, little sister. I am sure Mina would rather spend more time with myself than with you," interjected Montgomery as he threw me a wink. Regina gave him a restrained smile. Percival just watched, entertained by his two siblings.

"I am certain Mina would prefer female company to you," gritted Regina back at her brother, trying to make a fool of her.

"Princess Regina Isadora, I am sure if you had chosen to sit by Mina in the past, you would have a closer friendship," Queen Serenity added. Regina gripped her silverware tightly. While I definitely did not want Regina sitting by me, with what Queen Serenity and Montgomery had supplied for information, had Mother looking perplexed, and I could see the slight shock on Regina's face for being called out.

I watched as Regina's face crossed with a multitude of emotions just for her to finally respond with, "Ah, yes, but sometimes a chair was not always available by Mina." She smiled, trying to smoothen over her lie.

"Hmm." Queen Serenity paused, looking thoughtfully. "My vision must be going bad since I believe I have almost *always* seen a chair available by Mina." Her gaze leveled at Regina's. *Checkmate.*

Regina did not respond, and Mother, in the awkwardness, glanced between us all, trying to make sense of things. I highly doubted Mother would ever come to believe I was the unpopular princess. The only thing that could make this situation any more awkward was if Bay was here.

"Serenity," Mother finally said, breaking the silence, "do you have a free moment for us to catch up in a more private setting?"

Queen Serenity took a sip of her tea, looking at Mother over the tip of her teacup. It was an awfully long drink. I wonder if she wanted to escape from this table as severely as I did. Like Mother always did best, she was steamrolling over despite what had gone down just hours ago.

Finally, Queen Serenity set her teacup down on the saucer, "I am sure I can find some time in my schedule, Lydia."

"Oh, splendid! It will be just like old times," Mother squealed with a clap of her hands.

"I will send a servant with a note when I am available." Smiled Queen Serenity and I watched as Mother's face faltered just a smidge. Mother re-adjusted in her seat, plastered a big smile on her face, and replied with, "that would be lovely, Serenity."

Regina must have decided she had been quiet for far too long. Maybe her embarrassment from Queen Serenity was already forgotten since she chose to speak up now, "Lydia, will you be holding any more balls in the near future?" She smiled sweetly, even though I knew what she truly thought of Mother's balls.

"Maybe once the season is over," Mother replied sweetly. "No sense in hosting one with The Courting Season going strong."

"Tis true, Lydia." Regina picked up her teacup, ready to take a drink before she paused. Looking at me, she tacked on, "maybe I will see you there too." I just stared at her, understanding every implication she was getting at.

"Well, I hope not." Mother laughed. "By then, she will be married and no longer living at home."

"Oh, that is true," giggled Regina. I glanced over at Queen Serenity, who looked like she wanted to be anywhere else but included in this conversation. *That made two of us.*

"However, if she did have to come live at home, I suppose we could adjust to becoming a queendom," Father interjected. Mother glanced at Father, who looked at me and then towards Serenity. I perked up at this. While I knew this to be accurate, Mother had never once brought it up in our training. I wondered why. I was ready to hang onto the following words stated.

"Surely your kingdom would not be as accepting of change to a queendom." Smiled Regina sickenly sweet to Mother. I glanced at Queen Serenity, who now had her chin resting on her folded hands that were propped up on her elbows on the table. It was not the most table etiquette, but she was clearly interested in the conversation now, as was I.

"Oh, they will be fine. Mina has been taught in depth of Theorines's history and of the people," Father replied confidently, not caring to allow Mother to respond. "Plus, Theorines has flip-flopped back and forth between kingdom and queendom so often in history it should not be that difficult for the people to accept a switch again, considering it was a Queendon for a time when I was a child."

"That is true," Queen Serenity joined in, "Your grandmother had a difficult time giving up her power to your father, did she not?"

"Yes, she did." Father chuckled. Mother sipped her tea.

"Then why did you not originally choose for Mina to be heir instead of coming here to potentially give up her claim to your throne?" King Regalius asked Father now. Queen Serenity gave Mother an innocent smile. Everyone at this end of the table knew the answer, but how would my parents respond?

"Because," my father drawled, "we would rather see her marry a prince heir, next in line to rule their own country, than someone wanting to use her for her own crown." He leveled a gaze at Queen Serenity as he said it. That was a bold statement for him to state when my parents were doing the exact same thing, what they supposedly did not want done to me.

"What about her marrying someone like one of the Grewt'en Princes?" Queen Serenity ventured, looking over at the two brothers. "Surely, a prince who is not an heir would not be after Princess Persamina Rowena's crown when they grew up already in royalty . . . And I have seen the eldest Prince Montgomery Victory, show quite a bit of interest in Mina. Just think of the pros of uniting two queendom families together."

Montgomery sat up straighter in his chair with the statement Queen Serenity was proposing. My mind flashed images of a life with Montgomery as my husband. He was very handsome, and I bet he would look dashing in a tux on our wedding day. Warmth coursed through me from the thought of having kids with him. I shook the whole notion from my head; my imagination was getting the better of me.

My gaze fell on Regina for her reaction. Her face blanched as she was beginning to look more crossed by the second. I glanced at Montgomery, who winked at me with a devilish smile. Percival continued to watch in silence. A small part of me feared this becoming a possibility, so I focused back on Regina. I found entertainment in watching her facial expressions.

Father stroked his smooth chin, out of habit from when he had a beard, in speculative thought, and I noticed King Regalius regarded him with a quick glance to his wife before settling his gaze back on Father.

"We have thought of that aspect; they would make splendid candidates, but right now, with The Courting Season, we are seeing how it unfolds," Father replied evenly. "No offense to the children from Grewt'en," he tacked on as his gaze roamed over the three siblings.

"None taken, King Gideon," replied Montgomery. "Any man who married your daughter would be quite lucky."

"What about someone like my son, Prince Killien Knox?" King Regalius chimed in, ignoring Montgomery. I was unsure if Queen Serenity had talked to her husband since the rose garden conversation and how my mother had kept deflecting off the topic of Knox, but it was just too perfect.

Father blinked at King Regalius. "Yes, he would also be a suitable candidate to marry our daughter as well." Both kings maintained eye contact. King Regalius paused before responding, "Then maybe we should arrange it." My heart began thundering in my chest. There could be no way Father would agree to this.

"Why don't we wait until the end of the season? We did promise Persamina to try on her own," Mother quickly jumped in, and I caught her poor speech, "we all had our chance. It is only fair for her to have her own."

"We all did have our own chance, did we not Serenity?" Father stated, looking directly at her. I was not certain why he had addressed her in the matter. I assumed it was because Queen Serenity had risen in ranks from a lord's daughter up to a queen. I had never known

Father to be against lower-ranked people like Mother, but I was aware that Father treated Queen Serenity differently. When talking to her, he seemed quite cold at times. I questioned if it bothered him that Serenity had risen high in societal ranks.

Both King Regalius and Queen Serenity gave each other a sideways glance before dipping their head with a smile, not reacting to Father's statement.

"That we did." King Regalius nodded in agreement. "Then how about this: if your daughter and my son do not find a match by the end of the season, we will arrange their marriage."

"Our youngest son," Queen Serenity added quickly. "Considering Mina will rule her own queendom and Bay will stay here to rule our kingdom." Queen Serenity made certain Mother could not sink her claws into that loophole.

"Yes, our younger son, Killien Knox, to marry your daughter, Persamina Rowena," corrected King Regalius. My heart continued to race as the room began to spin. They were deciding my life as if I was not present. I felt like I was going to be sick. I liked Knox, but that did not mean I agreed to spend a lifetime with him.

"It is agreed upon." My father nodded his head. I could see my mother silently screaming within her own mind. All her years of planning and training me would go down the drain in this single conversation between kings.

"Were you all not in the same season?" Regina asked, changing back the conversation. Everyone at our end of the table just froze at her daftness of interrupting this very serious moment. Percival shook his head in annoyance at his sister while Montgomery looked up at the ceiling.

"Yes, that is how Serenity and I became best friends. It was during our season," Mother supplied, gritting her teeth.

"Yes, if it were not for the season, we would not have been

brought together," Queen Serenity joined in. Both kings leveled each other a gaze and then slowly began to talk about kingdom politics.

"But you both were not princesses?" Ventured Regina. If this girl were not next in line for her queendom, I would think she was making a grave mistake asking an insulting question like that. Both queens blinked at her in the same expression as I was thinking.

"One would think if one paid attention in her history lessons, she would not have to ask questions she already knew the answer to," I said. Regina shot me daggers at the dig I just gave her. I caught Queen Serenity covering a giggle behind her napkin as Mother looked at me approvingly. The rest of the dinner remained in silence.

I was thankful there were no after-dinner balls this evening as I excused myself and walked back to my private rooms alone. I would ask Eloise or Stella to grab me some food from the kitchens. With Bay not there to protect me, my stomach was angry in protest from the lack of food while under my mother's watchful gaze.

I made my way to the top of the stairs to my floor. Turning the corner to my corridor, I came upon Knox strolling towards me. He smiled instantly when he caught sight of me. I hesitantly smiled back. I was uncertain if Bay had talked to him or not about what he had overheard. I knew he would not have heard of our now pre-arranged marriage.

"Hi, Mina," he greeted me when we were standing in front of each other.

"Hi, Knox," I replied cautiously.

"Are you okay?" His happiness turned to worry. I glanced down before trying to give him a reassuring smile.

"It's just with my parents here. It is a bit more stressful, is all."

"Oh, I fully understand that. When my parents are in the same room as me, I become very stressed." He gave a half smile as he scratched the back of his head, shifting on his feet.

"Yeah, I will be happy when they leave," I relaxed a bit more, laughing. I felt more certain Bay had not talked to him.

"Oh, is that so?" Mother's voice asked icily as she came around the corner from behind me. My heart dropped, my eyes widening as I looked at Knox. His face was in alarm as well. I slowly turned around until I was facing my mother's glare. I took a step back into Knox as he took a step forward. He rested his hand on my right hip, and I leaned back into him for reassurance.

Mother's eyes darted back and forth between the two of us as she began to purse her lips. Father turned the corner a moment later, taking in the scene, he raised an eyebrow.

"Maybe Ol' Regalius was onto something after all." He stroked his chin in thought.

"Sir?" Knox asked, confused.

"Your father proposed a union marriage between you and our daughter Mina tonight." I felt Knox's hand squeeze, relax, and squeeze tighter on my hip. I held my breath. Father continued, "that is, of course, if neither of you matches with anyone else this season."

"Sir, I would be honored to marry your daughter." His hand squeezed my hip tighter. "But I refuse to force her into a marriage. That is for Mina to decide." I relaxed slightly. Father kept his gaze as Mother's eyes flitted back and forth between everyone. Despite Knox's nobility in the matter of my decision, there would be no overruling two king's decisions on the subject. Another conversation to secure what the kings had agreed upon. Another exchange to add to Mother's years of planning unraveling before her eyes.

"Marriage will serve you well," Father commented, "Lydia?" He extended his arm to her. She looked at us before taking his arm gingerly; we watched as they passed. He led her down the hall past my rooms before turning another corner to their rooms.

Once they were out of sight, I relaxed completely into Knox to help stabilize my balance. I felt his other hand come up to my hip, and both arms circled my waist, pulling me closer to him. He rested his chin on my head as I closed my eyes.

"That was intense," Knox's voice was low and quiet as I felt his voice vibrate against me.

"Very," I conceded.

"I can see now why you have been unnerved." He pulled me tighter to him.

"Mmh," I hummed, steeling myself for what I was about to ask him. "Are you okay with our father's decision?" He stiffened a bit against me.

"I always anticipated my parents would arrange a marriage for me," he commented quietly.

"Does it displease you that it's with me?" I asked, grateful he stood behind me and unable to see my face.

"I had always assumed they would pick someone I did not know," he replied, not answering my question. I was not sure what to make of that. If I pushed more, would I have a better answer? He had told me in the rose garden that I was his number one choice, but did that statement still hold?

"And?" I decided to push.

"Come along, Mina, I will walk you to your room," he said as he unwrapped me from his embrace; turning me around, he did not look at me. As I glanced up at his face, it was blank of emotions. We did not speak as he led me to my room, where he bid me a goodnight with a kiss on my forehead. I stood there confused.

Chapter 20

"You are leaving?" I asked my parents two days later. They had barely been here a week.

"Ah yes, well, we really could not stay long to begin with," Mother rushed out with a brisk icy smile.

"Yes, we just wanted to check in, Mina," Father supplied, patting my cheek. "And now that we have secured a hand in your future if you do not choose someone, our minds can be at ease." He smiled, assured of himself. I had never seen Father quite as happy as he had been these last few days. I had come under the distinct impression that my father had become very excited about me taking over when he stepped down. He also seemed on excellent terms with Regalius, so the prospect of uniting the families probably sounded like a fun idea to him.

I had a feeling their rushed departure had more to do with what Mother overheard me say to Knox and how much her plans were now ruined if I did not secure Bay's hand. Which, after what Bay had heard in the rose maze, I did not think there would be a chance for that anyway. Bay had been cold and aloof with me ever since that day. Queen Serenity did not treat me differently, making me uncertain if Bay had told her or anyone what he had overheard.

"It was nice having you both here," I forced out with a smile. The truth is it was nice having Father here, but not Mother. The relief of knowing they were already leaving would make my days easier again. I had thought they would be here for weeks.

I watched as they got into their carriage and left the castle grounds, my shoulders sagging when they were out of sight. Now, I have significant damage control to do with my relationship with Bay, thanks to my mother.

Tonight was another ball, and thankfully, my parents would be gone. I was pretty surprised there had been no balls with my parents here, but I had a feeling Queen Serenity made sure of it. She seemed to be more on my side than I ever realized.

I wore a soft peach dress; it was styled like an upside-down flower. It belled out at the bottom and had a mint green top half. It was not as extravagant as the dresses I wore with Mother in attendance, and I was grateful to return to my usual style of dresses. Eloise and Stella styled my hair in an elegant chignon with multiple tiny braids crisscrossing back and forth on my head before weaving about the chignon. We decided on simple pearl earrings with a simple pearl necklace.

As I entered the room, I could not find the twins anywhere about the room. During my parents' stay, I barely had time to talk to the twins, and now I desperately wanted to tell them everything that had occurred. It was odd not to see either one of them at a ball. I mentally shook off the worry; standing straighter, I made my way over to the wine table to grab a goblet before finding a suitable wall space to occupy. Surely, they are just running late.

Two hours later, I was confident they were not coming. Without the twins in attendance, it gave me time to reflect on everything that had happened this past week. It made me more nauseous the more I thought about it. A week ago, I had Bay as a friend with his kindness, and knight in shining armor. Mother ruined it all. If Bay did not inform Knox before the end of the season, I am positive he would do it when the kings announced the arrangement of my marriage to Knox.

The idea of marrying Knox did not turn me off. I had a friendship with him. I was unsure if I should feel guilt for what I had done with each brother. If Knox learned what I had done with Bay, I was worried about how he would react. However, I think I was more scared to rule a queendom than I was to be in an arranged marriage. I was never raised to rule, and this prospect frightened me.

I wondered if Montgomery's mother had been in attendance during that meal if my hand in marriage could have been arranged entirely differently. Could I have become pre-engaged to Montgomery instead? I questioned how much she would have a say in the matter compared to the two kings. Would she even care to interject in the issue? I didn't even know why my mind focused on that what-if fantasy. It was not like I even remotely had feelings for Montgomery; it was just that some things became a little too real too quickly the other night. Whenever I caught Montgomery's eye, he would wink at me now. I shook my head.

Alas, I would not be able to solve all of the problems. I would need to let time reveal what it had in store for me. Currently, time has revealed me drinking my wine alone. The nausea that had been formed from my worrying had only increased, and the wine did not help. However, it did help keep my brain fuzzy enough to make this ball bearable by myself.

I watched Bay dance with Regina. They continued to dance one after another on the floor without taking a break. I took another gulp of my wine. Knox had not shown up, and after the conversation we had the other night, I would have really liked to have seen him. While I know what he said to my parents, I would like to know what he really thought of the idea. Would he be okay marrying me? Would he be okay being a king in a queendom? Queendom's Queens did not have to be faithful to their spouses to produce heirs. Would we be faithful to each other? What if Knox could not sire an heir? Would he be okay with me finding another? I wanted to bury my head in my hands, but the goblet of wine prevented me.

I caught glimpses of Queen Serenity on her throne watching the dancers, but from across the room, I doubt she had seen me as I polished off another goblet of wine. At least with Bay keeping Regina busy, those two bullies left me alone.

"Drunk is not a good look on you, Mina," commented Montgomery as he grabbed his own goblet.

"Can you blame me after the other day?" I asked, raising an eyebrow. He chuckled to himself.

"I suppose not. Just think, it could have been us getting hitched," he joked.

"We barely know each other," I countered.

"And how well do you know Killien?" He challenged.

"More than I know you," I replied simply.

"We could change that." He gave me that devilish smile.

"You are incorrigible."

"You love it." He laughed outright, and I smiled. We stood there, silently sharing the space as we watched the others dance before us. It was not as awkward as I had been led to believe. I enjoyed standing here with Montgomery. I glanced up at him as he continued to stare out at the ballroom.

"Care for a dance?" He asked, not looking at me.

"Sure, why not," I replied. He offered me his arm, and I took it, heavily relying on him to guide us to the dance floor.

"This may be an interesting dance for me," commented Montgomery. "But certainly one I will probably forever remember."

"Oh? Why is that?" I inquired.

"Because it is apparent you have had too much wine, and I am going to enjoy watching you finally let loose." His eyes glimmered.

"Then I guess we will both have an excellent time." I returned, shaking my head. He put us in position, ready to start the next dance. We were further down from Bay and Regina, but I did not miss the feeling of heated glares upon us. I stiffened slightly. Montgomery leaned in to whisper in my ear.

"Do not worry about them. We are here to have fun, and I heard a rumor that Regina was spitting fire after Queen Serenity mentioned that you and I should marry." He leaned back, giving me a wink, causing me to relax a bit as I laughed. The dance began, and despite my mind being a bit slow to react, I did not make many mistakes as he glided us along, or at least I believe I did not. I was having a glorious time as he twirled and dipped me to bring me back up for more spins. It was probably from the wine, but I could not stop smiling and laughing.

"That's the spirit, Mina." Montgomery encouraged. When the dance ended, he asked me for a second dance, which I eagerly accepted. It was a bit slower pace, but he had fun throwing extra little spins and flares into it to lighten it up.

"May I ask you a question?" My boldness was surfacing.

"I will answer it to the best of my abilities," he jested.

"What do you see in me?" It was something I was gnawing on in the back of my mind for a while now.

"I see a strong princess who has been held down all her life.

Someone who has this brilliant light to do amazing things in life but only has ever had it extinguished by those around her. Mina, when I see you, I know you will do phenomenal things. You just need a little nurturing." He dipped me, and when I came up, I saw the reassuring smile on his face as he winked again. I blushed at his truthful honesty while wondering if he had ever become tired of constantly winking.

"Mont, I do not know what to say?" He made me at a loss for words.

"Mont? We truly are on our road to a close friendship with nicknames." He beamed.

"Is that what we are? Friends?" I pushed.

"Yup, were you anticipating more?" He pushed back.

"No! I mean," I stumbled over my words, "you are quite nice and attractive, but friendship would be wonderful, but I did not know. . .I mean. . ." I grasped at words. He began to laugh as the dance came to an end.

"No worries, Mina. I just want to be friends." He assured.

"I would like that a lot." I gave him a genuine smile in return.

"Good. Then, as your official best friend." *Did he just claim that title without permission?* "I suggest you head to bed. Get a glass of water and go sleep off this buzz before you wake up with a massive hangover." Montgomery went from someone I thought would try for my hand to a friend to apparently a doting parent. Correction-- best friend, since he slipped that right on in.

"Best friend, eh?" I quirked an eyebrow at him.

"Caught that? I wanted to claim dibs."

"What if I already have a best friend?" My mind flashed to Eloise and the twins.

"You wound me, princess." He placed his hand over his heart like I had stabbed it. I rolled my eyes; such a drama prince. "Now, off to bed, or I will carry you there," he threatened. I squeaked. Turning, I headed towards the double doors, but I was unable to make it to them. I felt a hand grab my arm and yank me to the side.

"I told you to stay away from my brother, you little bitch," Regina seethed, glaring at me. Olivia was standing behind her.

"It was just two dances!" I defended, my voice a few volumes louder than I had anticipated, causing a few people to look our way. I instantly flushed from the growing attention.

"A few dances, one too many. You are not marrying my brother," she hissed.

"Had no plans to," I tartly replied.

"Why? Is he not good enough for you? Not The Reclusive Prince that you are pre-engaged to?" Her hand squeezed on my arm, hurting me.

"Release your hand from my arm," I ordered. She cackled, giving my arm one more tight squeeze before roughly releasing me as she threw my arm back to me.

"Look who has grown a backbone," she continued to cackle as Olivia joined in with her. "Come on, Olivia." Regina turned abruptly and walked away with Olivia in tow. They came in a flurry and left in the same manner.

I shook my head, a bit shaken by the interaction. I was only a few paces from the wine table and marched my way over there for another glass. I downed it, not caring what the others thought. The previous buzz I had worn off with the dances returned almost instantly. My head began to swim as my face became quite flush. I quickly regretted downing that last glass.

I pushed out of the ballroom doors. My vision became slightly blurry. I crashed into a wall from losing my footing and leaned heavily on it for a second, taking an internal account of my body. I pushed off the wall and tried to make as quick of pace as possible back to my room. I just needed to make it to my room so I could retire for the evening. Mother would scold me for how much of an embarrassment I was to allow myself to ever be put into this situation. Except, she was part of the reason I was in this state.

Thankfully, the halls were primarily empty due to the attendance at the ball. However, it did not stop me from accidentally taking a wrong turn. It made me think of the bad directions I had given Montgomery, and now I wish he would have followed through with his threat. The wires in my brain became crossed, and I forgot what floor I was on. The sad part was that when I noticed my error, I realized I was still on the first floor. I sank to the ground, giggling and laughing to myself at my mistake. Leaning my head back against the wall, my face felt extremely warm. I really needed my bed. Water. . . I needed to remember to tell Eloise I needed to drink water.

I got back up to double back towards the staircase. My mind began to get away from me at the thought of anyone who currently saw me and what they would say. . . *"Princess Persamina Rowena is a drunk." "She cannot have Prince Bay, so now she is drinking her sorrows away." "She drinks to be able to tolerate the reclusive, cruel prince's company."* Why were people so vicious?

I made it to the stairs. Staring up at them, I already dreaded this ascent. I put my hand on the banister, knowing full well I was going to use it for all it was worth, so help me. It became more difficult to focus as my head began to swim more. With each step taken up the stairs, my feet began to drag from how heavy they felt. My tongue began to feel like sandpaper. I managed to finally make it to the top of the stairs. Only a couple of times did I accidentally lose my balance, causing me to step backward, down a step. I would immediately overcorrect, sending myself almost face-planting on the stairs in front of me. It was at those times I wished Montgomery would show up to carry me back.

I huffed heavily at the top of the stairs. Down the corridor and around the corner, I would be at my bedroom. I took a few tentative steps and then sidestepped until I stumbled into the wall, using it to keep me upright. I probably would have a bruise tomorrow. I just needed to make it to my room, and then I could collapse in my bed.

I felt like I was going at a snail's pace with each shaky step, both of my hands skimming along the wall to help keep my focus and balance upright. I finally cleared the corner and could see my bedroom in the homestretch. I heard giggles behind me, and I knew there was no way I would make it to my room before they spotted me. Well, let me just hope it was not anyone too malicious, but they were almost all vipers in their nest.

My breathing became more labored as I tried to pick up my pace to my room. The giggles sounded closer, and they must have turned the corner because then I heard, "Oh my! Is that The Poor Tower Princess?" Rushed by more giggles.

"How peasant-like to be so drunk," chirped another female voice. It sounded like Olivia, and I inwardly groaned.

"Prince Bay, why do you allow such royal trash to stay?" That was Regina and my stomach plummeted that Prince Bay was with them and witnessing me in this condition. But what was I to expect? He had been dancing with Regina all night long. He had overheard Mother and wanted nothing to do with me.

I tried to pick up my pace, but my shaky legs made me face-plant into the wall. More giggles erupted as they began to pass me. I glanced at Bay to see his cold, disgusted face.

He sneered, "How pitiful."

Both princesses on his arms giggling through their matching sneers. I tried to reach for Bay's back to remedy this situation.

"Bay," my voice cracked, barely audible as I lost my balance, stumbling to the floor, blackness taking over my vision.

Chapter 21

BAY'S POV

I did not know how to handle Mina at this point. Part of me wanted to be utterly disgusted with her by the conversation I had overheard between her and her mother and now to find her in this drunken state. There was a part of me that could not block out my feelings for her. The part that enjoyed watching her eyes dance when she ate sweets when she thought no one else had been watching. How she would pet every palace cat she passed and the kindness she showed everyone regardless of their social status. Then, the final memory passed through my thoughts: the feeling of her body, her lips, and her hands on me. The way my cock reacted to her.

I shoved the feelings away, trying to tell myself I needed to be repulsed by her. I needed to send her back to her kingdom and fast before she did something unforgivable. When Mother had talked to me, she informed me that Mina was pre-engaged to my brother, my fists clenching at the thought. To make matters worse, Regina recited the gossip multiple times about the conversation the kings had at the meal I decided to skip. I questioned if I could have done something different to change their future, but it would not matter . . . Mother made certain of that.

The two princesses accompanying me were annoying with their giggling and gossip, but Father stated it would be good to build relationships with the other monarchies. Regina was not the same girl I had played with as a child. She had changed into someone I barely recognized; the girl I knew surfaced at times, but then she would disappear again. We had been friends at one point. I knew she utilized that closeness to her advantage over the other princesses and ladies. Now, she was a stranger, and I missed the friend I had in her. She used to be sweet on Knox, but now she acted like he was a monster. I just did not understand what changed in Regina. Maybe it was the other princess, Olivia, that hung around her? I really did not know her too well, and from what I witnessed, I did not want to get to know her.

As we passed Mina, I wanted to yell at her for how she was acting. This was un-princess-like, but then I thought back to the maze and her mother's questioning. If I chose someone else, she would eliminate them by any means necessary. I wondered if she was trained in the art of poisoning. I felt fingers trail down my back, dropping my arms from the princesses at my side; I whirled to find Mina on the ground. Her face was flushed, and she was breathing heavily in huffs. The two princesses went into a hysterical giggling fit next to me.

"Silence!" I commanded, and they instantly stopped. I knelt down to touch Mina's face, and it was burning. She was running a fever. "Go find the guards and a royal physician," I barked. The two princesses just stood there, offended to do such a menial job task that was beneath their social status. "Are you disobeying an order from me?" I added to emphasize my position compared to theirs.

They stood a moment longer before scurrying away, hopefully, to do what I asked, or there would be consequences.

I rolled Mina onto her back. With an arm sliding under her legs and another under her back, I lifted her up to carry her the rest of the way to her room. She was a dead weight in my arms, but thankfully, her room was not too far off. I heard the guards coming up behind me. At least those two annoying twits did part of what I had asked thus far.

"Prince Rafael Baylor, do you want me to take her?" asked one of the guards, offering his arms.

"No, I got her. Just open her bedroom door, please." I did not want to pass her off. Despite everything, I did not trust anyone else to handle her. I should not care this much about her. I should just discard her, but I could not. The guard opened her door, and I walked in with the guards following me. I was taken by surprise.

When I had been here the last time, the room had been cloaked in darkness, with only the moonlight giving me enough light to see. I had been wholly focused on her that I had not given the room a second glance, but now, seeing it lit up it was quite sad to look at. I was expecting it to be overly decorated like the other princess's rooms, but it was quite simple. There really were not many of her personal items added to it.

"Oh, Prince Rafael Baylor," quivered a female jumping up from her chair, curtseying immediately. She must have been Mina's handmaiden. Her eyes darted to Mina and back to the floor, clearly worried for her princess.

"She is running a fever. Can you get the bed ready?" I asked as the handmaiden automatically started moving into action. I followed her through the doors to Mina's bedroom. The handmaid rushed over to the bed to pull back the covers. I laid Mina onto the bed as the handmaiden started undoing the clasps on Mina's shoes and removing them, taking them over to what looked to be the rest of Mina's shoes. It definitely was not as extravagant of a collection as the other princesses. There were only three pairs in total; I'm pretty certain the ladies had more shoes than Mina. I knew her kingdom was poor, but this was quite pitiful.

The royal physician came through the doorway with billowing robes. He tried to dress like he was older, most likely because he had recently replaced the now-retired, previous royal physician and his master. I am sure this one was trying to gain the trust of the people that the previous one received automatically when entering a room. I never learned this one's name. I just knew him by the billowing robes, crooked nose, spectacles, and sloppy brown mop of hair.

"Prince Rafael Baylor, I am going to have to ask you to leave. We will need to get Princess Persamina Rowena out of this dress, and that will be quite immodest." I may have been a part of this royal family, but the physicians were never afraid to bark orders to us. He was allowed to do so since he saved more lives and cured as many illnesses. The previous royal physician passed his knowledge on to his apprentice. I nodded and turned to walk out her door to wait on a couch in her entertaining room.

It did not take long until the physician came back out, "She is running a nasty fever. Rest is going to be critical for her recovery, and from there, we will need to wait it out," he said before shuffling off and then calling over his shoulder, "do not disturb her too much and try not to catch it yourself." I rolled my eyes before entering her room.

She was sleeping peacefully in her bed; her handmaid was smoothing out her hair as she adjusted a cold cloth on her head. She must not have seen me enter the room because she looked shocked when I was standing on the other side of the bed before dropping into a quick curtsy, "Prince Rafael Baylor, my apologies I did not see you."

"You are her handmaiden . . ." I trailed off, waiting for her to supply her name.

"Eloise," she supplied, curtseying again.

"Eloise," I repeated, "I never realized you were her handmaiden when the two of you walked about the palace grounds. I always just thought you were her friend from back home." I blinked. This caused her to blush. I had watched the two of them arm in arm, giggling over something silly. Eloise had always been dressed nicely enough that I was under the impression she was a lady. I never would have pegged her to be Mina's handmaiden.

"Please take good care of her." I nodded at Mina before turning back towards the door to leave. I didn't even make it five steps before Knox came crashing through the door. Panic showed on his face.

"Is she alright?" He panted, wild-eyed.

"She has a nasty fever, but the physician said she will be fine," I replied, trying to leave. I needed to get out of here.

"Is it true she collapsed on the floor?"

"Yes, that is true." Knox probably would not let me leave until he had all the answers.

"And you were there?" His eyes narrowed slightly.

"Yes, I was passing by with Princess Regina Isadora and Princess Olivia Jade when we saw her. She passed out as we walked by," my voice growing cold.

"And you did not think to help her prior?" He accused, venom filling his voice.

"I was under the impression that she was drunk," I spat back, becoming defensive.

"I heard she was stumbling along the wall, using it as support," he fired back. I stared at him as I cataloged in the back of my mind to deal with those two gossiping princesses later.

"I thought she was quite drunk, and given recent events, I have a duty to uphold that no longer involves her. So, take offense for my poor negligence of noticing her state as being anything other than a drunk. She is tucked in bed with her handmaiden taking care of her, as you can clearly see." I gestured back towards Mina and her handmaiden before purposely pushing my left shoulder into his to bypass him and leave the room in complete annoyance at his accusations. I honestly did not have time to deal with him as I pushed outside her room to retreat to my own.

Two days passed with still no progress on Mina's health. She had not been the only one who had fallen ill from the ball. She was, however, the only one who had yet to recover. She came in and out of unconsciousness and was completely delirious when she was awake from the fever.

Knox was becoming an emotional wreck from the state of his pre-engaged fiancee. He lashed out at servants, breaking things and barely consuming any meals. The servants practically had to beg him to eat. If Mina did not come out of this, I felt there would be no saving my brother. Mother's worry began to surface in our meetings.

I had never told him what I overheard Queen Lydia say to her daughter in the rose maze garden. Mother forbade me from telling him. He was entirely in the dark about the more extensive plans that were in play, I thought to myself. I took another gulp from my goblet with bloodshot eyes.

Chapter 22

MINA POV

I awoke, slowly taking in my surroundings. I found myself in my bed, feeling weak and my throat parched. What happened? I tried to shift through the haze in my brain as the memory of me trying to get back to my room and making a fool of myself in front of Bay came rushing back. I remember flashes of Knox's face and Eloise forcing liquids to my lips, but I could not latch onto the memories long enough before they slipped away.

I heard a light snoring to my right side and looked over to see a very rumpled-looking Knox, fast asleep. *Why was he in my room? What had happened after I passed out in the hallway? Oh no!* When I was falling, my hand grazed down Bay's backside. I am pretty sure I touched his buttocks as it skimmed. I was utterly mortified, but that did not explain why Knox was here. I just simply drank too much, is all, and it went to my head.

"Knox?" I croaked as my fingers played through his hair to wake him. He grumbled before looking at me and then popping up, grasping my hand.

"You're awake!" He practically shouted, causing me to flinch at the unexpected loudness.

"Uh, yeah?" I questioned uncertainly. My voice sounded gravely, "what happened?"

"You collapsed from a terrible fever, and it has been three days. I worried that I would have lost you forever." Knox moved from sitting on the chair to sitting next to me on the bed, stroking my hair as he looked into my eyes. I felt a tad overcrowded, but my mind was processing. I had been out for three days. *So, I had not drank too much; I had just been sick.*

"Can I have some water?" I asked quietly. He got up, running to the pitcher to fetch me a glass. Bringing it to my lips, I drank deeply before my empty stomach began to cramp.

"Thank you," I gasped. He took the glass away, placing it on the nightstand. Turning back to me, he gathered me into his arms. "I thought I lost you," he repeated, breathing into my hair. My heart fluttered, but I was still nervous he would pull back and away from me to become aloof again. I did not want my false hopes to be crushed because of a moment of worrying on his part. I heard a tray crash.

"Mina!" Gasped Eloise as she stepped over the tray with broken porcelain and food towards me. Grabbing my hand with tears in her eyes, she said, "I was so worried you would never wake." I cupped her cheek, smiling.

"I could never leave you behind." My thumb stroked away her tears. Her eyes shone as a smile graced her lips.

"I need to go let the physician know you are awake!" She stood up, running and jumping over the tray again. "I will send someone to clean that up!" She called over her shoulder. The door slamming behind her.

I turned back to Knox, not knowing what to say to fill the silence in our conversation.

"I was very worried," he repeated.

"I am sorry to have worried you," I replied, a bit uncomfortable. I did not know how to respond to anything in this instance.

"When I heard you collapsed and had a fever, I rushed to your side without question . . . I . . . I realized how much I did not want to lose you." He took my hand in his. "And then Eloise began to explain things, and more things began to make sense. Princess Regina Isadora and Princess Olivia Jade have been sent back to their respective monarchies. You need not worry about them anymore," he finished. I was a little confused about what Eloise said to him that made sense. I would need to ask about that later. I felt my eyes begin to fill with tears from his concern. I may have a chance of a genuine future with Knox.

My bedroom door slammed open, causing Knox and me to jump startled. There was Bay breathing heavily with his hand bracing himself on my doorframe, staring at me. His clothes were wrinkled, and his hair a mess. I did not know what to say, and before I could think about it, he was striding towards me.

I was barely aware of Knox still beside me as Bay tilted my chin up towards his face and crashed his lips onto mine. I was so utterly taken aback that I could not even react. By the time my mind caught up to the kiss, he had already broken it. Knox was gripping my hand very tightly.

Bay pulled back just enough, holding my face in both his hands, our noses barely touching. I noticed the bags under his bloodshot eyes.

"If you ever do something like that again, I will never forgive you." He pulled away and turned on his heel, walking over the abandoned tray and slamming the door behind him. I stared at the closed door for a few seconds until Knox broke my thoughts.

"What was that about?" He seethed.

I turned my head wide-eyed to look at him, "I do not know, myself?" *How could I explain something that I had no knowledge of?*

"Well, it looked like he kissed you quite passionately, and you did not fight my brother off," he gritted out.

"First off, he took me by surprise," I defended. "Second, I just woke up after being sick, and I am still very weak. Thirdly, what right do I have to deny him in his own home?" I knew it was a low blow to Knox, but it was the blatant truth in the matter. Bay would always trump Knox for being born first in the Royal succession. I could not be blamed for something I had no control over.

I watched as the hurt flashed through Knox's eyes as a wall slammed down between us. He distanced himself as he stood and took a step back.

"Very well, I understand." He bowed his head and started walking towards my door.

"Knox!" It is not like that! I promise!" I called from behind him. I was too weak and indecent in just a nightgown to chase after him. He halted but did not turn to face me.

"You just made it very clear how it is." He continued to my door, closing it softly behind him.

I glanced down at the still abandoned tray with its broken teacups and plates. Tea was staining the carpet as the pastries were mixed in with the broken shards of porcelain. They were being completely forgotten, as I felt right now.

Chapter 23

KNOX'S POV

I paced my room, trying not to destroy things and trying hard to keep my temper under control. *How dare he kiss her and right in front of my face, no less! Has he no shame? He certainly has no respect for me!* This was a complete outrage, and I could do nothing about it. My fist slammed into the wall, causing the drywall to crack and dent inwards. He did not even care about Mina prior to her fever; he acted like she was dead to him. He did not bother to visit her room once while she was unconscious for the last three days. I blamed Mina for his actions when, deep down, I knew she couldn't have controlled that kiss. She was innocent in this whole mess.

I threw a vase, and it smashed against the wall. So much for reigning in my temper as my arms slid across the top of my desk, throwing all the books and items on it to the floor. Turning, I ripped the curtains off the rod from the window and growled when they fell into me. I became tangled in the fabric and, in my frustration, yanked the curtain fabric until I heard it ripping apart. I threw the shredded pieces to the ground.

No matter what I did in life, I would always be the cruel, reclusive prince unworthy of love and unworthy of even being anything more than second place, if not completely forgotten. I was the spare.

Chapter 24

BAY'S POV

I kissed her. I ran my right-hand fingertips over my lips, letting my fingers lightly touch where her's had been. I never intended the kiss when heading to her room. When Eloise passed me, rushing for the physician saying she had awoken, I immediately moved into action to make my way towards her. To verify that it was true, that she was alright.

But the moment I entered her room and my eyes landed on her, I saw her and nothing else. It was as if I had no control over my body or my reaction to seeing her awake. It was not until after I had kissed her and then threatened her that I realized what I had done. I barely had been aware of my brother's presence at that moment. He had witnessed it. The worst part of it all was that no matter how much I needed to deny it, I could not lie to myself because I wanted to kiss her again. I wanted to do so much more to her.

Chapter 25

The physician made me spend the rest of the day in bed, and I could join for breakfast the following day if I so chose. He had informed me a vicious illness had circulated around the castle, and I was the last to recover from it. Many of the other guests felt better after a day, while mine had dragged me under for three days. Eloise had been at my side caring for me, and I knew I was in good hands. I felt a tad wobbly on my legs at first, but nothing was too worrisome. I just walked a bit more cautiously than I normally would.

Eloise was at my elbow, helping guide me and being there if I needed to lean my weight on her. I had not seen either brother again yesterday, and today was a new day. I honestly did not know how I would react to seeing either of them. Bay would be the easiest since there was an expected societal way to respond to him, and he could direct the conversation in any way that he wanted to. I would just simply need to follow his lead.

Knox, on the other hand, would be a whole other beast. Even

though he was also a prince, there was still a bit more leeway, especially as The Reclusive Spare Prince and all. Most people paid no heed to him. But I had a feeling when it came to me, all eyes would be on us, and there really was no escaping that, especially with him being my pre-engaged fiance. At the very bare minimum, at least Regina and Olivia were gone from the castle, and I would not have to deal with them or any altercations that came with their meddling anymore.

Eloise and I entered the breakfast hall to see a decent number of guests, but Bay and Knox were absent. I breathed easier, knowing I would not have to confront either of them just yet, which set my mind at ease. But in the same breath, it also meant eventually, I would have to face them, and when I did, hopefully, it would be in a less populated location. Thankfully, the physician ordered Eloise to be at my side for at least today, and then I could decide if I needed her to attend events with me for the following days.

I ate breakfast, and people whispered amongst themselves while giving me pointed looks. I was becoming used to this treatment and tried to ignore it as best as I possibly could. It was a shame Eloise could not sit directly by me as she stood along the wall behind me. It would make this a tad less lonely of an experience.

"We were worried about you," chirped Iryse as she sat down on my right.

"We missed you," Tearani said in her monotone voice as she claimed the chair to my left.

"I apologize, but I am alright," I replied a bit self-consciously, looking at both twins.

"You are to come to our room after breakfast so we can catch up on *everything*." Iryse waggled her eyebrows, causing me to laugh slightly.

"Ah, Mina, I see you are feeling better." Montgomery pulled the chair out from across from me. "I blame myself for not escorting you to your room."

"Montgomery? I thought you would have been sent home with your sister?" I asked, surprised.

"What? And leave you without your best friend to fend off these wolves, I think not." He leaned back in his chair, winking at me with that familiar, devilish grin.

"Ahem, best friend?" Iryse raised her voice a bit; her eyebrows shot up into her hairline. Montgomery came back down on all four legs of his chair to lean in across the table at her.

"You heard it, Irysey," he challenged. I shifted a bit, uncomfortable in my seat, as I hid a smile behind my napkin.

"Don't call me Irysey," she scoffed, crossing her arms. Montgomery chuckled before focusing his attention on Tearani.

"Tea, good to see you as always," he said, dipping his head at her. She blinked at him before looking down at her food to take a bite. He chuckled some more. It dawned on me that he had grown up around the twins like Regina had. The only difference was they must have all gotten along, unlike Regina regarding the twins.

Neither brother showed up for breakfast, and I made my way to the rose garden with the twins while Eloise followed behind. Eloise thought I should take it slow and easy, but Iryse argued that fresh air would do me good first, and then we would spend the day in their rooms. And without Regina and Olivia here, I could officially relax and enjoy the sunshine.

We chose a table to sit at; it was still early, and the area was free of people. I immensely enjoyed the sereneness of it all. Eloise went to fetch tea for us.

"Do you two mind if I take a quick stroll through the maze before Eloise comes back?" I asked the twins.

"We will be here," Iryse replied, waving her hand for me to go on ahead. Tearani just blinked before looking over the gardens. I knew Eloise would scold me for doing so, but I had the twins to tell her where I had gone. I was kind of hiding behind Iryse in that sense. I knew she would make Eloise back down. I took a deep breath of the heavenly scent of the blossoming roses. I wished I had grown up with something like this, but then I probably would not appreciate or enjoy it as much as I do now.

I wandered through the twists and turns of the maze. I did not have the maze's patterns memorized, but I tried to remember which way I had come from. I found a bench and took a seat. I was not entirely worn out, but the break was nice. I sat there, letting myself to collect my thoughts, finally alone and able to breathe.

What was I going to do? Bay stormed into my room without a word just to kiss me in front of Knox, and then Bay left as fast as he came. And now Knox was nowhere in sight and refusing to accept any letters I sent him. I had no control over Bay's actions. Regardless of my attempts, Knox would not listen to reason. I realized that Bay had seen me with Knox physically, but Knox had never seen or known about me with Bay. And here I am alone, sitting on a bench in the rose garden maze.

I was not bold enough to attempt the East or the West wing to run into them, so that left me to wander the rose maze and plan to walk the castle corridors later. I would wander aimlessly with Eloise in hopes of bumping into them. At the very minimum, I needed to fix things with my pre-engaged fiance. I did not want to start a marriage full of loathing.

I saw one of the friendly white fluffy cats approaching me. I leaned down from the bench to pet it as it came running for ear scritches before I ran my hand down its back and up its tail.

"Where were you off to?" I asked, knowing I would never receive an actual answer. The feline did a few more back-and-forths under my hand before walking the same way it had initially been headed. I decided to get up from the bench to follow the white cat. What harm could come from it? I had nothing else planned to do for today.

Every so many yards, the white fluffy cat would look back to ensure I followed it. We kept going deeper and deeper into the maze than I had anticipated. I hoped I would not become lost as I stumbled over a brick that was not even. The feline paused, waiting for me, before continuing.

We ended up back at the desolate, ungroomed fountain that Knox had first brought me to, but we were not alone. Queen Serenity was sitting on the bench, looking at the fountain. The white feline jumped into her lap and settled down.

"I see Sugarplum brought you to me," she said casually, and I was beginning to realize Queen Serenity loved naming the castle cats after foods or ingredients.

"Yes, I decided to follow her, and she brought me here." I curtsied.

"Very well, I did have a matter I wish to discuss with you." Her face was void of warmth, and I gulped.

"What are your intentions with my sons?" I took a step back, unsure of how to even answer that question to myself. If I could not answer it to myself, how would I even know what to tell their mother?

"Queen Serenity," I replied softly, trying to gather my thoughts and also to stall.

"I am already aware Killien stayed by your bedside while you were sick, and Rafael came in and kissed you before leaving without saying a word." *Oh, he said words,* I thought to myself. "Now, neither of my sons are talking to each other, and they are a terror to be around. The common denominator is you." Her blue eyes turned icy, cutting right through me deeply. I wanted to turn and run away. *Why did I have to follow Sugarplum here?* I could have avoided all of this. "You who are already pre-engaged to my youngest, meanwhile my oldest who cannot have you is being reckless."

"To be honest, I am still puzzled over Bay- - I mean Prince Rafael Baylor's actions, and Prince Killien Knox will not answer any of my letters." Honesty, to the best of my abilities, was my only hope currently because I was beyond confused.

"I already know you are informal with them. No sense of keeping up acts now," she chided. "However, you expect me to believe my son Rafael kissed you once you awoke, unprovoked, when he was a tyrant smashing everything around him and was holed up in his room while you were recovering?" Her eyebrow quirked at me, waiting to continue down this path of my story.

Part of me felt elated that Bay had been worried about me, but the other part of me became all the more confused. After the conversation he had overheard between my mother and me, I did not think what we had shared prior mattered to him anymore.

"Queen Serenity, all I know is Bay wanted nothing to do with me prior to collapsing, and then when I woke up, he rushed in and kissed me." I smoothed down invisible wrinkles in my dress. She hummed, mulling this over a bit in her mind. I wanted to twist the rings on my fingers but kept my hands clasped in place in front of me.

"With the way your Mother played the game," she finally said, pausing before continuing with, "I would not put it past her to have raised you to go after both of my boys. Rumors or naught," she surmised, giving me a leveled stare, challenging me to defend against her statement. I straightened and squared my shoulders.

"Queen Serenity, like the majority of the females here, I was raised to marry a prince, and that is why I am here."

"Bay told me what he overheard when I had left you and your mother in here. All of it," she challenged back.

"You know my mother from your season with her and witnessed her in action here. What choice did I have for my own safety other than to parrot what she wanted to hear." I curtsied and turned, dismissing myself.

"And that is why I played against her." Queen Serenity's voice came from behind me. I paused, turning to look back at her. "I watched you closely to see if you were anything like Lydia. Imagine my surprise when I found you were nothing like her. It is very evident Gideon is your father." I was not sure how to feel about that last statement. Queen Serenity did not give me time to think as she continued, "you formed a friendship with Killien free will, and the cards fell naturally with Rafael. . ." She paused to think out her next words carefully, ". . .When I said I would enjoy you as a daughter-in-law, I meant it. Preferably with Killien." Her eyes sliced right through me.

"That will be up to Knox at this point." I dipped my head and walked away. I half expected her to prevent me from leaving, but she let me go. When I believed I was far enough away, my footsteps picked up as I tried to leave the rose maze as fast as possible, lest I be entrapped in another conversation with Queen Serenity.

I found Eloise sitting at the table with the twins, who were sipping on the tea she had gone to fetch. Eloise watched me emerge from the rose maze, not saying anything until I approached the table.

"I see you decided to stroll the maze. . . If you had not come out in the next five minutes, I would be dragging these two twins in with me to come fetch you." She did not sound happy. Iryse rolled her eyes, and I witnessed Tearani's lips twitch a fragment before returning to a straight line.

"Apologies for running off. I just wanted to think things through," I said in response.

"And did you think things through?" She was a bit cool. I knew the twins were listening intently to add to their treasure of knowledge on people.

"I ran into Queen Serenity." All three pairs of eyes widened at that.

"What?" Eloise gasped at the same time Iryse demanded to know what happened. Tearani watched me. She blinked slowly as she stated, "let's take this to a private room."

The four of us made our way back into the castle. We ducked into an unoccupied entertaining room and shut the door behind us. When we were all seated, they sat there waiting expectantly for me to tell them the details.

"She was in the maze," and then I continued to tell them what had occurred, leaving out the details of our conversation about Knox and my pre-arranged engagement. They listened quietly the whole time, and when I finished, there was a pause before any of them responded.

"It may be rumors, but I have heard from the other older servants who were here during Queen Serenity and Queen Lydia's time that they say Lydia followed Serenity around like a nuisance," Eloise finally said first. I leaned in to hear more. "Lydia was desperately after Regalius and flocked to Serenity's side and stayed that way until Queen Serenity became engaged to King Regalius, and your mother took the next best option, your father, King Gideon." Eloise paused, letting it sink in until she continued with, "supposedly your father had been quite sweet on Serenity their whole time here and when Regalius announced his engagement to her, your father found solace in your mother, they announced their engagement mere days after Regalius and Serenity," she finished.

"Our parents had told similar stories while we were growing up. They may have mentioned your mother possibly sleeping around as well," chimed in Iryse. "Our parents were in an arranged marriage, so they only attended the season to form alliances during their engagement." I had forgotten the twin's parents were placed in an arranged marriage. I wonder how that had fared for them?

All these years, Mother's stories may have only been half-truths. Had my mother been sleeping around with other males? While Mother was here during her season, had she thrown herself at Regalius? When Serenity announced her engagement, did she settle for Father? I thought they had been completely in love, but by this new truth, it sounded like my father had agreed to marry her while nursing a broken heart. Was his heartbreak severe enough for him to agree to marry someone he didn't love when his crush became engaged to another?

I decided I was too exhausted to spend the afternoon in the twin's bedroom and that I needed to rest for a few hours. The twins made me swear to come to their room later that evening to catch up on all the details. Eloise guided me back to my room to lie down. Thereafter, it took a bit of convincing from Stella and myself to make Eloise agree that I could go to the twin's bedroom by myself when the time came.

Chapter 26

I shut my bedroom door quietly behind me to head to the twin's bedroom. As I turned in the hall, there was Bay lounging against the wall, watching me.

"Bay," I said, startled. I dropped into a curtsey, not knowing why he was waiting down the hall on my floor. He shoved off the wall and strode towards me, not saying anything. He reached his hand out and grasped mine.

"Bay?" He did not respond as he began leading me towards the East wing. His wing. My heart began to race. He took us up staircases and down corridors, lefts, and rights until I knew I would not find my way back if I tried.

We came to a very intricately carved door that he pushed open to what I could only assume were his rooms. The walls were in light gray tones with darker gray curtains that led out to a balcony. The furniture was soft creams and beiges. His main room was very simplistic and sophisticated.

He did not stop at the first room, pushing through the double set of doors to his bedroom. The bedroom was nothing like the main room. The walls here were dark teal, with black curtains hanging down the large bay window. The canopy bed was massive with dark mahogany wood. Tall wooden spindles came up to almost touch the ceiling on all four bedposts. The top of the canopy was all wood with matching crushed velvet teal drapes coming down the sides. There was a dark mahogany writing desk in the corner strewn with papers about it. It was probably the only untidy thing in his whole living space.

We got halfway to his bed before he stopped. I did not know what to say, so I stood there silently, awaiting his next move. Finally, he turned to look at me, and everything else melted away, just like in the library when our eyes locked.

"I don't know what it is about you, but I cannot get you out of my mind," he stated. My heart hammered in my ears, excitedly anticipating what would happen next. My eyes searched into his as he looked back into mine. He leaned into me and softly kissed me. I closed my eyes as he deepened the kiss and dipped me. My arms wrapped around his neck to keep my balance, bringing him closer to me.

He brought me back up to him, pulling me close. I was uncertain what had come over Bay. He had not talked to me since the day he kissed me. Knox had not been around to talk, and now I was alone with Bay in his bedroom. My heart began to race at what this could mean as our kisses deepened.

He lifted me up, and my legs wrapped around his waist. My dress bunching up between us. Kissing me even deeper, he began to take steps toward the bed. Running my fingers through his hair, I was confused about many things regarding the T'Lovoness brothers, but I believed I was ready for this. After all, I could be entering a loveless marriage shortly enough, so why not feel something with the brother who was showing me affection?

He lowered us both down onto his bed, with him staying between my legs. His hands trailed from behind my thighs to the front, gathering my dress further upwards.

He broke the kiss. "Let me get you out of this dress," he suggested, and I nodded. "May need a knife to undo the corset laces." He smiled, leaning over to his bedside table; he procured a beautiful blade with jewels encrusted in its handle from the bits I could see.

"Roll over," he commanded.

"You will need to get off of me," I replied shyly. He chuckled and got up to stand over me as I rolled over onto my stomach. I felt his warm hand on my shoulder and then slipped it under the back of my dress to lift up the fabric. I then heard the material being cut away down my back as it became loose and easier to breathe. The sound of the last bit of the fabric being cut away ended.

"I want you to get off this bed, stand up, and hold your now ruined dress before me," he commanded as he stepped to the side to make room for me to follow his order. I slid to the edge of the bed, holding my ripped dress to my chest. I got off the bed with my back facing Bay. I heard the bed creak as he sat down. Peeking over my shoulder at him, he sat there with his arms resting on his knees, his eyes admiring my exposed back. I blushed as the butterflies went crazy in my stomach.

"Turn around, Mina," he commanded, and I slowly turned around, still clutching my dress to conceal my nakedness. He dipped his head, and I dropped the dress, letting it pool on the floor at my feet.

He drank me in, and then he unfolded his hands to crook his right finger at me. My heart pounding in my ears, I nervously stepped out of my dress, taking a few steps forward, and made him sit back to look up at me in between his legs.

His fingers came up to my panties, not breaking eye contact as he slid them down until they dropped to the floor. I stepped out and kicked them off to the side. His hands came back up and firmly grabbed my ass, forcing me to stumble into him a bit; my hands landed on his shoulder for balance.

"You are breathtaking," he murmured. He pulled me closer as he leaned back onto the bed, rolling us and guiding me until I was lying on my back with him on top of me. He kissed my neck as he started unbuttoning his shirt. Shrugging it off and throwing it out of the way, he began to work on his pants.

Bubbles of excitement and nervousness fluttered in my stomach as I watched him slide his pants off, letting them drop to the floor. He situated himself on top of me, and I felt his hardness against my right inner thigh. His hand ran down my right leg as he yanked it up higher. His chest rested on mine as he began kissing me again. His other hand came to cup my left breast. Breaking the kiss, he growled, "I want to taste you on my tongue." My stomach clenched instantly.

He began peppering kisses down my chin and neck. They continued down over my collarbone before pausing to suck on my right nipple as his right hand gently pinched my left one. I arched up into him, moaning. His lips left my nipple to continue his descent. Butterflies were going crazy within my stomach as he kissed my left inner thigh. I looked down at him, his blue eyes meeting mine as his head lowered to kiss my clit. A full shiver coursed through my body, causing me to arch myself into his mouth.

His tongue began to swirl around my clit, causing me to moan. I raked my fingers through his hair, grinding against his mouth. He trailed his left hand down my body, over my hip, and down my ass. He adjusted himself until his finger was at my entrance. He slid his finger into me and began to form a rhythm between his finger and his tongue. I gripped his hair more tightly, breaking eye contact as I threw my head backward against the pillow, arching more from the pleasure. I could feel myself building as he picked up the speed. I moaned louder, grinding against him as I chased my own release until it finally came crashing through me, and I was moaning his name. He did not stop as each wave of my orgasm kept coming.

The pleasure was beginning to become too much as I tried to escape away from the overstimulation, but he followed my body. He locked me in to keep receiving the pleasure from his mouth. I begged him, crying it was too much pleasure. I was shaking, still trying to escape his strong arms that kept me in place as he continued to suck my overly sensitive clit. My hands dug into the bedsheets, now trying to ground myself. I continued to beg him to stop. He did not listen. I was a squirming puddle of a mess when he finally released me.

"You will be done receiving pleasure when I deem so," he growled. He pulled himself up and wiped his mouth on the back of his arm before kissing me hard on my mouth. I tasted myself on his lips. I appreciated that he did not kiss me with a wet face.

I felt the head of his cock at my entrance, with his hand guiding himself in. I tensed, and he broke the kiss. "Relax, I will be gentle," he promised softly, kissing me. I felt him slowly pushing inside and a slight pain and discomfort that accompanied it. I hissed a breath inward. He paused and pulled back out, re-adjusting his hips. As he pushed back in, I whimpered from the sensitivity still coursing through my body. He pulled out and pushed himself all the way in.

"You are perfect," he breathed as he began to grind against me, slow at first, and then picked up his pace. I began to move with him, and he yanked my right leg up higher, causing him to go in deeper. I yelped from the newfound depth he reached. He picked up his rhythm, going faster and harder.

"Bay," I moaned out as I felt him hitting all the sensitive spots from him grinding against me. He moaned back in response as he fucked me harder. "Bay." I cried his name. He continued going faster until he was panting and yelling my name. Then, finally, he collapsed on me.

Breathing heavily and sweaty, I could hear my heartbeat pounding in my ears. I was still wrapping my mind around the idea that I was laying here naked with Bay still sweaty on top of me. I was no longer a virgin.

We lay there for a few minutes as he began kissing my neck. I felt him hardening again. Then he was kissing me, sliding back into me for another round. I was a bit tender and sore, but I wanted to please him desperately that I did not complain. I did not want this moment to end.

It was after the third time that I began to lose steam. Nestling into him, I fought sleep while curled up at his side. I dozed for a while until he woke me up with more kisses in the middle of the night for a fourth round. After we finished, I was exhausted, begging for no more and that I needed rest now. I was falling in and out of sleep this last time and thought I heard him whisper, "you are mine forever." Before falling asleep.

I awoke the following morning with the light streaming in through the windows. I was sore but beyond comfortable, and I did not want to leave this bed. It was when I shifted that I realized I was not alone, and it all came back to me. I was wrapped up in Bay's arms, and I felt him softly breathing on my neck as he spooned me. I shifted again and felt his arms tighten around me, and my heart fluttered.

"Mmh." He nuzzled into my neck. "You smell heavenly in the morning." He pulled me in even closer, and I felt his hardness pushing into my backside. I smiled, not knowing what to say. He kissed my neck, causing me to shiver.

He began rolling us, with me ending up underneath him. I looked up to see one of his rare smiles. His legs nudged mine apart, and he began to kiss me. His hands slid along my side, down my hip, and then trailed in between my legs, stroking my clit. His fingers slid into me. With an overly sore and pleasured body, I moaned into his kiss.

"Bay, I don't think I could handle another round," I pouted, exhausted. He chuckled darkly.

"I want to have my fill of you, that you will only ever want to be consumed by me." He promised. He withdrew his fingers and replaced them with the head of his hardened cock. He glanced at me, and I nodded in confirmation. Pushing into me, he took his pleasure from my body, grinding and kissing me until I was orgasming on his cock.

"Hey, Bay?" I asked, uneasy.

"Yeah?" he replied, buttoning up his shirt.

"I know we did not discuss this, but are you on a tonic?" I became nervous because I had never taken one to prevent pregnancy, and I was hoping he was.

"Yup, you will be fine," he said casually. While it answered and eased my mind of one question, it caused more questions to pop up as to why he may be on the tonic. Did he do this with other females often? I decided I was not going to press the matter. I was not ready to end this good mood.

"I do not have anything to wear out of here." I twirled my hair, not knowing how I would not get caught in a ripped dress if I left this room.

"Do not worry," he said confidently.

"What do you mean?"

"I sent my handmaid to fetch yours and to bring a dress with her," he replied, finishing the last button.

"Oh, thank you." I had not anticipated him already thinking ahead. He pulled on his pants.

"Of course." He smiled at me as he began tugging on his boots. He walked to me, still in the bed, leaning down, and kissed me on the lips, "I have somewhere to be. I shall see you later, Mina." He smiled before leaving. I was not going to dwell on where Bay needed to be nor allow myself to feel guilty for what I did last night. I tried not to think about why he may already be on the tonic, knowing the obvious answer as to why. I attempted to keep the barriers up in my mind against the thoughts of just being a number on his list. My elation began to plummet the more I mulled it over.

Minutes later, both Eloise and Stella entered my room with a mint green dress in hand.

"Mina," hissed Eloise in complete surprise and amusement at what she walked in on with me still wrapped up in bedsheets in Bay's bed. Stella tried to hide a knowing smile behind her hand as she ducked her chin into her shoulder.

"Eloise," I countered as I smiled, attempting to be unashamed.

"Men do not marry those they sleep with prior."

"Nor do women," I countered. Out of the corner of my vision, I saw Stella take a step back like I had physically slapped her. It was not meant to be insulting towards her as a person but to validate my point to Eloise.

"That is different." She had a warning tone in her voice.

"If the porcelain shoe fits." I shrugged nonchalantly.

"Maybe I should leave," Stella offered, beginning to turn away.

"No. Stay Stella," I ordered. I rose from the bed with the bedsheet around me, and Eloise gasped, looking at the bed. I hindered a glance there to see the blood stain.

"Eloise, I have been controlled all of my life." I walked towards her. "You have been my friend the whole time. . . Let me make my own decisions for once." Her gaze leveled with mine before she broke into a smile.

"It is about time you gained a backbone. I was becoming afraid it would never grow," she finally said before glancing at Stella. "Help me get this dress on her before people start noticing her absence."

"I already missed enough events since arriving, and I am certain this will be no different."

"Nonetheless." She began tugging the dress over my head. "Let us dress you so when Prince Bay sees you; you still take his breath away after last night." I liked the way her mind worked.

"But what about Knox?" Stella asked, causing the whole mood of the room to change.

"I am not sure," I replied uneasily, looking at the floor. Eloise's hands moved faster, smoothing down bits of my dress.

"Let us not worry about it now," Eloise clipped out. I could hear the warning tone in her voice towards Stella. This launched Stella into action to begin helping Eloise with getting me laced up into the dress.

Chapter 27

Eloise had Stella check to ensure the coast was clear in Bay's wing before she let me emerge, just in case someone would pass by and see me leave Bay's room. There was a bit of a thrill in sneaking around. It made me both excited and scared if someone were to catch me right now. Especially if that someone would be Queen Serenity or Knox. Thankfully, I managed to leave his wing without anyone passing me by, and I headed straight to breakfast. I spotted the twins and made a direct beeline to them, claiming the empty chair across from them.

"Where were you last night?" Iryse asked instantly when I sat down at the breakfast table.

"I will tell you both after breakfast. This is not the right place. . . Too many ears," I replied, glancing around the table. Tearani simply blinked at me while Iryse pursed her lips.

"Alright, but you better show up this time," threatened Iryse.

"I will. I will. We will go straight to my rooms after breakfast." I would have suggested their rooms, but I did not trust their maids to keep a secret like Eloise and Stella would. The less that they know currently, the better. Bay did not show up for breakfast, which made me wonder what sort of thing he had to attend to.

Before we could say another word, the empty chair to my left was pulled out, and Montgomery sat beside me.

"Good morning, my best friend." He smiled as he leaned back, balancing on the chair's back legs as his arm rested on the back of my chair for support. Iryse tightened the grip around her fork.

"Good morning, Irysey, Tea." He nodded his head at the twins. Iryse narrowed her eyes at him as Tearani nodded with a blink.

"What is the good word for today?" He asked, ignoring Iryse's reaction to him.

"We are going back to Mina's room for a girl's day," Iryse snipped out.

"Can I come?" He asked, not missing a beat.

"No. Girls only. No boys."

"What if I pretended to be a girl?" He countered, batting his lashes at her.

"No." She took an aggressive bite of her food.

"But, but," he pouted, coming back down on all four legs of his chair. He rested his elbows on the table, clasping his hands to rest his chin on them, "I could make a very pretty girl. I will even wear a dress, you could braid my hair. . . I want a friendship ankle bracelet."

I was taking a drink of water when I about choked on it. My eyes widened as I looked at him, trying not to laugh at the idea of him wearing a dress.

"How did you know about the ankle bracelets?" I inquired.

"Oh, come now, I have seen you all wearing one. It was not hard to put two and two together." He leaned his chair back onto two legs again. "As your best friend, I want one too."

"You. Are. Not. Her. Best. Friend," gritted out Iryse.

"Oh, really? Who is?" He asked as he looked at his nails, completely unphased. I found it hilarious how he taunted her.

"We are," Iryse replied in a tone that meant the end of the discussion. Montgomery looked at me.

"Is that true, Mina?" He gave me the most enormous, saddest puppy dog eyes. I hid my smile behind my hand.

"I can have more than one best friend," I replied. I was trying to make everyone happy at the table. Iryse gave me a look of *really* with a raised eyebrow. Tearani continued to eat her food without looking up from her plate. Montgomery gave me that devilish smile with a raised eyebrow.

The empty chair to my right was pulled out as Knox plopped down next to me. I was startled by him not sitting in his customary spot at the head of the table by his parents. Our last encounter ended with him storming out of my room, pissed at Bay for kissing me. Now, he was casually sitting beside me as if everything was alright. This unnerved me a bit. I felt like I was on shaky ground, and if he discovered what had occurred just last night, I knew he would blow up.

"What are we talking about?" I did not miss a beat of his eyes lingering on Montgomery's arm, resting on the back of my chair for balance.

"That I am Mina's number one best friend." Montgomery cockily replied as he gave Iryse a wink. With the way she stabbed the food on her plate, I thought the silverware would go right through the plate and pierce the table. Knox gave Montgomery a confused look, probably not expecting that reply.

"Umm, okay?" Was how Knox replied.

"Iryse and Montgomery are having a pissing match about who is Mina's number one best friend," Tearani filled in as she paused her eating. "Do you care to join in the matches of pissing for the title of best friend?" She blinked, looking at Knox.

"Uhhh, I think I am good," he replied. Iryse's glare at him crackled, daring him to even try.

"Good, good. One less competitor since Killien will not be joining." Smiled Montgomery. Knox shifted slightly in his chair. I was unsure if it was due to him not joining in on being my number one best friend or that Montgomery so casually called him by his first name. "Killien, we should go do some manly stuff today since the girls here are having a girl's day, and they will not permit me to join." Montgomery threw a pouting look at Iryse. Knox shifted again in his chair. I questioned if he regretted taking a seat by me.

"What did you have in mind?" Knox asked Montgomery cautiously.

"Whatever our hearts desire, maybe we will give each other friendship bracelets too." He was definitely hung up on that one.

"Friendship bracelets?" Knox asked, uncertain.

"Fine. Friendship daggers because we are manly men."

"Stating that you are manly men does not, in fact, make you manly men," Iryse stated.

"So hurtful." Montgomery put a hand over his chest dramatically as if she had stabbed him in the heart. I glanced over at Knox to see how he was doing. He had a small smile on his face, and when he caught my eye, I smiled at him, giving him more reassurance.

"So, girl's day, huh?" Knox asked the twins.

"Yup! It has been a bit since we caught up with Mina because she was sick and whatnot," Iryse replied. I did not miss the slight scowl that crossed Knox's face briefly.

"That was quite scary for a bit," Knox added.

"Most dreadful," Montgomery replied melodramatically, "for I could not eat or sleep knowing my best friend was unwell." He draped an arm over his eyes to emphasize his point.

"That is a lie! I saw you at every meal eating away!" Accused Iryse. "Besides, Knox never left her side," she tacked on to make her point as she nodded her head towards Knox. Montgomery dropped his elbow to look at Knox from behind me.

"Oh, how much of a chivalrous white knight you are." Montgomery's arm that was resting on the back of my chair moved until he was resting a hand on Knox's shoulder. Knox looked at the hand, confused, then back to Montgomery, probably questioning the audacity to be touched at all. "Please, Killien, please take care of my little girl," Montgomery pleaded in earnest.

"Little girl?" I asked, giving him a confused look. He talked as if he was my father.

"I only want what is best for my best friend," Montgomery replied, looking at me before turning back to Knox. "You have my blessing, Killien. Love her well."

"You do not have a right to give her away!" Interjected Iryse in a huff. It was amazing that no one else was sitting close enough to us to pay any mind to this little soirée that was occurring.

"Then who does?" Montgomery demanded as if he was ready to challenge them for the right.

"Her parents!" She glared at him.

"They already did," Knox replied sheepishly, causing me to blush. Montgomery and Iryse both instantly reacted to that. Montgomery came down on all four chair legs as Iryse stood up, her hands slamming down hard on the table.

"What?!" Iryse exclaimed; she looked at Montgomery. "And you already knew, didn't you?!" Montgomery gave her a shitty grin. I wondered how life became this complicated and how Regina had not spread rumors of my pre-engagement to Knox. *Did I miss being the wallflower with no friends?* At this direct moment in time, yes, yes, I did. I buried my face in my hands, trying to hide from the looks all my friends were giving me.

"Our fathers agreed that if we did not find a match by the end of the season, then we would be engaged in an arranged marriage," Knox replied.

"But the end of the season is in three days!" Cried Iryse. My stomach dropped. I completely forgot we were closing in on the end of the courting season. I had too many strings I needed to tie up between Knox and Bay. *Did Bay even want to marry me after last night? Was I okay with marrying Knox?* Three days. I had three days to find my answer.

Knox rested his hand on my leg, giving me a small squeeze. "Three days," he said. I dropped my hands from my face to look over at him. I took him all in as I weighed if I would want to spend my life with him. There were so many things I did not yet know about him. We had too many hiccups. Last night with Bay added to all the more confusion. *How would I ever tell him what happened? Would I ever tell him?* No, I did not think I could tell him. I gave Knox a small smile.

"Alright, to your room now. We need to have a word with Mina," Iryse ordered, breaking up the conversation. Tearani stood up and began to lead the way out of the breakfast hall without looking back to see if we were following.

I stood up as Knox's hand dropped from my lap.

"You both have fun doing your manly man things," I jested with a wink before following the twins out of the room. None of us spoke as we made it to my bedroom.

My rooms were empty. Eloise and Stella must have been off doing something with their time together. They probably already realized they may not have much more time together. We would be heading back home to Theorines. I was unsure if I could take Stella with me on that trip or if she would want to come to a poverty-ridden kingdom just to follow Eloise.

"Alright, catch us up," Iryse demanded when we all sat down by the bay window. Tearani stared at me, waiting to hear everything. It was a bit unnerving with her attention solely on me and not looking out the window.

I began to tell them everything. The conversation Bay had overheard in the rose maze with Mother. How I collapsed in front of Bay, waking up to Knox by my bedside. Bay kissing me in front of Knox, causing Knox to storm out. The convenient parts I had left out of my story with my conversation with Queen Serenity in the rose maze garden. My confusion over Knox at breakfast today, acting like nothing had happened. I finally ended on the ultimate confession of why I never made it to their rooms last night. Tearani barely reacted to what I said while Iryse hung onto every word. When I finally finished, there was a moment of silence.

"Are you capable of marrying Knox and ruling a queendom?" Tearani was the one to break the silence. I twisted my fingers in my lap, playing with the rings.

"I am not certain. . . My heart is confused. Knox . . . Knox is complicated." My stomach knotted. "One minute, he is nice, and I am enjoying my time with him, and then the next minute, he is a complete stranger and is pushing me away." I fiddled with my rings. "And every time I am having a moment with Knox, we are interrupted. . . maybe destiny doesn't want us together, but yet every time I am with Bay. . . every time I am with Bay, things just fall into place easily." I sighed, mulling over Tearani's question that I had not answered. "I think I may be afraid of entering a loveless marriage while simultaneously needing to rule a queendom with no training."

"Then we may be in the same boat." Tearani nodded with a

blink. I was a bit perplexed; this was the most I had ever seen Tearani becoming even remotely close to having ruffled feathers. Iryse was quiet a moment longer, pondering all the implications before she finally spoke.

"So, how was it with Bay?" Iryse twirled her hair, picking at an invisible lint. It was obvious that she was trying to play off how curious she actually was. I was grateful for her to change the topic away from my fears.

"Wonderful," I gushed. I had no one to compare it to, but I could only hope it was like that every time. It made me question if it would be like that with Knox if we ended up marrying.

"If you end up marrying Knox, would you tell him?" She pushed.

"I plan not to," I replied. With the way Knox had reacted to Bay kissing me in front of him, I could not even begin to imagine how he would react if he knew Bay and I had slept together. Let alone if he found out Bay had taken my virginity.

"Probably for the best. . ." Iryse agreed.

"Enough talk about me. Who is your secret person, Tearani?" I asked. I was quite curious about who had caught the princess's interest, and I had never been able to ask her. Tearani blinked at me, letting a very long pause occur. It became rather awkward, and I regret asking her the question.

"It no longer matters. We ended things. They were not comfortable with being a consort while I ruled a queendom." Tearani did not seem ruffled by this.

"I am sorry to hear that. Are you okay?"

"I will be fine; it was just a summer fling." She shrugged. I decided to change topics to the second half of what she had said.

"Your parents decide to change officially?" I pushed.

"Yes, we just received the letter yesterday." She blinked at me.

"This is very exciting!" I squealed, happy to have a close friend being an allying monarchy to me.

"Very much so." She agreed with a nod. I noticed Iryse had not said a word as she still fiddled with the invisible lint on her dress.

"How do you feel about it, Iryse?" I pushed. She looked up at me with a shrug of her shoulder.

"I am very happy for my sister. It also takes more pressure off my shoulders to find a spouse." She looked out the window. "It makes my future plans of traveling potentially easier with all the focus on Tearani, and my sister has agreed to allow me passage to travel."

"That is great, is it not?" Since the beginning, Iryse had made it abundantly clear that she wanted to travel and not be some little housewife.

"It is," she sighed. *Why did I get the feeling she was not as excited about these plans as she had been when she initially told me at the start of the season?*

"Is something wrong?" I asked.

"No. Everything is alright." Iryse stood up abruptly. "I need to be somewhere. Please excuse me." She stalked towards the doors and left. Tearani and I both watched, neither of us able to say a word with how quickly she had exited.

"Is she okay?" I asked Tearani, a bit shaken from Iryse's reaction. Tearani let out a sigh as she looked out the window.

"Iryse is not ready for change."

"Change?"

"We are twins. We grew up together by each other's sides. With me becoming queen and to rule our country, it will separate us."

"But she always mentioned on wanting to travel?"

"Yes, which for her was great when she was imagining it. Now it is fast approaching, and reality is catching up to her dreams." Iryse was not ready for her life to be flipped upside down. I wondered if that was why she was less happy and had been snappier, and maybe why she let Montgomery antagonize her over silly little things such as number one best friend. Because within a year, in reality, probably within a few months, everything will have changed.

"When will your parents be announcing you as heir?" I asked Tearani.

"The same day as you announced your engagement. In three days." She blinked. My stomach dropped at the reminder. In three days I could be announcing an engagement, but to which brother I was uncertain.

Chapter 28

After my conversation with Tearani yesterday, I lounged about my rooms for the rest of the day. My anxiety grew with each passing thought on what to do next. How much my life was going to change in two days. *Would I be queen to Bay, and my kingdom be left into the hands of some stranger? Or would I be queen to my home with Knox by myself?* I loved both brothers in their own ways. Maybe love was a strong word to be using in this current state of things.

Maybe I loved the idea of each brother. Knox had become my first friend here in the castle. He was reclusive and had a bit of an anger issue, from what I had witnessed. Although his shyness and unsureness of things made me adore him. The night of us dancing on the floor for the first time had been fun. We both really began to trust each other. A trust that I would not hold up to by keeping secrets about myself and Bay.

Which led me to think of Bay. When we locked eyes, nothing else mattered. He had become my knight in shining armor. He made me feel better. He definitely knew his way around my body. I had gone far further with him than I had with Knox. He knew what Knox and I had done because he had walked in on us. There would be no secrets to break our trust because he already knew. By marrying Bay, I would have completed everything I had been raised to do. Mother would be proud of this. The only problem was that I was pre-engaged to his brother, and Bay had never once given an indication of wanting to marry me. Since there were two days left to decide my fate, I was going to go to Bay's room to get my answer. I believe I knew the way. Leaving my rooms, I headed straight there.

Okay, maybe I did not know the way. I became lost a few times down the corridors and the stairs. When I finally reached his overly intricate double doors, I was a bit out of breath and very embarrassed. I knocked.

It took a few seconds before the door was opened by Bay himself. He looked at me, stunned that I was standing on the other side of his door. I was surprised that he had opened his door instead of a servant.

"Can I help you, Mina?" He asked in an indifferent tone. I was a bit taken aback by this. It was as if the other night did not happen between us.

"May I come in, Bay?" I asked a smidge awkwardly. He stepped back and swept his arm out to allow me to pass through. He was alone, which explained why he was the one answering his own door.

"What is this about, Mina?" He asked after he closed the door behind him. When I realized he had not taken a step away from the door to follow me to the chairs. I turned around to him.

"I wanted to talk to you about the other night," I began. He watched me patiently. "What does it mean for our future?"

"It means absolutely nothing," he replied almost instantly, striding forward until he was standing directly in front of me.

"But, Bay?" I asked, completely shocked at his blunt reply and the lack of personal space I currently had from him being this close. My heart dropped as I felt my body warming up. Tears threatened to form in my eyes.

"Mina, while you are a very wonderful girl and I do think highly of you . . ." Bay trailed off, thinking of his next words as he reached his hand up to play with a section of my hair in between his fingers. ". . . I have no intentions of marrying you. You are better off marrying my brother."

I inhaled a sharp breath at the hurtful words. I thought the wonderful night we had together meant something to him, at the very least.

"But I thought . . ." I started before he cut me off.

"That you were special? No, Mina, not in that sense. I have taken dozens of girls prior to you to my bed." His words cut right through me. "I will cherish you as a sister-in-law but nothing more," he said point-blankly.

"What am I supposed to tell your brother when I am no longer a virgin?"

"Knox is very open-minded; just do not tell him it was me." Bay shrugged, letting my hair drop from his fingers.

"Then who am I supposed to tell him it was?" My voice began to rise as I fought the tears back.

"You are clever enough. Figure it out. Just remember words have consequences."

"Consequences?" My eyebrows furrowed, my vision blurring.

"If you tell him it was the stable boy or a lord's son, well. . . Either the stable boy could be beheaded or thrown out of the palace, and a lord's son. . . You would have to marry, or if rejected for your lies, you may lose your chance of marrying at all. . ."

I curled my hands into fists. Bay thought he had this all figured out in a nice, neat little bow for me. "As a ruling Queendom, I would have more say than Knox on who I named."

"You would, once your coronation," Bay countered.

"So you are saying that if I claim it was you—"

"I would reject the notion."

"But why?"

"Because, if I accept yours, then what about all the girls before you that have schemed and tried to force my hand into marriage? Knox wants you. Our fathers agreed upon it, and I would rather have you as a part of my family as a sister-in-law than just some washed-up girl who tried to use me."

"Fine," I replied, feeling a crack spreading within me. My submission caused Bay to give me a perplexed look.

"Just fine?"

"Yes, I would also prefer to keep an amicable relationship with you than have you be someone I thought I knew. . . I rather enjoy your company," I surmised, squaring my shoulders with gritted teeth. Aside from emotions, I had no level ground to stand on against Bay. I had no angle to win in this. I wanted to rage, I wanted to scream, I wanted to fight, but where would it get me? The answer was nowhere.

"I am glad we are in agreement." Bay gave me that devilish smile he was so well known for.

"You are going to get me into trouble," I rolled my eyes, another crack splintering within me as I tried to maintain my composure. It felt like needles pin-pricking my body as I fought back every emotion I tried to hold in.

"Most likely, yes. . . But I would also like to have your queendom be an ally of mine as well. We would make great business partners." It was obvious he had been already thinking this all through.

"You know I have no training in that regard," I replied, letting my shoulders sag.

"Mother will train you."

"My mother never had any intentions to."

"Not your mother. *My* mother," he countered, and I looked at him, confused.

"Queen Serenity would train me?" I questioned, astonished. He was volunteering his own mother.

"We had a chat. Knox will come with a sizable dowry that will pay off your soon-to-be queendom's debts. . . But it will come at the cost of Mother being the one to train you to rule a queendom." I gulped. His family had everything figured out. *Was I just a pawn in their game?*

"Is Knox on board for this?"

"Like I said, Knox wants you," he replied as if I should have already known the answer to that question. "I suggest you go find Knox. Why drag out the inevitable?" I nodded woodenly, walking past him and towards the doors.

"Mina," he called my name, causing me to stop with my hand on the door handle. I glanced over my shoulder at him. "I wish you the utmost happiness in your life." I left without a reply.

Closing his door behind me, I pressed my back against the wall. *I would not cry. I would not cry.* The pain began to prick at the back of my eyes. I looked up at the ceiling, trying to prevent the tears from falling. My lips quivered as I closed my eyes, trying to count my breaths. I gave myself a few more minutes, grateful the hallway stayed empty, and Bay did not leave his room to find me.

What was I going to do? That is a very dumb question, Mina, and you already know what you are going to do next. I pushed off the wall, squaring my shoulders. I swiped at my eyes, clearing away any tears that had escaped. Taking a deep breath, I shoved my heartbreak and feelings for Bay down to the deepest part of my mind and locked it in a tiny little box as I prepared myself for what I was about to do next.

I hurried down the halls towards the library, not allowing myself to change my mind. I needed to find Knox. I would do what Bay said and not drag out the inevitable. With two days left, I had no intentions of marrying anyone else in this castle now that Bay had cleared the air between us. From what I surmised from breakfast yesterday, Knox did not have anyone either. It would be the two of us. So why not announce our engagement before the season ended?

I would mend my cracked heart later. I would grieve at the revelation of Bay's true nature. I knew in the moments when I would be alone, I would unlock that tiny little box, and my mind would be flooded with memories of Bay. But right now, I was going to chase my one chance to a possible future happiness. I was not going to dwell on what could have been, what I had hoped for . . . after all, there was a man who I believed wanted me, and at one time, secretly, I had wanted him too.

I turned the corner for the hall of the library, and there he was, walking towards the library doors by himself. I had guessed correctly where he would be. This was far easier than trying to locate his bedroom in the wing opposite of his brother's.

"Knox!" I yelled at his back. I started running towards him as he began to turn around. I threw my arms around his neck, catching him off guard.

"Mina?" He gasped in surprise, his hands automatically falling on my waist to support us.

"Do you like me, Knox?" I asked seriously.

"What?"

"Do you like me?" I repeated. I didn't think I could handle another heartbreak of rejection.

"Yeah, why?" His eyes were searching mine.

"Good, because I like you too," I replied, kissing him hard. I knew I was forcing myself to feel these things. I was only telling him a partial white lie. It took him a second for his brain to catch up to what I had said. He pulled me in tighter, kissing me back. I pulled back to continue with what I had anticipated to say.

"I want to marry you, Knox. Why should we wait two more days to announce our engagement? Our fathers already approve. Why not just make it a thing now?" I rushed out, not allowing my head or heart to talk reason with each other.

"Are you for certain?" He asked eagerly. I felt his fingers dig into my sides. *No, I was not certain.* But with what Bay had stated, I wanted to start my future out with Knox on a good note. Ultimately, whether we announced it today or in two days, it did not matter. We were still walking down the same path together. I would say I dreaded the consequences I would receive from Mother over this, but there was not much that could be done. Both kings had agreed upon this, so announcing two days prior would not change anything.

"Yes, I am certain." I forced myself to smile at him. He crashed his lips to mine as he twirled me around the corridor in his arms. Placing me back down on my feet, he broke the kiss and took my hand. I tried to pretend to be as happy as he was.

"Let us tell my parents at once!" He decided as he began to drag me towards wherever he believed his parents would be. He ended up dragging me into a private room along the corridor, telling two servants to go fetch each of his parents to meet us there. When I was confused by the room, he informed me that the royals could use multiple rooms throughout the palace on a whim. One of such rooms was a door down from mine, and that was why I had seen him exiting it my second day here.

Queen Serenity arrived first, taking us both in before she took her seat at the round table. King Regalius was not far behind her. He had a glimmer in his eye, knowing what would come next.

"Go on, Knox, tell us what this is about, even though I am sure your mother and I already know," began King Regalius.

"Father. Mother," he looked at them both as he squeezed my hand. "Mina and I have decided to marry. We decided why wait two additional days to announce something we already know is true now." He looked at me with shining eyes. I only hoped that I would be able to reflect to him the same level of happiness that he felt.

"Congratulations, dear boy. Celebrations will need to be arranged." The King clapped his hands, and a servant appeared immediately at his side. "In two days, I want to have an announcement celebration planned for Knox's engagement to Mina."

"Do you not think Gideon and Lydia should be here for their daughter's engagement announcement?" Interjected Queen Serenity.

"They knew this was coming. They will be here for the wedding in a month."

"A month?" I asked, alarmed. I had not been prepared for this.

"Yes, I am not getting any younger and would like to see my lineage continue. Considering Rafael did not settle on a female this season," King Regalius huffed out. I picked up that The King was a bit disgruntled by this. I tried not to allow myself to feel pleased that there was no one else for Bay.

"You boys go on ahead. I would like to talk to Mina about little female conversations for the planning." Queen Serenity winked at her husband and son, waving her hand to make them leave. *Why did I have a sinking feeling about being left alone with her?*

Knox leaned down to kiss me, calling me his fiancé as he and his father left the room. I took a breath and looked at Queen Serenity, who was watching me.

"We are going to have our work cut out with you, are we not?" She asked, matter of fact.

"What do you mean?" I jerked back in my seat.

"You were never raised to be the ruler of a queendom. I will be preparing you to do so, and you will not break my son's heart." Once again, her frosty demeanor took over.

"Break his heart?" I questioned. *We just agreed to marry*. I did not understand.

"I already know about your little rendezvous with Bay. Knox cannot find out, or it will destroy him. I need you to keep your time with Bay a secret from Knox. I may be fond of you and thrilled about you becoming my daughter-in-law. . . What I said before still stands true. But a mother is always protective of her children. Do you understand?" She gave me a leveled gaze, awaiting my response. I nodded my head slowly. I did not understand how she already knew about Bay and me having sex. How could she have already come by this information?

"Good." She clapped her hands together. "You will not be attending the itinerary activities. We will begin wedding planning and your training at once. I will send a letter to your parents as we send out letters to everyone to attend your wedding in a month." I nodded again, trying to take this all in. Queen Serenity stood up, concluding our private meeting, and walked towards the door. She paused before opening it, looking over her shoulder at me.

"Remember, Mina, do not hurt my children."

I gulped.

She walked out the door, closing it softly behind her.

Chapter 29

"Creams or beiges?" The wedding planner asked as we walked down the hall.

"Uh, creams?" I answered, uncertain if there was a difference between the two colors.

"Good choice, now mauve or burgundy?"

"You are just making up colors now," I stated.

"No, I am not." He held up a dusky dark pink. "Mauve" before waving a darker red-purple color. "Burgundy."

"Burgundy then," I sighed.

"Excellent choice to pair with the cream!" He complimented. Wedding planning was exhausting. This has become my life since the announcement of our engagement a week ago. Every day of, every waking moment of every single hour was wedding decision-making or training to run a queendom. If I was not being critically judged by the wedding planner when I did not make the right choice, I was being drilled by Queen Serenity on how to rule properly. At this point, the only time I have seen Knox was at meals.

I was beginning to pick up on the wedding planner's cues. If I did not make the best choice, I got a hum of slight judgment. If I chose the second-best option, he would say "fair" in a very disinterested tone. Only when I made the best choice, in his opinion, did he compliment me with a smile in his voice. This was not my wedding; this was my wedding planner's wedding.

"How is my beautiful soon-to-be bride?" Knox asked, wrapping his arms around me. I sank into him, feeling the full weight of fatigue from wedding planning crashing down on me. The wedding planner glanced over, raising an eyebrow at us before he sniffed and took a few steps away to give us our privacy.

"Ready for this to be over," I groaned.

"Uhh. . . Not the answer I expected to hear from my fiancée?" He hesitantly joked, uncertainty entering his voice.

"It is not you," I smoothed over, meeting his eyes to reassure him. "It's just this wedding planner. Every choice is a test." I sighed.

"Wedding planning is a test?" He quirked an eyebrow.

"Join me with wedding planning, and you will see," I joked.

"Alright, I will walk with you and see these so-called tests." He pulled me tighter in his arms, and the reassurance of him being with me to decide things helped relieve some of the stress. We walked to the wedding planner hand in hand. He glanced at our hands, back up to us, impatiently waiting.

"Prince Killien Knox." The wedding planner glanced at me with a raised eyebrow and then back to Knox.

"Knox said he wanted to join me in planning our wedding. I told him that would be an excellent idea, especially since we have not had much time to spend together with all the planning." I smiled through gritted teeth as I held my breath. The wedding planner gave his unamused expression, looking down his nose at us. After a very long, awkward pause, he finally started walking, and I began to breathe again.

"Very well, now onto flowers. Lilies or roses?"

"Lilies," I replied.

"Hmm," he hummed.

"Um, roses?" I asked, trying to remedy it.

"Yes," he agreed. *I personally would prefer lilies over roses, even irises over roses, but what could I do?*

"I beg pardon?" Interjected Knox. I looked at him as the wedding planner halted in his tracks to turn to face us.

"Is there a problem, Your Highness?" The wedding planner inquired with his usual quirked eyebrow expression.

"I believe my Mina wanted lilies over roses," he boldly stated.

"Roses are a better choice, Your Highness," countered the wedding planner, turning to keep walking.

"She wants lilies. What my soon-to-be wife and queen wants, she will get. Last I knew, we paid you, so unless you want to be replaced with someone who gives her what she wants. I suggest you mark down lilies." Knox stood firm, both of them staring each other down.

"Very well, lilies it is," sniffed the wedding planner before turning again to proceed walking. "White Casablanca lilies, pink stargazer, or tiger lilies?"

"White Casablanca," I responded instantly. I just loved how big they were.

Knox made the wedding planner go through the whole list that we had covered in the last week to ensure I got everything I wanted for our wedding. It was exhausting, but Knox sat there with his arms crossed, ensuring the wedding planner did not bully me into his preferences. I was finally beginning to breathe a bit and felt something inside me stirring again for Knox.

"As a queen, you will need to fix your queendom's problems," incited Queen Serenity as she walked back and forth in front of the room, teaching me how to be a ruler. I sat at the table listening to her. "Now your home is in a lot of debt. By our agreement to you marrying Knox, the dowry coming with him will be helping to pay off that debt. . . Please note the stipulation is for you and Knox. It will not be going to your parents." She looked at me to emphasize her point.

I nodded.

"Meaning, when your parents relinquish the throne to you, then you will start receiving the funds."

"What if they do not step down for decades?" I inquired, a smidge worried. I could not see Mother relinquishing her title from Queen to Queen Mother.

"Then you will stay living here until they do so."

"Is that not like being a prisoner?"

"Either be a prisoner in luxury or be a prisoner in a crumbling home. Either way, as royalty, you are a prisoner one way or another. The choice is yours and Knox's." She picked her nails as she stated this indifferently. I may have grown up in a crumbling home, but Knox did not.

"I could not subject Knox to that kind of poverty lifestyle," was my reply. The corner of her lip quirked a bit at this before she began drawling on with more lessons. My head swam with the constant dump of information. She was attempting to cram all this training in before the wedding in the event my parents did step down from the throne immediately for me. On the off chance they held onto it longer, Queen Serenity planned to take her time training me more thoroughly.

Chapter 30

"I think your dress should be ice blue," Iryse chimed in as I stood on top of a block as the dress designer draped creams and gold dress swatches around me. Iryse was lounging in a chair, in a very un-princess-like manner, while eating chocolates.

"I think pink," Montgomery chimed in as he, too, ate chocolates, leaning back on two legs of his chair.

"You should not even be here," Iryse stated, throwing another piece of chocolate in her mouth.

"Best friends' duty to make sure Mina does not walk down as a complete travesty," he shot back. Tearani, Iryse, and Montgomery were here to help me figure out my dress. It took me some warming up to Montgomery being in the room during my wedding dress fittings, but he added a certain sass level that kept me laughing. I needed it. We had two weeks left until the wedding. Mother and Father would be arriving any day now. The more I had planned prior to Mother's arrival, the better.

"She would look best in a wedding dress of cream with accents of royal blue, blood red, and accents of silver and gold to honor both the kingdom and future queendom," Tearani said while looking out the window.

"Silver and gold? Come on, Tea, one or the other. Not both." Montgomery threw another chocolate into his mouth. The way he and Iryse kept eating those chocolates, we would have to roll them out.

"No. Together. Take two chords and twist them together. It will be perfectly balanced harmony." Tearani did not turn her head away from the window when she replied. I looked at the dressmaker with a questioning look. She simply nodded, taking the fabric swatches with her to collect what Tearani suggested.

The dressmaker was a short, little old lady. Her head barely came up to my shoulder. Her ebony black hair was streaked with silver, and she wore it in a simple bun perfectly centered on the top of her head. She had sharp red eyes with tints of pink. The color was unique on its own, not that I could talk much with my violet eyes. She had porcelain white skin that was peppered with beauty marks that almost looked strategically placed on purpose. Like the one by her right eye and left lip, I noticed another one on her right breast above her fabric line. Even now, I knew she was a great beauty, concealing it with her humbled mannerisms.

The door opened, and Eloise and Stella walked in with fresh refreshments. I spied the blueberry rosemary lemonade, and I could not wait to have a drink from it. I stepped off the block, making my way to them to grab a glass.

"Perfection," I said after taking a drink. Ever since the wedding planner had us try beverages for the wedding, I could not get enough of this lemonade. I craved it. It was so heavenly.

"It is an excellent choice," saluted Iryse as she took her own drink. Tearani left her lemonade untouched. I noticed she was not much of a sweets person. I wondered if Iryse had taken all of the sweet teeth and left none for Tearani. The two did balance each other out when they were together.

The dressmaker came back with the swatches that Tearani suggested. I handed my lemonade glass to Eloise as I resumed my place back on the block. The dressmaker wrapped silk that felt like butter over my shoulders and around my waist. She layered the swatches around with a cord to give an idea. Queen Serenity walked in at that moment.

"Oh, that will look absolutely, splendidly beautiful on our Mina." She clapped her hands, strolling towards us. She took a glass of lemonade off Stella's tray. Taking a sip, she paused to inspect the contents of the lemonade.

"It is blueberry rosemary lemonade," I replied. She glanced up at me, tilting her head back and forth as if weighing something in her thoughts before taking another sip.

"It is good," she finally concluded.

"Are we thinking A-line like the rest of your dresses?" The dressmaker spoke up in a melodic voice, her words flowing together whimsically as she interrupted my focus on Queen Serenity. I had not expected the dressmaker to speak during this whole fitting. When I inquired about her name, she simply rushed out in a low voice, "Dressmaker is good enough." Before she started pulling multiple fabric swatches from her trunk.

"Yes, A-Line fits me best." I smiled at her. She must not have been used to royals directing their smiles at her. Her eyes had widened a fraction as her eyebrows lifted before she went back to work, a bit more ruffled. She began taking measurements of my body.

"Okay. I have my daughter draw up some designs. I come back in two days. You tell me your thoughts on designs, okay? Okay," she spoke so fast in that whimsical, high-pitched tone that I could barely tell apart the words. She began putting fabrics back into her trunk before I could even respond. I blinked, and she was out the door, hauling the trunk in tow like it weighed nothing. I looked at the now-closed door and back to the group left in the room. The Queen let out a chuckle.

"That is Esame for you," Queen Serenity replied to my confusion in an endearing tone.

"Her name is Esame?" I asked.

"Yup. Oldest royal dressmaker in the monarchies." Queen Serenity smiled. I looked back at the door, wondering how old the lady was. I had seen her gnarled hands, the wrinkles on her face, and how she was slightly bent over. I thought it intriguing when the dressmaker arrived as an older lady and not someone young like my wedding planner.

"Does she design your dresses?" I inquired.

"Some of them, yes." Queen Serenity smiled. "I have a few dressmakers on hand for various dresses. Esame is very talented and skilled, but I like to ensure she is happy and has breaks in life, too." I knew The Queen was known for her kindness. I just did not realize it reached these levels when it came to the royal staff.

"Queen Serenity, do you have any dressmakers for myself and Tearani? We would love to have new dresses for the royal wedding," Iyrse inquired. Tearani did not respond to this request.

"I can send Tiviola for you, Iyrse, and I believe Myrese would fit Tearani's style." Queen Serenity nodded her head.

"You ladies have all the fun with new dresses. What do I have? Tuxes that I could change out some jackets to and bow tie colors" complained Montgomery.

"Why are you here, Montgomery?" Queen Serenity asked him.

"Oh, Queen Serenity, did you not know? I am Mina's *number*

one best friend," he said, and I watched as Iryse clenched her hands into fists. Queen Serenity did not miss a beat either as she softly smirked.

"How fortunate for Mina to have five best friends in this room."

"Five?" Montgomery quirked his eyebrow, puzzled by who she was all including.

"Of course, she has you three, but I am quite certain her handmaids are also her best friends as well." Queen Serenity nodded her head in their direction before she added on, "I will be saddened to see you leave, Stella."

"What? Your Highness?" Stella asked, completely alarmed. She probably thought she was being let go. I spoke up to give her the good news.

"I asked Queen Serenity if you could come with me to be my handmaid when I ascend my throne as a queen." I walked towards Stella, reaching my hands forward to take hers. She instantly put the tray of lemonade glasses down on a nearby table. Wiping her hands on her dress, she brought her hands up for mine to take them. "That is, of course, if you would like to stay my handmaid?" I asked. I watched as multiple emotions flashed before her face-- confusion, shock, and surprise until she settled on happiness with tears forming in her eyes. She gripped my hands tightly to steady herself.

"Oh, Mina. . . I would love that," she finally replied, tears beginning to stream down her face. Eloise had put down her lemonade tray to approach us, softly touching Stella's arm. Stella dropped my hands to throw her arms around Eloise, hugging her tightly as she began to cry. Eloise held Stella tightly, swaying back and forth as she mouthed a *Thank you* to me. I nodded, letting them have their moment.

Two days later, the dressmaker returned with stacks of designs of wedding dresses that her daughter had drawn. It was a bit overwhelming. I was surrounded by my friends, each of them collecting their favorite wedding dress designs they believed I should wear.

"Oh, Esame. I do not know how I could simply choose between all these wonderful designs. Please give your daughter my regards," I replied. Esame gave me a startled look, probably for knowing her name this time. There had to be over fifty designs to choose from. How did her daughter have that much time to draw this many dresses? No two dresses were even remotely identical. They were all unique in their own way.

"I believe she should have a ruffled dress; just look at how this cream tulle layers in ruffles with beautiful satin trim at the edges," commented Montgomery, holding up a drawing.

"That dress is perfect. . . for a soiree, but for a wedding?" Iryse wrinkled her nose. "No, she should wear something like this!" Iryse slapped the dress design down on the table. It had red lace sleeves, a sweetheart neckline bodice, and trailed down to a long train with royal blue scalloped edges.

"I believe this one," Tearani replied, calmly placing her pick down on top of her sister's. It was a two-piece wedding dress. The top of the bodice was blood red, with the bottom piece being cream that faded into the royal blue. It had two slits on each side for the legs. Iryse rolled her eyes.

"That is something you would wear." She whined, exasperated.

"I think we finally agree on something, Irysey," said Montgomery.

"How am I ever going to decide?" I placed a hand over my eyes, leaning back in my chair. I was utterly overwhelmed by all this. I had to pick today. The wedding was now less than two weeks away, and they would need to begin making this dress immediately. My parents still had not arrived yet, which caused me to be anxious every second of every day. I was just waiting for Mother to slam open the door.

"What about this one, Mina?" Eloise said quietly as she handed a design to me. I took it from her, looking over the design. It was simply stunning. The top bodice was filled with cream scallops that overlaid royal blue material. The scallops trailed down various places onto the bottom half of the dress. The train was layers upon layers of soft pinks and cream tulle. I already knew if a breeze captured this dress, it would billow beautifully in the wind. Woven amongst the scallops were silver and gold chains.

"Eloise, this is perfect," I breathed, still gazing at the dress with adoration. The others got up from their chairs to gather around behind me to look at the dress, even Tearani. They all murmured their agreements. I looked up to Esame, giving consent that this was the chosen dress. She took the design, gathered up the rest of the sheets, and left without saying another word.

Chapter 31

Hands came up to cover my eyes, causing me to jump. I had been enjoying a quiet pause in my life in the gardens. Somehow, there had been a gap in my schedule from wedding planning and queen training. I was going to take complete advantage of it and enjoy the fresh air before someone wrangled me back for more.

The hands dropped from my face, and I turned to find Knox standing there with a smile. I smiled back easily in reply, tiptoeing up to kiss him on the lips as was expected by me. He returned the kiss, wrapping his arms tightly around me.

"Hello there, my beautiful fiancée." He kissed me again.

"Hey there, yourself." I kissed back.

"We never seem to have a moment of alone time for ourselves anymore," he joked.

"Imagine if you did not help me with the wedding planning with the planner; we would probably only see each other during meals," I jested back. He picked me up, causing me to squeal as he twirled me around in the air. Giddiness began to rise within me.

"Come on then, let us go." He did not put me down as he began walking.

"Where are we going?" I laughed.

"To the rose maze garden, where else? I want some privacy with my fiancée." He continued walking toward the rose maze garden, still carrying me.

"You know, I can walk. My legs are able to do that."

"Yes, but I feel like carrying you there."

"You are carrying me like a child or an animal by just holding me up by the waist." Before I knew what was happening, Knox swung my body weight around to reposition me, his arms now supporting my legs and back.

"There, now I can practice for after we say I do." He winked. I blushed. With each moment we spent together, I found Knox coming out of his shell. He was not as reclusive as he was that first night. Every so often, I would see that scowl come out, but he would calm down with a simple touch of my hand.

The tiny little box that I had locked deep down in my mind creaked open as my thoughts began to drift to Bay and what we had shared. A small part of me felt guilty that I would keep that secret under lock and key. I dreaded our wedding night when I did not reveal to be a virgin. I still was uncertain what I would say if he took notice.

The only time I saw Bay now was at meals if we were both in attendance simultaneously. We barely passed in the halls, and if we did, we greeted each other as if nothing had occurred. The tiny little locked box would break open and tear at my heart each time, but I made my peace and my future as I would tuck it back into place and relock it. I had to remind myself that regardless of my choice, my fate had already been agreed upon to end up with Knox.

I was thankful that I had found a friendship in Knox prior to our father's agreement. I questioned how rocky our life would be if we were to get married and then get to know each other. Granted, I could have multiple lovers, but I really did not know if I wanted that lifestyle either. I had a feeling Knox was a one-and-done for monogamy. I had never really thought about it prior. I had to be honest with myself; I never allowed myself to think about a lot of things before coming here. The twins, Montgomery, and many others helped open my eyes.

"There she is! Our darling daughter!" My mother's voice was like nails on a chalkboard to me as I slightly cringed in Knox's arms. "And with her fiancé nonetheless! How charming!" She purred, but I could hear the venom in her voice. I knew a storm was brewing.

Knox turned us around to face my parents. Father looked pleasantly pleased at seeing us together. On the other hand, Mother had a smile that was a little too big and had no warmth in her eyes. Father's walk was leisurely while Mother practically stalked towards us. I felt Knox grip me a little tighter, protectively.

"I hear congratulations are in order," Father said. There was a twinkle in his eye. When he reached us, he clapped a hand on Knox's shoulder. "Happy to have you as a son-in-law."

"Now, now, dear. They have not said 'I do' yet; let us not get ahead of ourselves," Mother interjected, patting Father on the arm.

"Schematics, Lydia. In my eyes, these two are already married." Father brushed Mother off of him. It was not until being here that I realized how coldly distant my parents were with each other. With what the twins and Eloise had informed me about the true story of their courtship, I was surprised Father had not just divorced my mother and started anew.

"Thank you, King Gideon, that means a lot to me." I felt Knox's chest puff out a bit. It was becoming a bit unsettlingly warm with still being in his arms and out in the sunshine. Mother was staring a hole right through me. I would need to get ahold of the twins and Montgomery to ensure they always stayed by my side from here on out. Eloise and Stella would not be enough; Mother would overrule me until they handed the throne over.

"Where are you two off to?" Mother asked, her face smoothed into an innocently wide-eyed expression.

"Just stealing away a private moment with my soon-to-be wife." Beamed Knox.

"Oh, I was hoping to have a moment with her." Mother began to put on her pouting face. I felt Knox begin to shift a bit on his feet.

"Come now, dear, we were once young. We did not want our parents around. Let us go catch up; I heard some of our friends started arriving early for the wedding." Father began to guide Mother before she could protest. We stood there watching them leave.

"I cannot be left alone with my mother," I said quietly to Knox.

"We will make sure you will not be." Knox began to walk us towards the entrance of the maze. We made it a couple of steps in when I caught Bay walking towards the maze entrance towards us. My heart flipped.

"There is the happy couple," Bay said by way of greeting.

"Hi, Bay," I greeted, ducking my head to try to hide my emotions.

"Hey brother, I have a favor to ask of you." I turned my head to look at Knox curiously.

"What is it, Knox?" Bay raised an eyebrow.

"Mina's parents are here. We cannot let Mina be alone with her mother for one second. Can you please help make certain of that?" My heart did not know whether to drop at the implication of Bay chaperoning me places or to swell at the kindness of Knox looking out for me. Bay's face went from ease to concern immediately.

"We cannot have that. Let us gather everyone involved to devise a plan to make sure that does not occur." Bay became serious as I could see his mind begin to work. Knox began to lower me until I stood back on my two feet again. Bay watching intently.

"Let us go round up the others." Knox took my hand to lead me back to the castle. Bay came up to take my other hand; my heart flipped again. I looked at him, and he shrugged nonchalantly and kept walking.

Chapter 32

The night before my wedding, I sat in my bathroom tub alone. I sank lower in the warm, sudsy water. I was not confident I could pull this off. I became doubtful with Mother in attendance that things would go correctly. I knew she would try to ruin something.

I would be lying if I told myself that my feelings for Knox had not grown since our engagement. I had not witnessed him shut down once, and I wondered if I had exaggerated all those interactions. I knew I had not, but he had been nothing but doting.

I pulled my knees up to my chest, wrapping my arms around them. I rested my head on the top of my exposed knees from the water, ignoring how they made my face wet. I was not sure I could contain that tiny little box anymore. I had found myself alone with Bay in the last week and a half more than I cared to admit. The tears began trailing down my cheeks, blending into the water of the tub. I couldn't stop myself as the sobs racked through my body.

Chapter 33

I began to march up the aisle, all eyes on me. It was overwhelming. *Do not trip; do not stumble—slow, steady steps.* I took as many deep, slow breaths as I possibly could. I became grateful for having a veil covering my face. It helped block out some of the view of every pair of eyes on me. *Please, just do not stumble.* They were calling this the wedding of the century. The last thing I needed to be documented was myself tripping.

The wealthiest kingdom's prince marrying the poorest kingdom's princess. Then, the impoverished kingdom's princess turning her own kingdom into a queendom. Two parents who were friends from their courting season uniting their children when the time came for their own courting season. All the monarchies were attending. I glanced down at my bouquet of Casablanca white lilies and smiled to myself. I looked back up.

The crowds of people blocked my view from seeing Knox at the end of the aisle, but I knew he was there waiting for me. Each step brought me closer to him. Closer to my saying 'I do' to being his wife and launching the next step of my life as queen to my future queendom. I may not be ready to rule just yet, but the guidance and wisdom Queen Serenity has given me this past month has helped immensely.

My eyes landed on my parents. My mother still did not have a chance for alone time with me since the day they arrived. I knew it infuriated her, but friends stepped up to protect me. Tearani especially was quite comical a few times. I noticed that Mother became quite unnerved when dealing with Tearani and avoided trying if the twin was in the room with me, which became quite frequent.

Tearani's parents announced that they would relinquish their throne to her when she was ready to rule it as a queendom. I like to think that Mother avoided Tearani because the twin unnerved Mother with her silent, emotionless stares. It probably did not help matters with Tearani ascending to be queen; she now outranked Mother as more than just a current princess.

I kept taking steps, keeping my balance so as not to trip until there he was. He shifted on his feet. The moment he caught sight of me, the biggest smile I had ever seen from him broke upon his face. I almost tripped, slightly stumbling as I caught myself. I heard a few surrounding guests' gasps, my cheeks inflamed. I hoped this veil blocked my face out as much as it blocked them out.

I ascended a couple of steps to stand directly across from Knox. He looked rather handsome in his tux. He had cast aside his standard black attire to adorn his kingdom's colors. His tux jacket was blood red and accompanied by royal blue pants. The jacket was full of golden swirls of intricate designs that trailed from the waist up and began again from the sleeves upwards. His regular long, shaggy hair was swept back away from his face. He shifted on his feet again before he leaned in slightly.

"You look beautiful," he whispered to me. I warmed from his compliment.

"You look handsome yourself," I whispered back. I looked past his shoulder to see Bay standing there, watching me, and my heart missed a beat. Internally, I shook my head, not allowing that tiny little box to come unlocked again as I directed my focus back to Knox and our wedding. My mind began to wander, not focusing on the wedding, and the next thing I knew, we were reciting our vows.

"I, Princess Persamina Rowena of Kingdom Theorines, take thee, Prince Killien Knox of Kingdom T'Lovoness, as my lawfully wedded husband. To love, to hold, through sickness and health," I recited.

"I, Prince Killien Knox of Kingdom T'Lovoness, take my beloved, Princess Persamina Rowena of soon-to-be Queendom Theorines, to be my lawfully beloved wedded wife. I will love and hold you through sickness and health, through any struggle that we may endure. For I am your beloved as you are mine," Knox incited. I did not realize he took liberties to make his wedding vows to me to be more personal.

Knox lifted my veil for us to share our first kiss as husband and wife. His lips were soft on mine. The applause around us became a deafening roar. I broke the kiss, ducking my head to my chest, blushing.

"Come on," Knox whispered encouragingly as he grabbed my hand to lead us back down the aisle. He began to pick up pace until we were running out the doors. It was not very princess-like, but it caused me to giggle and be slightly less nervous as giddiness took over.

We slowed our pace in the hall, his hands circling my waist as he picked me up, twirling us around. I looked down at his smiling face as he looked up at mine. Slowly, he brought me down until my lips were on his, and he kissed me back. We had mere moments until the rest of the guests would be filing out into the hallway. I needed this moment of us time to help ground me before the ball.

Knox broke the kiss and took my hand, beginning to walk as I followed him. "Come on, let us get to the ballroom to claim our place at the head table. Our guests can get a head start on congratulating us, then we can enjoy our time together sooner, wife." He smiled. He led us to the ballroom, and when the servants opened up the double doors for us, it took away my breath. All the decision-making this past month was worth seeing it decorated like this. It would never have looked this beautiful if Knox had not stepped in to ensure I had gotten my way.

Everything was gold with white Casablanca lilies and white fluffy ostrich feathers sewn about in arrangements. The banners and sways were in a light lavender coloring with mint green weaved within the designs. There were little pops of sapphire blues. The room looked like something straight out of a fairytale, with the pastels balanced with the bold colors.

Knox walked us to the head of the table to claim our seats. Fresh blueberry rosemary lemonade was brought to us immediately, and both of us took a refreshing drink.

"This is simply marvelous," complimented Knox.

"Trust me, I know. Ever since my first taste of it at our beverage tasting, I have been craving it every day. I am pretty certain at this point the kitchen staff has a pitcher made of it at all moments for me," I joked. Whenever I asked Eloise or Stella to fetch me a glass, they were back rather quickly compared to my other requests from the kitchen.

"I can see why," he commented, taking another sip. That seemed to be the resounding response to my choice of drink. It pleased me that I had picked something everyone else enjoyed.

The guests began milling in, and I hardly recognized anyone who had not been a part of the courting season. I started putting together parents to their children that I knew. They extended their congratulations and best wishes to us as they passed by.

I caught sight of Regina trailing behind her mother, Queen Fairness. I shifted in my chair uneasily. I had not seen Regina since the night I passed out in the corridor. I felt Knox's hand rest on my leg, giving it a light squeeze. As Queen Fairness gave us her congratulations, it became evident that Montgomery received his flamboyant personality from his mother. She made me want to become her best friend instantly. It made me wonder how Regina turned out the way she did. Queen Fairness passed by, and Regina stood directly before us.

"Congratulations to the happy newlyweds," Regina bit out. We nodded at her in our way of thanks. Montgomery was directly behind her with his dashing, devilish smile. I could only hope when he found a spouse, they would make him eat their heart out. He needed someone to give him a run for his money.

"Mina, you look absolutely magnificent," he complimented, his eyes flicking to Knox. "Knox, please take care of my precious Mina." After a month of Montgomery hanging around Knox and wedding planning, Knox seemed to have grown used to Montgomery and his mannerisms. He did not bristle; instead, he chuckled.

"You need not fret; I will take exceptionally good care of her," he promised Montgomery.

"Good, good. Congratulations to you both. Just please make sure Mina and I still have our chocolate and wine nights." Montgomery winked before following suit of Regina, who had already disappeared from our table.

"He will always keep us on our toes, will he not?" Knox asked me.

"You have no idea," I laughed.

The guests kept coming through with congratulations, and I became more nervous about our first dance. Knox and I had been practicing for weeks on a specially choreographed dance. Our dance would be solely unique to us and our wedding, and everyone would be watching in awe of what it would look like.

As the last guest came through for congratulations and everyone was seated, our food was brought to us. I felt nauseous. The moment we stopped eating, Knox would be leading me out to the center of the dance floor.

"You will do fine," Knox said as he leaned over to me. He knew how nervous I was. "Just focus on me like we have done in each one of our rehearsals. Everything will just melt away, and it will just be the two of us." I nodded my head, forcing myself to take another bite of the food.

I felt like I blinked and then Knox was leading us out on the dance floor.

Deep breaths, Mina, deep breaths. My breathing became shallow and quick. I can do this. Think of how beautifully this dress will flow with each twirl and spin from Knox. We arrived at the center of the dance floor as the musicians began the song created for this dance.

"Deep breath, my beloved Mina," Knox whispered before he raised my left hand to above our heads for me to walk under, following through into a circle as I came to face him. His left hand extended straight out behind him, and I rolled up into his right arm. His left hand came down on my shoulder as he cradled us with a slight rock before he unrolled me from his arms and led me immediately into a three-spin twirl. Catching my right hand, we began our in-sync steps. Three forward, one backward, with twists, turns, and twirls mingled within. We sped up pace with the rise of tempo and then slowed down as the music slowed to rise back up again.

Knox had been correct; everything had melted away as my body fell into muscle memory from all the practices we had done. When the last note dropped, we stopped in the middle of the dance floor with each other breathing heavily, facing each other. Both of us were smiling at what we had accomplished. The room fell into silence. I bet we could hear a pin drop, and then the applause and some cheers broke out. I recognized Iryse's cheer amongst the crowd.

Realization sunk in that I was officially married.

Chapter 34

As the evening of our wedding concluded, Knox and I walked back to his rooms hand in hand. We decided to live in his wing of the castle until we moved to Theorines. My items would begin being moved into his rooms this week. *I guess I should start calling them our rooms.* I would also need to memorize the pattern of how to arrive to his chambers. I had never stepped foot into them. I was uncertain of what I would expect.

A servant stood outside what I presumed would be Knox's rooms, opening the door for us. The room was in shades of black, gray, and dark blue. The wood furniture was stained black and had either black or dark smoke-gray cushions on top of it. Even the curtains were dark gray with swirling black patterns weaving up them. One wall was lined with bookcases filled with books; it was like Knox had a personal library within his own room.

"You can change it if you do not like it?" He offered, scratching the back of his head as we paused at the entrance.

"It is fine, and I am sure we will make it our own. But it has been your bedroom your whole life, and I am not about to overhaul it," I responded.

"Our bedroom, I am willing to make the changes necessary to make it ours," he countered. I warmed in happiness at him, trying to make me feel welcomed. We could be living here for weeks, months, or even years. Father never let on when he would relinquish the throne. I already knew he would decide it on his own without even telling Mother. We all would be caught unaware when he chose his moment to make the announcement.

He continued to hold my hand as he led us to the bedroom. I was nervous and tried not to slow down in pace to reflect it. His bedroom looked identical to his main room, all grays and blacks, with more books in bookcases. His big bay window curtains were closed, cloaking the room in what would have been complete darkness if not for the main room's light filtering in through the door behind us. The bed was massive, bigger than mine or even Bay's. I was utterly astounded.

"Your bed is quite large," I commented. He chuckled.

"I actually requested to have a larger bed for us to share. . . I knew it would probably be awkward with us sharing a bed at first, and I did not want us to be sleeping on top of each other." He scratched the back of his head.

"That was . . . kind of you, Knox." I smiled up at him. Despite the darkness, I was pretty certain I saw him smiling in return.

"Do you need help getting out of your dress?" He asked nervously.

"Yeah, you just need to undo the corset and buttons in the back. It will come off easy enough from there," I replied, letting go of his hand to turn my back to him. I felt his deft fingers struggle to undo the back of my dress. I stood there waiting patiently, with my nerves building with what would come next.

Ten minutes later, I could finally breathe with the dress loose enough to step out of. I draped it over a chair lest it become wrinkled. I removed the crinoline and hoop skirt until I wore only my black wedding lingerie and black silk tights for Knox. I had argued with a few about the color choice, but I knew Knox would appreciate it.

I clasped my hands behind my back as I turned back to face him. I had not heard him take steps closer to me; the thick carpet must have muffled the noise. He stood before me, and I had to look up into his face. I bounced up and down on the balls of my feet to release some of the nervous energy that was forming. He had removed his tux jacket and shirt. He stood there bare-chested. I never realized how muscular Knox was under all his clothes. My stomach clenched.

His hands reached up to cradle my face as he leaned down to kiss me on the lips. I kissed him back softly as desire began to course through me as he deepened the kiss, raking his fingers through my hair. I wrapped my arms around his neck before he took a step back, and I followed him step for step toward the bed.

His fingers left my hair to trail down my body, slightly bending us, his fingers gripped into my upper thighs as he hauled me up. I wrapped my legs around his waist, his tongue sliding into my mouth, and mine danced back. I anticipated us falling onto the bed, but he braced me against one of the spiraled bed pillars closest to us instead. With one hand still holding me, his other hand worked to undo his pants, letting them drop to the floor. I felt flesh on flesh. It startled me that he had been without undergarments this whole time.

"Sorry," he mumbled, breaking the kiss. "I do not like wearing undergarments. . . I hope that is not a problem?" He gave me a slight grin, and I felt his fingers squeeze a bit harder into my thigh.

"That's okay, it just took me by surprise, is all," I rushed out. My voice was higher pitched than I had meant for it to be before a nervous laugh escaped me. He slightly chuckled in return. Slowly, he lowered me back down on both of my feet.

"I am not certain what came over me, heat of the moment?" He offered, standing naked against me.

"Well, I currently feel a bit overdressed compared to you," I teased, trying to lighten the mood. His eyes sparked.

"I do like the black," he commented.

"Would look better on the floor," I flirted back, noticing his cock twitch at the thought as he gulped. His fingers began undoing the lingerie. It was a bit clumsy at first, but I was now naked against him, only wearing my silk black stockings.

"Leave those; I like those," he requested. I nodded my head, my breathing coming in a bit quicker.

"Should we resume on the bed?" I asked hesitantly.

"Yeah. . . yeah, we should." He watched me crawl onto the bed first before he crawled onto it next to me. "I have never . . . I have never done this before," he confessed. In the dim lighting, I could see him blushing profusely.

"That is okay, it will be okay," I said, trying to comfort his nerves. "Truth be told, I am just as nervous as you are." My confession seemed to have calmed him. He rolled over on top of me, kissing me. *I guess we were done with talking.*

I repositioned my legs to be around his hips and felt the head of his cock barely touching my entrance as he kissed me. He deepened the kiss, and as he did so, the head of his cock slid up my folds, and he grinded against me, moaning into my mouth. He continued grinding, creating a friction of pleasure on my clit with each pass from the head of his cock. He pulled back a bit too far that when he pushed forward, I felt the head of his cock pushing into me. I gasped, breaking the kiss.

"I will take it slow," he whispered, promising me. I inhaled, preparing myself as he pushed himself into me more. I felt the stretch from his cock, and I whimpered. "It's okay, Mina, it's okay," he continued to whisper. He was unaware that this was not my first time. I found it sweet that he was trying to comfort me.

He pulled slightly back out, causing me to relax from the sting of his girth. "Mina, I need you to relax; the pain will be gone in a second. Just trust me," Knox promised. I nodded my head, relaxing, not prepared for him to thrust fully into me. I cried out from the unexpected intrusion within me.

"There, there, sweet Mina, give it a few seconds," he comforted as I adjusted to him being fully seated within me. I took steadying breaths, trying to relax again. "Are you good? Do you feel okay?" He asked. I nodded my head in response. He kissed my forehead before pulling slightly out and pushing back in.

"Mina, you feel amazing. I am not going to last with how tight you are," he gasped as he picked up his rhythm. He trusted a few more times before stilling with a gasp. *Was it over?* "That was amazing," he moaned, collapsing on top of me and breathing heavily.

His cock softened, withdrawing from me, and I felt his warm hot seed begin to leak out of me. He rolled off of me, and I lay there trying to make sense of everything, trying desperately not to compare him to his brother.

"Your turn," he chirped.

"What?" I asked, startled out of my own thoughts.

"Your turn to orgasm." He smiled at me before shimming his way down my body, with his head in between my legs. I was not expecting this, hoping for it? Absolutely, but I thought we were done.

His tongue began to trail in between my folds; finding my clit he began sucking hard. His teeth grazing and nibbling. I jerked into his face, not anticipating the feeling. My orgasm began to stir against his mouth. I started grinding my hips, chasing the build that was growing. My hands dug into the sheets as I arched my back. He nipped again, and I came undone. Wave after wave coursing through me. *I have never cum that fast.*

Pleased with himself as my orgasm subsided, he crawled back up alongside me. Knox rolled us onto our right sides as he snuggled me to him. His arms wrapped around me tightly. "You are magnificent, my wife," Knox complimented. It was not long until I heard his breathing slow down, and he was asleep.

I managed to untangle myself from his arms. I slid out of the enormous bed, and finding a black robe of his, I shrugged it on before heading out to the main rooms. The servants must have dropped off a pitcher of my favorite lemonade as I poured a glass. I took it over to the enormous armchair by the big bay windows that led out to the balcony. Looking out the window, I let my mind wander.

I did not know what I had expected with Knox. My only experience was with his brother, which may have set the bar a bit too high in some respects. I was sore from Knox's cock. His girth and length would take some time getting used to. Something was missing. I did not want to admit it to myself. Squeezing my eyes shut, I tried to block it out. But not even in the darkness of my mind could I keep out the vision of blue eyes.

Chapter 35

Three days later, Mother cornered me in the library. Being newly wedded to Knox had made it easy to always have someone with me. However, today, Knox had to run to do something, and I thought if I snuck to the library, it would be a place she would never think to look for me.

"Mina, I would like to have a word with you," Mother stated in a flat tone. My stomach dropped as my fingers paused on the book covers I had been trailing them on.

"Yes, Mother?" I asked, not facing her. I concentrated on the books in front of me, trying to read the titles on the spine, but I couldn't focus.

"Turn around to face me when I am speaking to you, or have you forgotten all your training," she jabbed. Dropping my hand back to my side, I slowly turned around to face her. My toes curled and uncurled in my shoes as my stomach clenched.

"You have been avoiding me," she stated bluntly.

"I have not," I countered. She narrowed her eyes at my lie.

"Do not lie to me. I am very well aware that you always have an entourage surrounding you."

"Are you mad because I have friends who want to be with me?" I shot back at her. She rolled her eyes, shaking her head.

"Friends? They are just using you as a means for entertainment and to get a stake in the wealth you now hold. They do not want anything to do with the real you." She laughed with her sharp words. A small part of me considered listening to what she was saying, but I knew it could not be further from the truth.

"You are wrong, Mother." I boldly stood my ground. She cocked her head, probably not expecting me to speak up against her.

"Oh? Just make sure that Grewt'en boy does not get you impregnated with his child," she shot back. I shook my head in startlement—*the audacity she had*.

"Excuse me?! What is that supposed to mean?!" My voice rising.

"Exactly as I stated. You are to be married to Bay. We do not need any Grewt'en brats running amongst us as imposter heirs," she spat back.

"For your information, I am *not* sleeping with Montgomery. He is my friend and nothing more," I huffed out a breath. Mother hummed with another roll of her eyes.

"Fine, keep your little lies to yourself. But a mother always knows the truth." She cocked an eyebrow, daring me to deny her statement.

"Since I am now destined to become Queen of Theorines, I can have as many brats from whichever lover I so choose. Or have you forgotten the way a queendom works, Mother?" I mirrored her expression. *I would not play this game.* Her eyes narrowed more with pursed lips.

"Now, you have had your fun with the spare prince. That time needs to come to an end," my mother seethed, taking steps towards me. My back was already pressed against the bookcase. She stood directly in front of me, glaring. "Terminate your marriage. You were raised to be married to Prince Rafael Baylor, the heir of T'Lovoness."

"I will not, Mother!" I gasped. The wheel had already been set into motion for my life, and I needed Knox's dowry to save my home. "Your dreams with my future are over. I am married to Knox, I will rule Theorines, and I will repair what you have destroyed during your reign, Mother," I spat back at her. There was nothing Bay could do for my home. There was nothing he could do for me. *Lies.*

She took a step back, her eyes widening. I had never talked back; I was frightened of her as a child. I would no longer allow her to ever hurt myself or Eloise. We were protected here and would continue to be when I ascended the throne into my new title.

"How dare you, you ungrateful little brat. I did everything for you. I gave up everything for you. And this. . . This is the thanks I receive?" She threw her hands up in the air, accusing me.

"Everything for me? Gave up everything for me?! You threw our kingdom into bankruptcy over your own gluttony!" I fired back the truth at her. The redness in her neck crept up to her face. I knew from experience this was pure rage.

"After every single thing I have done in *my* life and the sacrifices I have made . . . the things I gave up against my will . . . I do not know what I did to deserve a daughter like you!" She tried to make a jab at me, but I disregarded it.

"Maybe you should take a look in your mirror. I care for Knox, and I will stay married to him. When Father decides to hand the throne to me, I will ascend and become Queen. You will just be the Queen's Mother, and I will have a say in your future. So, mind your tone." I leveled my gaze at her as I took a step forward.

"Pfft, you would have a far better life with the older brother." It was only momentarily that fear flashed before her eyes, but she covered it up with a roll of her eyes. "You don't know what you are settling for. You're blinded. Deluded."

"No, you're the deluded one, Mother." I took another step towards her. She stood her ground. I kept taking steps until I was standing directly in front of her. "No matter what you say to me, it will not change my mind. I am married to Knox, and that is final." I moved to walk past her, but she halted me as she gripped my wrist tightly, yanking me back to her.

"You will regret this, little girl," she threatened, digging her nails into my skin.

"Release me," I gritted my teeth from the pain she was causing me.

"Mark my words; if you don't marry Prince Rafael Baylor, you will regret everything I have worked for." She gripped my arm even harder. I tried to jerk out of her grip, but my attempts were feeble.

"I don't know why you are so hung up on this, but you need to let it go. Now release me," I warned, trying to shake out of her grip again.

"You wretched child, I don't know where I went wrong with you," she spat, "I will find a way to end this. Mark my words." She raised her free hand. I squeezed my eyes shut at the same time and flinched, bracing for impact. The strike never came. I waited a second before hesitantly opening my eyes up to see Bay standing beside me, her hand in his grasp. When we made eye contact, I felt his hand come up to rest on my hip with a soft squeeze to check if I was okay.

"P-Prince Rafael B-Baylor," Mother stuttered.

"I would suggest you release your grip on Mina." Bay's voice was cold and hard as steel. Mother looked at her hand on my arm. She gripped it tighter one last time before dropping it, letting her nails drag down my arm. I hissed from the pain, jerking away into Bay's body. The hand on my hip wrapped around my waist, pulling me closer to him in a protective hold.

"Release your grip on me, Prince Rafael Baylor." Mother squared her shoulders, tilting her chin upwards to exude her authority. Bay scoffed as he threw her hand to the side.

"I suggest you turn around and leave this room." Bay may have suggested it, but it came out as a direct order. Mother's eyes widened a fraction, her eyes bouncing between Bay, myself, and Bay's protective arm wrapped around my waist. I knew she was getting the wrong idea. She nodded and left without a word. I relaxed a bit into Bay.

"Your mother is . . . intense," he finally said. I laughed.

"You have no idea . . . That, however, is the worst I have ever seen her."

"You know I heard everything," he stated calmly and quietly. I tried to move away from him, but his grip tightened on my waist, trapping me to him.

"Bay!" I began to protest with more struggle.

"No. I want you to listen to me," Bay said in that same calm and quiet tone next to my ear. When I stopped struggling, he slightly loosened his grip. "I will make sure you are never unprotected like that again. I promise you, you are none of the things your mother stated about you. You are so much more."

"Bay?" I questioned him, turning my head to look up at his face. His eyes catching mine.

"I promise."

"That seems like an impossible thing to promise when you will not always be by me."

"Do not worry about that, Mina." I was uncertain of how to respond. *How could I not worry about the bold statement and promise he gave me.*? He gave me one last squeeze before he released his hold. I stepped out of his arms, turning to him.

"Bay. . .?" I questioned, looking at him, confused.

"I lied to you the morning after. I apologize for that," he said, not breaking eye contact as my heartbeat began to accelerate. The tiny little box cracking open.

"You lied?" I questioned, hope bubbling within me.

"About wanting to marry you." We watched each other cautiously with his confession. I bit my lip, not missing how his eyes tracked the movement.

"Bay, I . . ." I did not even know how to respond.

"I am not trying to start anything. I just wanted you to know that is all. Your happiness is all I want." Bay nodded his head as he turned and walked out of the library, leaving me to stand there alone.

<h1 style="text-align:center">One Year Later</h1>

I sipped on my blueberry rosemary lemonade while enjoying one of my life's rare peaceful moments. Someone always needed me for something any more, and the silence was beyond welcomed at this point. I heard the door to my future library open, and I shut my eyes, preparing for what would be needed of me now.

"Queen Mina, you should not be in here!" admonished one of the men we hired to help with the reconstruction of our castle. His name was Max, and he was a good work hand with the construction, but I was unable to break him of the habit of calling me 'Queen.' I was still becoming used to the title, myself. . . But at the very least, I was able to convince the majority of the people to just call me Mina.

Knox's dowry was being put to good use; we were bringing my queendom out of debt. We paid our workers exceptionally well to help with their future. This had all been put into motion when I had announced my pregnancy to my parents. Father did not hesitate to hand the throne over to me to rule. He wanted to see a new generation be brought in. Mother stood by with pursed lips; I had anticipated for her to put up a fight. Some days, I still anticipate her to, but they were on an extended vacation, traveling and visiting friends. I chose to gift Father some funds to, at the very least, get out of my hair.

"Very well, Max. You have been doing exceptional work." I bid him to have a good day as I left the room to head to the nursery. My pregnancy had not been a complicated one, but it brought new fears of its own with it. My daughter had been born in the dead of night one month too soon. She was healthy, with a strong pair of lungs on her to let the world know she had arrived. I already knew she would be keeping my hands full.

I reached the nursery and opened the door. There sat Knox, rocking my whole world in his arms. He glanced up at me, his green eyes in a state of wonder, awe, and love. Every time he looked at her, it was as if he was looking at her for the first time. I made my way towards them. Placing my hand on the familiar butterfly flutters in my stomach, I smiled down at my precious baby girl, my Rohanna Myrcella.

Sneak Peek!

Come read a sneak peek into Book 2, *A Queendom of Heartbreak and Sorrow*. The story of how Serenity went from a Lord's daughter in love with a stable boy to being The Queen of the largest and wealthiest monarchy. Coming Spring 2025!

A Queendom of Heartbreak and Deceit

CHAPTER 1

Giggles filled the rafters of the stable. I knew we ought to be quieter, but I could not help it. He had me wrapped in his arms, and I could not stop smiling when I was with him. Anyone passing by would easily hear us if we kept it up, and if Father heard about it, my plans would be for naught.

I knew Father would not approve of my wishes to marry a stable boy, but I have been determined in my research to convince him otherwise. Despite Father's ambitions for there to not be a divide between the common people and us, I was certain he would never allow his eldest daughter to marry so lowly beneath her social status as a lady.

"You know it's true." Theo joked. His golden-brown eyes danced with laughter. I loved how when the sunlight hit his eyes, they turned a warm honey shade. Another laugh escaped my lips before I could stop it; I was certain he was teasing.

"I highly doubt Millie is visiting Crogs Hallow." I shook my head; it was an absurd idea. Crogs Hallow was a rough neighboring village; it was more of a traveler's stop than anything else. It had a tavern attached to an inn with a stable and a tiny bakery. Many of the villagers set up stands along the road to sell their wares to travelers. Every time we passed through it, I only noticed the smell of dead fish and dampness.

I never understood why anyone would want to set up a business in the location, let alone live there, when Fayers Village was just a little bit down the road from it. Fayers had brick-lined roads and businesses in abundance. Unfortunately, for us to get to Fayers, we had to travel through Crogs Hallow. I suppose sellers making a quick coin had better luck selling at Crogs Hallow since there were no market stands in Fayers.

Theo brought my attention back to him. "She sneaks out any chance she can get. It's why her mannerism has become quite . . . Interesting."

"That is just the way Millie is, she has always been . . . interesting," I argued. Millie was a nice girl, but she was definitely peculiar. Frequently, I caught her spacing out or not paying attention. Once, while she had been sent to pick apples, I had been riding by on my horse to see her dangling upside down in the tree, just swinging away for fun. She did not have a care in the world to show off her underlings. Anytime I tried to talk to her, she would blatantly ignore me.

"Kitchen life is not enough for her; she wants to perform."

"Perform what?" I inquired. It made me wonder what a simple kitchen servant could perform. Would she perform baking or cooking for the citizens of Crogs Hallow? Father kept the village well supplied and protected, but it was not lavish. It was nothing compared to Fayers, Dentriea, or Altura.

Twice a year, Father would escort the family through Crogs Hallow to attend the Spring and Winter Solstice in either Dentriea or Altura. He would make a purposeful stop in Crogs Hallow for a bit; he claimed he wanted us not to be strangers to the common people. He wanted to teach us humbleness and hospitality, things we could not learn within the manor as Lord's children. As a child, I enjoyed the trips. Now, at twenty, I attended out of expectation.

"She performs by dancing and singing," Theo responded seriously.

"Singing? Where did Millie learn to sing?" I asked, astonished.

"At the local tavern, *The Sandy Hook,* which is also where she performs, by the way," Theo tacked on. This started as jesting and joking, but I was beginning to realize Theo knew quite a bit more, and it made me wonder how he knew this much about Millie.

"Let us change the topic, shall we?" I was growing weary of hearing about Millie. Theo and I only ever received stolen moments together lest we spend the stolen moment talking about another female or trivial things that did not matter.

"What shall we change it to M'lady?" Teased Theo. I smiled, rolling my eyes at him as I pretended to push out of his arms. Despite all the times I have told him not to be formal with me, he still did it to ruffle my feathers. "Does M'lady have a topic in mind . . . or maybe." Theo's hands began trailing down my hips as he took a step closer to me. "Maybe, M'lady would like me to please her." Theo leaned down and kissed me softly. I wrapped my arms around his neck to pull him closer to me and deepen the kiss. I did not understand how I had not noticed Theo all these years past, but he had become all I had known for the last year.

A horse neighed outside the stable, and we instantly pulled apart. I ran to my chair, grabbed the book, and pretended to read from the light streaming through the window. Theo grabbed the pitchfork and began mucking the horse stalls. Seconds later, Father was strolling through the stable doors.

"There you are, Serenity," he said by way of greeting. I looked up at him with an innocent smile as if I had been reading here all morning. "Theo." He nodded his head as way of greeting, passing by Theo to stand before me.

"Father, how are you today?" My heart raced from the

exhilaration and fear of almost being caught. Thankfully, the watch horse neighed in time, a few seconds later, and we would have been caught. There was a time when the watch horse annoyed me with its constant neighs every time someone passed by, but now I was grateful.

"I am quite well, Daughter." He glanced at my book before looking around the stable and back at me. "I will never understand why you choose to read in the stables when there is a library and other places within the manor to read." He glanced over at Theo, my heart quickening before he looked back at me. I doubt Father would suspect.

"I like the smell of the horses, Father,"

"Really?" He took a deep breath in, his nose wrinkling a bit.

"When the stables are fully cleaned." I laughed. Theo had become quite distracted in his chores when I arrived. Usually, the stables smelled far better than this. I loved the smell of the horses mingled with fresh hay and the leather saddles hanging on the wall.

"I suppose so." He nodded, accepting my response.

"Was there something you needed, Father?" I asked, wishing he would go away. I tucked my bookmark between the pages of the book, letting it rest on my lap.

"No, no. I just had not seen you about the manor and wondered where you had run off to," he replied, eyeing my book. "What are you reading today?"

"History of the Six Monarchies by Ser Rylei Doaka of House Kalka. I only began it today." I stood up, preparing to preen under Father's compliments.

"Ah, a dull read but the most accurate on the topic. Bit of a long read as well." He glanced at the book again as I held it in my arms, squeezing it to my chest. The book was relatively thick at over eight hundred pages, filled with in-depth knowledge along with beautifully penned illustrations for house banners, symbols, plants, and whatever the artist desired to draw.

"I don't know if I would call it dull. It can be quite fascinating," I countered.

"Fascinating?" He chuckled. "Only you would find it fascinating. Tell me, why are you interested in reading all the historical texts? Your sisters prefer their romance novels, and your brothers do not read at all unless I forced them to."

"I like comparing the texts. It helps me see similarities and where each author focuses their efforts. For example, Taurok focuses more on the way of living for the classes, while Blaisi takes an interest in trade. Kakda has a fascination with the death of each royalty and houses; she goes into a bit of detail on even how to make the specific poisons . . ."

"Should I bar you from the kitchens? Will you be making your own poisons, Daughter?" Father raised an amused eyebrow at me. I laughed, shaking my head.

"No, no. As I was saying, Father, each historian has a predominant focus, some in-depth, other's surface level. I am collecting each reading to layer together. I want to understand the ultimate history of them all." I felt the passion bubbling up within me. This little task began at first for finding Ladies who married below their rank, but now it has turned into a more enormous feat.

"And what do you plan to do with the knowledge of all this history that no one has done prior to you?" It was evident I was Father's favorite amongst his five children. I was the only one who took an interest in historical texts like him. I enjoyed philosophical banter, and I have never disappointed him.

"I want to write the most completed history book of all time with a combination of all of these texts, minus the fluff," I replied.

"Fluff?" He questioned, his expression amused to see where I was taking this.

"Blaisi goes on and on for paragraphs to sometimes pages about what the trader's travels were like. I am not interested in the great details of the storms that prevented sea travel or how broken wagon wheels came about. That Father is fluff."

"Ah, I see now. Yes, Blaisi can be quite extensive in his details, but what better way to understand the issues that merchants, traders, and travelers deal with on a regular basis? I am a Lord in Grewt'en; you have been fortunate to be born my daughter and not have to know these struggles.

"I suppose so, father," I replied, pretending to mull it over. "Is there anything else, or may I resume my reading?" I asked. I wanted him to leave, but I did not want him to suspect it. He eyed me thoughtfully for a moment and then shook his head.

"No, I just had been wondering where you had been. Come along, let us head up to the house. Theo has chores to do." Father commented, offering me his arm. I withheld my sigh as I repositioned to holding the book in my left arm while sliding my right arm into his.

As we walked past Theo, I looked at him longingly. He smiled with an understanding look. Someday, and I hoped soon, I could have him all to myself.

Hello Reader! I am beyond happy that you have made it this far! I wanted to leave a little note about my debut novel *A Kingdom of Promises and Lies* from my series *The Courting Seasons*. When I first began writing *A Kingdom of Promises and Lies*, I had full intentions of it being a standalone novel when I first put pen to paper (literally) on March 5, 2023 to write the scene of Chapter 4. I am not certain why of all the scenes I had to first get out of my head was Eloise giving Mina advice to create a distraction to gain Bay's attention, but sometimes you just have to roll with the punches, lol.

It was not until I was writing more of the love triangle between Bay, Knox and Mina mixed in with Mina's parents visiting that I realized I wanted to write more to the world. I wanted to give all of my characters more depth, more hidden motives and personality. I wanted to flesh out the side characters and not allow them to be 2-D like. I wanted not only myself, but for readers to know my character's quirks when they read their books. I, at one point, thought about making Mina book 2 or 3 to flesh out a different character, but I still feel she is a good neutral starting point to the world.

My intentions for each book are, they can be read as a standalone . . . but there will be some loose strings to each one. Book 2, *A Queendom of Heartbreak and Deceit* is Serenity's story (Bay & Knox's mom). There will be some loose strings tied up in that one, but also more strings created for other books. Serenity's book is also where you will have a deeper dive into the history and cultural of this world. I have always loved world building books, but hated the boring info dump that can occur, hoping I did a decent balance with what I felt the reader needed to know in book 1.

I already have plans in the works of which character book 3 and 4 will be and have been arguing with myself about who I believe should be book 5, lol. That is as far as I have gotten for the order, even as each character has a little shelf in my mind for ideas with their story. Fun Fact, I have majority of the last book in the series wrote, but I won't tell you whose book it is. Mind you, I still cannot believe I decided to take a standalone novel idea and create this very complex series, but yet here we are.

Thank you once again for taking the time to read my book, you will never know how much it means to me to have another individual know about the world and characters I have created!

-N. F. Schmitt

Acknowledgments

Thank you, everyone, for reading Mina's story in my debut novel, A Kingdom of Promises and Lies, part of *The Courting Seasons* series. I hope you fall in love with reading this series as much as I have fallen in love with writing and creating it.

Cody: Thank you for being a wonderful husband and best friend through the years. From being my high school sweetheart to the person I love to spend time with daily, your constant support means everything to me.

My Parents: Thank you for being the two to support and encourage my love for reading since childhood. Especially you Mom for being the reason I fell in love with historical romance in the first place. (I blame you for my love of Fabio covers as well, lol!)

Erica: Thank you for giving me advice through this journey, regardless of how crazy I have come out of left field at times. Your support and friendship have meant the world to me, I am glad I never listened to the advice of "don't make friends on the internet", otherwise we wouldn't have met via TikTok, lol. P.S. Thank you for reading my girly, princess book even if it is not in your genre realm for books!

Kyle: Thank you for being my biggest cheerleader and for allowing me to bounce all the ideas off your head even when they were complete spoilers for not only this book, but the series in general. I definitely know I sounded like a crazy conspiracy theorist as I went off with my obsession. I'll forever be your sledgehammer if you'll be my hammer.

Amy: Thank you for being beyond supportive as I began this journey. Knowing how much you took time out of your busy schedule as I talked about the writing process of this book has meant the world for me. Especially when I would fan-girl gush over Bay & Knox. (and thank you for making my mini books! They are beyond adorable and perfect! luckyjo423@msn.com if any other authors are interested!)

Bookish Sirens: Thank you, Admin (Dana, Kyle & Maggie) and Moderators (Hannah & Kylee), for being some of my first cheerleaders when I decided to start telling the world about my book. This group of girls has become like a second family to me; please check them out and support them on Facebook, Instagram, TikTok, and more!

Alex: Thank you for being with me through the beginning process when I was first beginning to figure out the layout for my book and how I wanted to plot it. Thank you for being one of the first people to read through my book.

Thank you to the friends who read it before I hit published! You have all helped support and encourage me and helped make this book the best possible version of itself that it could be! You all have been an important part of my life in one way or another.

Social Media

Keep in Touch with N.F. Schmitt

Website: www.NFSchmitt.com
Add me on Facebook: www.facebook.com/n.f.schmitt
Facebook Page: www.facebook.com/NFSchmittAuthor
Instagram: www.instagram.com/n.f.schmitt
E-Mail: NFSchmittAuthor@gmail.com

Want to discuss my books and other fun shenanigans with like-minded readers? Join my reader group:

www.facebook.com/groups/nfschmitt

About the Author

N.F. Schmitt is a born and raised Iowa girl, living in the country with her husband and all their pets. When she doesn't have her nose in a book or head in the clouds, you can find her ATVing most weekends on a dirt bike or sports quad, video gaming, drawing or planting a new tree in her yard (the local plant nursery know her & hubby on a first name base from all the indoor/outdoor plants they buy).

www.ingramcontent.com/pod-product-compliance
Lightning Source LLC
Chambersburg PA
CBHW070610300726
48975CB00006B/1776